M.E. SAMM

Golden Boy

Cover design by: GetCovers

First edition

ISBN: 9781068972249

This book was professionally typeset on Reedsy.
Find out more at reedsy.com

Contents

Preface

About This Book

Golden Boy is set in the same universe as the *Judgement* series by Mex Tate, with permission. *Judgement, Part 1* is available on Kindle and Kindle Unlimited. *Judgement, Part 2* is currently available on Archive of Our Own under the author name Mex Tate.

Content Notes

This is a coming-of-age journey where mistakes are made and trust is mislaid; where not every relationship is the right one but the happy ending may be found where it's least expected.

Includes:

- Queer normative, near future setting
- Large age gap (not romanticized)
- Mild power dynamics
- Addictions
- Low spice
- Adults behaving badly
- Rich people behaving badly
- Childhood friends to lovers

Acknowledgments

Many thanks to my kind, generous and helpful beta readers: Kay M. Woodgreen, Will Flynn, K. A. Smock, S.S. Genesee, and Danny.

Part I: Chapter 1

I remember the solid *thunk* of the football as I trapped it in my hands, the way my arms flew backwards with the momentum of the throw—a long-bomb from my brother Lance, my first really good catch. Then the rough rubbery feel of the faux-pigskin hugged into my chest, a glimpse of Tiran surging toward me as I wheeled around to begin my sprint, the hard *thump* of his outstretched hands against my shoulders, and finally the unexpected *thud* as I met the ground, the sprawling tangle of our bodies.

After that, there's a series of freeze-frame images—the flattened lawn beneath me, the high bold blue sky above, a red polo shirt and the fleeting chafe of fabric against my arm; the broken blades of grass releasing their fragrance as I skidded across the ground, landing finally with Tiran beside me.

Just a regular friendly football game on a late summer day, boys against the adults; my dad, Jimmy, too busy working to join us, as always. We played two-hand touch, not tackle, since we boys were so much smaller then, but a helter-skelter leap could still pull anyone to the ground. Probably not the first of these games, and certainly not the last, but the one for some reason I remember most clearly.

As Tiran, standing again, reached out a hand to haul me to my feet, I heard faint cries from my little sister somewhere on the sidelines and turned toward her instinctively. She was playing in the sand pit with the other kids too little to join our game.

"Mary-Dee—" I began, taking a step toward her, but Tiran caught my arm.

"It's okay, Barry," he said. "The nanny's there, remember?"

Yes. The nanny was responsible for the little ones now, not me. Maybe that was the day I really understood that the chaos and uncertainty of my old life had ended; my new role as young princeling was underway.

* * *

My mother hadn't been in our lives much even before she died. Some combination of illness, addiction and a restless spirit kept her from settling down, I guess. She never mentioned the man or men who helped with our creation. Her mom, and her brother, Jimmy Hawkins, had been our constants. Grandma did her best for us, but we were always moving from one tiny apartment to another in our small hometown, trying to scrape together some kind of life. I have vague memories of my mother stopping by to visit us, but I doubt any of my younger siblings remember her at all.

We lost grandma a few months after mom died, when I was six. Then only Jimmy was left—nineteen years old and suddenly responsible for his sister's five tiny children. I'll always give him credit for stepping up, and I can hardly blame him for being confused and overwhelmed—he was probably terrified. For the next couple of years, things were even more precarious than before.

Who knows what would have happened to us if not for Tiran Marx? It was just luck that we all came from the same small town, and Tiran grew up to be a megamillionaire. Jimmy wasn't especially close to Tiran but they had some mutual friends. I always assumed the friends talked Tiran into hiring Jimmy out of sympathy, since Jimmy had no particular talents. Whatever the reason, when Tiran moved out to the west coast he offered Jimmy a job managing his new property, and Jimmy accepted.

And so, in 2083, when I was eight years old, we all picked up and moved to Tiran's large, lovely estate on the Pacific coast. Our new and infinitely better life began.

* * *

"C'mon," I said, "Rick's setting up the new cambots today, let's go watch!"

Lance and Steve, two of my younger brothers, didn't look away from their game on the big screen. I tried to get their attention by standing directly in front of it. "Don't you wanna see?"

"Get out of the way!" Lance craned his head to look around me, and Steve glowered without pausing.

"What about me?" Randall piped up.

"Sure, you gonna hang out with me?" I said, scooping him up into the air. The youngest of my brothers, he was barely seven at the time, but at least he wanted to leave the house. I glanced over at the other little kids. The nanny had them working on some craft which no doubt bored Randall but seemed to entertain the other two. Best to leave them be.

"Wanna see the new bots," Randall agreed.

"Okay then, let's go, buddy."

Technically the nanny was responsible for all of us, but I was eleven by then and had no need of her. I had the run of the estate and loved it. It was so hard to fathom why the other kids wanted to stay in one place.

Randall and I set off under the high west-coast sun. Rick lived just a couple of houses away from us, but he was installing the new bots on top of one of the cliffs overlooking the ocean.

As we walked toward the water, I saw Jimmy on the central lawn, standing motionless while one of the outside workers gesticulated forcefully at him. When Jimmy first told us he was going to be Tiran's *property manager*, it had sounded like a made-up position to us—how could looking after someone's property possibly be a full-time job? Back then we'd had no sense of the scale of Tiran's estate, but poor Jimmy now seemed in way over his head. We barely saw him these days.

Unlike Jimmy, Rick never let anything bother him. He was one of the mutual friends who had probably advocated for Jimmy. Affable and competent, he'd originally been hired as Tiran's bodyguard but quickly risen to head of security on the compound. Like a lot of rich people, Tiran tended to trust the people he'd grown up with, which was why he'd brought Rick along with him when he moved out west.

I liked to follow Rick around because he had the coolest gadgets, and didn't mind explaining things to us. We kids especially liked his roving band of camera bots that showed feeds from all over the property; even Lance and Steve would sometimes pry themselves away from their games for the thrill of spying on everyone we knew as they went about their business.

"Now these guys'll be covering the ocean perimeter," Rick told us, as Randall and I watched him put components together and punch buttons on the command panel. "Along with the drones, of course. This one stays up top. There's another'un that goes underwater, and that last one'll patrol the shoreline, right here below us, just in case something gets inside."

"Bad guys?" Randall asked.

I elbowed him lightly. "There's no bad guys here." I understood by now that rich people like Tiran needed to be protected, but unlike Randall I remembered the old days, the succession of decrepit apartments in questionable neighbourhoods, before we moved here. That was when I'd actually worried about bad guys.

"Well, all the upheaval's caused some instability," Rick said, though he didn't sound too concerned. "Lots of displaced people. But more'n likely we'll just pick up one of you boys sneakin' down there where you're not allowed."

"We don't go in the water alone," I assured him. "Only with a grown-up. You can ask Tiran." We all knew Tiran had one literal superpower—he was an infallible human lie detector—so *ask Tiran* had become our standard assurance of honesty. In later years, I wondered if that superpower had something to do with the immense fortune he'd built. "The waves are too big," I added. "I make sure the kids stay away."

"Oh, you do, huh? You in charge of the kids?"

"Well, I'm the oldest." It seemed self-evident to me. Even now, standing near the top of the cliff with Rick and several of his workers around, I was tightly holding on to Randall's hand, just in case.

"Okay, well—" Rick closed the panel door and pushed a button on his control device. "That'll do it for me. I gotta go work on the new kid's details."

"New kid? Oh—Curtis."

Rick gathered up his tools as we watched the small bot whir quietly to life and begin its slow promenade along the cliff top. I spied a set of calipers in Randall's small fist, pried them out and handed them to Rick.

"Is he getting here today?" I asked.

"Not sure when," Rick said. "I just gotta make sure all the protocols get done."

"C'mon," I said to Randall, happy for a new diversion. "You want to meet him, don't you? Let's go find out!" I tugged his hand and raced off, back toward the houses, pulling him along with me.

"Wait up, Barr," Randall said plaintively, the cry of little brothers everywhere, and I forced myself to slow down a little on the path so as not to leave him behind.

When we reached the right house, I banged on the front door briefly, then led the way to the back patio when no one answered. "Pat, Dell, are you—Oh, Dell, there you are. Hey, is he here? Is he coming today?"

"What?" Dell looked up from her sun chair, using a tablet to shield her light eyes against the sun. "Who?"

"Curtis. Is he on his way? Is Pat out picking him up?"

"Oh." She glanced back at the house. "No, Pat's just inside getting drinks. Curtis should be here tomorrow, we hope."

"You hear that, Randall? We'll get to meet him tomorrow." Pat and Dell had also grown up with Tiran, and he'd invited them to live on the estate around the same time as us. It seemed like they'd been working on these adoptions for years. Their first son had arrived last year, and now Curtis would be his younger brother.

Pat came outside carrying two glasses and passed one to Dell. "You guys seem pretty happy about this."

"Yeah," I agreed. "We like getting new kids."

Dell sat up, hesitating a little, and put a hand on my arm. "I'm glad you want to meet him, but...you'll be careful, won't you? He's very young."

"We're afraid this could all be kind of—overwhelming for him," Pat added.

"Oh no," I said, almost surprised they needed the assurance. "I'll be there. I'll look after him."

"We know you will," Pat said, taking a long drink from his glass. "It's the rest of the boys we're—"

"There's so many of you…" Dell put in.

I waved my hand. "I'll take care of them. It'll be fine. Don't worry."

Dell was a kind woman, not very complicated. I could see her smile grow more relaxed. "Thanks, Barry," she said. "I know we can count on you."

"Yeah, it's gonna be okay."

Pat, a solidly-built man with dark hair and tanned white skin, still had worry lines on his forehead. Something was going on with him that I didn't really understand; something to do with Tiran. Everyone on the estate was here in some way because of Tiran, but Pat didn't seem to work for him, like Jimmy and Rick did.

Pat took another gulp and glanced back toward the house. "I gotta get going," he said to Dell.

I went over to collect Randall, who had wandered off into the backyard. "You want me to come by tomorrow then—after lunch maybe? I can take Curtis over to meet everyone."

"That would be lovely," Dell agreed.

"Hey, Barry—" Pat asked, swirling the remains of his drink and looking down at it. "Did you…happen to see Tiran on your way over here?"

"No." I looked up at the sky, gauging the time from the sun's position. "He's probably just finishing his workout now, then he'll head down to the ocean for his swim." To reassure Pat, I added, "He'll go around the back of his house. You'll be safe walking from here to the garage." I didn't know what was going on between them, but I knew Pat tried to avoid Tiran these days.

Pat looked embarrassed. "Thanks," he mumbled.

Drops of sweat trailed from my eyelids to my lashes, and as I rubbed them away I thought about the cool of the ocean. "Think I'll join him for the swim," I said. "C'mon, Randall."

"You'll be careful, won't you?" Dell called behind me as I led Randall out.

The side gate let us out near the house next door, where Dusty and Kat lived with their son Pasha. Dusty was another of the mutual friends from back home. He'd always aspired to be a movie star, and when Tiran, who was a bit older than the others, moved west to start dabbling in vid production, he'd naturally brought Dusty along with him.

Since Randall was too little to go in the ocean with me, I planned to drop him off at home. But Dusty's collie, Scout, lay sleeping in the shade of a willow tree, and we stopped to say hi first. Randall buried his face in her silky soft hair, as he loved to do, while I scratched her neck the way she liked it. With Scout and Randall both content, I glanced around the yard and found Simba, the cat, hiding under the steps, as he always did when Scout was outside. I went over to give him some scratches and comfort. He was missing his collar, which usually happened after a tussle with Scout.

"Hey, Barr," Dusty said, stepping out the side door with a towel around his neck. He must have just finished working out with Tiran. "Do you know—"

"He's at our place with the nanny," I said. Dusty was always worrying about Pasha. I didn't get it at the time, though later I wondered if it had something to do with Dusty's career in the vid industry. Anyway, Pasha was so sheltered we hardly saw him when we first arrived at the estate. It had taken a couple of years for his parents to lighten up and let him hang out with us occasionally.

"Oh, okay. Do you think—"

"I'll bring him back with me. I'm going over there now to drop Randall off." I spied something gleaming under a holly bush near the fence and went over to retrieve Simba's collar. "Did Tiran go for his swim?"

"He was just heading over when I left." Dusty towelled off his fine straw-coloured hair absently. He also had some kind of deal with Tiran, but unlike Pat he never seemed stressed about it.

I went over to hand him the collar. "Scout's been scaring Simba again. You shouldn't leave them outside alone like that."

"Oh, poor Simba." Dusty looked guilty. "I just thought—while I was at the gym—"

"I'll take her with me," I said, grabbing Scout's lead from the hook on the side of the house. "So Simba gets a break."

Randall, Scout and I crossed the wide, open lawn that separated the two main clusters of houses on the estate. The whole complex sat on a kind of peninsula, surrounded by ocean on three sides. Tiran's mansion, the largest structure, dominated the eastern headland, at the top of a series of cliffs towering above the ocean. From there the land sloped down gradually to the west, giving way to a stretch of gentle beaches before rising again to a small wooded area.

The houses we'd just left were grouped in a semi-circle above the beaches, facing Tiran's house and the ocean beyond. My family lived in the second group, on the other side of the lawn, where the houses mainly faced the shoreline to the south.

I dropped off Randall, changed into my swim trunks, and told the nanny I was taking Pasha home on my way to the beach. Unlike Randall, who usually zoomed ahead or wandered off as the mood struck him, Pasha never left my side; he followed wherever I led, like Hansel following Gretel into the woods. His hand in mine looked impossibly pale, especially against the rich amber of my own. He was kind of an extreme version of his father—where Dusty had a sandy, all-American boy appearance, Pasha almost looked like he'd been bleached.

I delivered him safely to his parents, and picked up Scout's water bowl so I could take her with me to the beach. There were a few different places to swim in the ocean, but the best spot was what everyone called "Tiran's beach". Loping down towards it, I bumped into another one of the adults, heading in the opposite direction.

"Hi Barry," Paul said, stopping to give Scout a few scratches. "Didn't see you this afternoon."

Paul lived next door to us, near the small wooded area by the shore. Tall and lean, with a shock of dark hair that contrasted with his skin, he took long walks around the estate most days. I often joined him, half skipping to keep up with his long strides, when there was nothing more entertaining to do.

"Naw, Rick was setting up the new cambots," I explained. "And tomorrow Curtis is coming, so...maybe I can walk with you in a couple days."

"Sure," he said. "You going for a swim?"

"Yeah...well, Tiran should be around. I'm allowed in the ocean as long as there's a grown-up."

He gave a brief nod and said shortly, "He's just getting there. See ya later then."

Paul must have left the beach when he saw Tiran arriving. He worked for Tiran, in a job I didn't really understand—something about managing money for him. They were old friends, and they'd grown up together, but for some reason Paul was always tetchy about him.

It seemed like everyone here had some kind of reaction to Tiran. They might like him, like Dusty, or not, like Paul; they might be afraid of him, like Pat, or grateful to him, like my dad. Back then, he seemed like any other grown-up to me; the only thing that set him apart was the way other people saw him.

When I reached the beach, I tied Scout's lead to a tree on the shoreline, where she'd have some shade, set her water bowl down, and ran through the burning sand toward the waves. Tiran was already working on his laps, methodical strokes pulling him back and forth between the buoy markers strung out across the water. When I got to the water's edge he glanced over and gave a wave to show he saw me.

The beach here was set in a small bay and slightly sheltered, with waves that were big enough to play in but not scary. I found a paddleboard on the edge of the shore and made my way through the shallow tide.

When the water reached the top of my legs I plunged in, diving under the rolling spray to fully douse myself. Once in, I set up a rhythm with the board, paddling out a little deeper and following the tide back in, letting the waves toss me around and the current drag me against the sandy floor. After a few minutes, Tiran finished his work-out and headed back to shore, sprawling on a lounge chair to recover. I stayed in a while longer, riding the waves on my little paddleboard while the seabirds cawed overhead, until I'd swallowed enough saltwater for the day and made my way back to the beach.

Scout waited patiently under the tree. I brought her over to the deckchairs, where I took the one beside Tiran and she lay on the sand between us, accepting languid caresses as we dried in the sun.

"So how's things going, Barry?" Tiran asked eventually, turning toward me, and I recognized the look of mild bemusement behind his dark glasses. He always seemed out of his element with kids, kind of looking at me like I was someone's pet frog he didn't want to accidentally step on.

"It's okay." I tossed a piece of driftwood for Scout to chase. "Curtis is coming tomorrow."

He nodded. "That's right, I heard. Is that good news for you?"

"Sure. We like having more kids around."

"I know it's kinda boring for you guys," he said, like he was trying to sound sympathetic. "To be trapped here. I'm really sorry about that."

This was an old theme with Tiran. We weren't literally trapped; it was just that all the security made it a big production to leave the estate. When we first arrived, Tiran had hired an on-site tutor so we didn't have to go through security every day on our way to school. I thought that was nice of him but he always acted apologetic about it.

"It's fine," I said, which was true for me. Lance actually whined all the time about not getting to hang out with other kids, but that wasn't Tiran's problem.

"How's your dad doing?" Tiran asked after another moment.

"Jimmy's okay. We don't see him much."

"Really?" Tiran turned to look at me again. "How come?"

"I mean, he works a lot. He's busy."

"Sure, but I didn't realize…I guess I should get him some help."

Scout brought back the driftwood and I threw it for her again. "Maybe."

"I mean, I don't want to keep him away from you guys."

I shrugged, watching Scout scramble away over the sand. Jimmy had done so much for us, but I didn't really feel like there was any more I needed from him. The younger kids, though—Randall and Mary-Dee—they'd probably like to see him around more often. "Sure," I said, more encouragingly this time. "The little ones would love that."

By the next week, Jimmy had a full-time assistant working for him. Maybe that's when I started to get the idea that I could make things happen through other people.

Chapter 2

Curtis arrived the next day, very different from his older brother. Phillip had been seven when he joined the Van Mertz family, calm and self-contained, with steady grey eyes and a serious look. I'd kept an eye on him, of course, but Phillip could hold his own with all of us. Curtis was younger, with chaotic moods and frequent outbursts. I did my best to help him adjust, though I often had to step in to keep the peace.

Over the next few years, we grew into a pretty tight circle—the five of us Hawkins kids, Phillip and Curtis Van Mertz, and Pasha St. Vista. Occasionally other employees had a child who would join our gang for a while, but workers who didn't live on the estate tended to come and go, and their kids went with them. With minimal outside contact and mostly benign neglect from the adults, we relied on each other for entertainment. While Lance rarely left the house, Steve could sometimes be coaxed away, and there were enough of us for many elaborate games and adventures.

We spent our days either in the makeshift playroom in our basement or wandering the estate. By this time, I knew every leaf and crevice on the grounds—the caverns and boulders at the bottom of the cliffs, the sandy paths through the little wooded area, the sports fields, even the tunnels that ran underground, left behind from initial construction or added as part of Rick's security planning. As the oldest child by a few years, I pretty much ran the show, leading the kids from basketball games to secret hideouts and everywhere in between.

At some point Tiran must have noticed the sizeable gang we'd grown into as we roamed the grounds—or maybe someone else pointed it out to him.

In any case, he had a kind of club house built for us, just behind our house and near the western edge of the complex. It was more like a small cabin than a house, with one big room and various activity spaces—but Jimmy let us help him design and furnish it, and for a group of young kids it was a kind of paradise.

* * *

The estate was self-contained but not exactly isolated. A small, middle-class town called Whittier neighboured us on the east, and to the west lay a public beach used often by the locals. We were about forty miles north of New Ellay, the large metropolis where the vid industry had reformed following the coastal collapses.

Tiran sometimes used a small hovercraft to get around, but he also collected cars. He had a large garage full of them, along with a full-time mechanic who doubled as chauffeur. The collection included a few fancy imported models that only Tiran and the mechanic were allowed to touch, as well as a bunch of regular cars available for anyone's use. Dusty had his own pretty little convertible coupe, which I greatly admired, and the other adults used the every-day cars when they needed to get around.

Enrico, the mechanic-chauffeur, generally drove us kids to doctor's visits or similar appointments. Occasionally I could persuade Jimmy and Enrico to let me pilot one of the self-driving cars as far as Whittier. But we didn't go anywhere very often. That was partly because of the security hassles but also because we didn't know anyone outside of the estate. We had everything we needed at home anyway.

Between the other kids, our little paradise, and my almost unfettered freedom, I couldn't imagine anything else I might want at first. It was only after we'd been on the estate for a few years that I started to notice the gap between myself and the younger children. Lance, the closest to me in age, was almost two years younger and we didn't have much in common; Steve, the next oldest, could be easily led, but if I didn't actively steer him in my direction he tended to gravitate to Lance. And the other kids were even younger.

In some ways, I felt like a bridge between the child and adult worlds of the estate. Keeping Jimmy reassured and out of our way was one of my regular functions, and I could usually negotiate with him for anything we might want. I enjoyed running my small fiefdom with the kids, but when I grew bored of our usual games I'd join Paul for one of his walks, or play tennis with Tiran and his friend Rocky, or hang out with Pat and Dell in their backyard. I knew all the grown-ups and their routines, and eventually I began to notice their interactions as well.

It was around this time, when I would have been thirteen or fourteen, that I started to figure out what was going on between Tiran and the other adults. My understanding was imperfect but what I did pick up rattled me a little, and my confusion made me irritable in a way Jimmy eventually noticed.

It must have been a weekend, a day without tutoring, when he broached it with me. I remember being a little annoyed as he stopped me while we headed over to the club house after breakfast.

"Hey, Barry," Jimmy said, as I got up. "Can you hold on a sec? I want to talk to you."

"What is it," I said, trying to hide my impatience.

"C'mere." Jimmy waved me back over to the table when the other kids were gone. He still seemed a little harried, even with the extra assistance, but I had started to realize that was his natural state. "Sit down. I just want to check in with you. Is everything okay?"

"Sure."

"Because I feel like you're not as happy as usual. It seems like something might be bothering you." Jimmy paused, resting his arms on the table and watching me intently.

Maybe he wanted me to tell him everything was okay, so he could go back to worrying about maintenance schedules and the gardening staff. In retrospect, maybe I should have just kept my mouth shut. Like most kids, I wasn't too eager to share my concerns with a parent. But I guess my mind was so full it couldn't help overflowing.

"I saw Dusty with Tiran a couple of days ago," I said finally, shifting the cutlery around randomly on the table. "And, um...Dusty was, like...in front of Tiran. I'm pretty sure he was, uh...kissing his hand."

"Where was this?" Jimmy asked sharply. "Did they know you were there?"

He was missing the point. I shook my head. "No, course not. They were at the bottom of the cliffs, and I was coming out of one of those tunnels that ends there. They didn't see me."

"Was anyone else with you? Any of the other kids?"

"I mean, Steve and Pip were behind me but I stopped them before they came out. They didn't see anything." I looked up at Jimmy. I hadn't wanted to talk about this, but I really needed to know. "Tiran's a Dom, isn't he?"

I'd picked up a few basics about adult relationships by this time. Like everyone, I knew orientation and gender identity were fluid, and it was outdated to expect people to fall at one extreme or the other. I knew monogamy was an old-fashioned concept. But other topics weren't openly discussed—*kinks* they used to be called, though that was considered a slur now. I'd vaguely heard of Dom/sub dynamics, mostly because the media would sometimes make sly references to powerful people as Doms or use "sub" as a kind of insult. It all made me a little uncomfortable, but also, to be honest, slightly intrigued.

"Barry..." Jimmy lifted a hand to his forehead and shut his eyes for a second. "You shouldn't be asking about this. You're too young to know anything about it."

"No I'm not." My irritability grew. Why ask what was bothering me if he didn't want to hear the answer? "You can't say that when I've already *seen* it."

"Well, you shouldn't have. These things are for adults only. I'll tell them to—"

"I'm old enough. Why can't you just tell me what's going on?"

"Because you're too—"

"Is that why everyone's here? Does Tiran—like, *own* you all? Is that what he does with his money?"

"Jeeze, Barry!" Jimmy seemed stung by the questions. He stopped and took a long slow breath, but I kept my insistent stare on him.

"Okay," he said finally. "Look. I mean, sure, he's a Dom. But not for everyone here, just—just for some people. And it's not like he *buys* them."

"Dusty, right? What about Rick—or Rocky? And Pat—that's why he's always so scared, isn't it?"

"Look, Barry, I told you, you shouldn't even know about this. I'll speak to them about—"

"I want to know who. You say it's not everyone here but who is it?"

At first Jimmy kept his mouth closed, and I thought he might not answer me. He got up and started the dishbot to begin clearing. I watched him, feeling the anger rise in my throat.

"Not Rick," he said at last, with his back to me. "Dusty, yes. Pat and Dell. His houseboy. A few others."

"What about you?" I asked, almost afraid of the answer. "What about *us*?"

"*You*?" He sounded appalled. "Why would—" He turned around, his forehead creased with anxiety. "Of course not you. You guys are *children*, this has nothing to do with you. You shouldn't even know about it."

Adults always seemed to think kids would never figure things out, when it was only a matter of time. "But you?" I asked, hearing the bitterness come out in my voice. "Is that why he brought you here? And what about when we grow up—"

"*Barry*." Jimmy cut me off and returned to the table, seizing my hands as he threw himself into the chair beside me. "Not me, and *of course* not any of you. Not now, not ever. You know, he doesn't—"

"You're not a sub?" I asked, not interested in the explanations. It would have explained so much.

And he paused; he did have to think about his response. "I'm not a sub for him," he said finally. "And to be honest, Barry, my personal life is none of your business. I don't want any more questions about that." It was unlike him to be so firm. "The only thing you need to know is that this is for adults only. It doesn't have anything to do with you guys, and it doesn't have anything to do with us living here." He shook his head like he couldn't believe he was saying this.

"He just gave you a house out of the goodness of his heart?" I found it hard to believe in Tiran's benevolence just then.

"Yes. Really. I know that might not jive with what you think you know about him..." Jimmy let go of my hand and sat back, frowning. "But it's the truth." The worry lines that never left his face seemed to deepen, like I'd added one more problem for him to stress over. Sometimes I wondered why he didn't just leave. "Listen, Barr," he went on, more uncertainly. "Do you think I did the wrong thing by taking him up on his job offer? Because if you do..."

"No," I said quickly, wanting the conversation to end. I'd gotten all I needed from it. I stood up, keeping my hand steady as I picked up the dishes in front of me. Now it was time to manage Jimmy, as I so often did. "You did the right thing. It's fine."

He stayed motionless in the chair, his back rigid, watching me while I helped the dishbot finish up. "So...you're okay with all this?"

"Yeah." I wasn't sure about *okay*, but I wanted to take it back off his list of anxieties. "As long as we're not involved...and we don't have to see it."

"I'll talk to them about being more careful." His shoulders dropped a little and he got up to help me load the bot. "Are you feeling better now?" he asked as we finished.

I nodded. "Sure. Guess I'll go join the others now, okay?"

"You won't say anything to them, will you?"

"Course not. See ya later, dad."

That conversation actually did help me get over my initial discomfort. I wondered occasionally about Jimmy—was it Rick, maybe? Or Paul? I never found out for sure. But he was right about us kids being completely left out of whatever games the adults were playing. I still noticed little things, like Pat's constant heightened anxiety around Tiran, or the way Dusty quietly deferred decisions to him. After a few years the other kids started figuring things out as well, and I'd sometimes hear gossip and speculation. I always cut it off immediately, treating it the same way we'd treat the idea of our parents having sex—*gross*, and something we didn't want to know about. I kept my growing curiosity to myself.

* * *

CHAPTER 2

I guess everyone starts off thinking their childhood is normal. While life on the estate differed wildly from what I'd known before, it hadn't occurred to me it also differed wildly from the rest of the world. It was only after I figured out Tiran's deal with some of the other adults that I started to realize how far from normal things were for us.

When I started paying attention to the popular media, I found plenty of talk about Tiran in it. That's how I learned he wasn't just a rich Dom, he was one of the wealthiest men on the planet. And he wasn't just a central figure on the estate, he was famous—or perhaps I should say infamous—around the world. He didn't seek out fame but lived a life of complete hedonism, doing exactly what he wanted with no concern for how he might be perceived. While it was still considered vaguely impolite to refer to Dom/sub relationships in the media, Tiran's proclivity was an open secret. That, along with his money and his influence in the vid industry, made him the subject of endless gossip and fascination.

It seemed impossible at first to reconcile the constant scandals and escapades I heard about in the media with the regular guy I saw around the estate, doing his laps in the ocean or playing football with us on the lawn. Eventually I realized how deliberate that was. Tiran chose to keep the decadent stuff mostly outside, and treat the estate—his home—as a kind of sanctuary of normalcy. I suppose that's why I'd been fooled for so long.

While what I learned about Tiran intrigued me, Dusty St. Vincente had a more immediate impact on my life. I'd always heard him called an actor but only realized how exciting that was once I started seeing him in vids on screen as I got older. And if that didn't impress me enough, I eventually realized he wasn't just an actor, he was a leading man—a heart-throb, a bona fide *movie star*.

I saw his celebrity in action once when he took me into New Ellay with him for some reason. He likely had an errand to run and by then I'd grown curious enough about the outside world to tag along when I could.

Downtown New Ellay had been built quickly over a short period on the new coastline that emerged after the original disasters. It gloried in its lean, inter-connected high-rises, climate-control technology, vanity towers, and synthetic greenspace. I never passed up a chance to marvel at it all.

This time Dusty's business took us to the suburbs, where real people lived and the heat had chance to disperse over sprawling low-rise commercial buildings. We'd been in a store or a bank, and when we stepped outside a woman on the sidewalk happened to recognize Dusty. I saw the sudden amazement and adulation in her face as she stopped in her tracks and gasped, "*Dusty St. Vincente?*"

"Good afternoon, ma'am," Dusty said congenially. "Yes, that's me."

"*Oh my god!*" The woman turned to her companion, and the next thing I knew Dusty was scribbling his name on small scraps of paper and posing good-naturedly for selfies. In a moment a small crowd had grown around us, a ring of comms in the air snapping photos and people beaming, whispering excitedly to each other or calling out his name. I stood beside him, watching in surprise and somehow basking in the second-hand glory.

"Does that happen to you all the time?" I asked as we drove home, after he'd deftly steered us out of the crowd and back to his convertible.

"Ehh...not all the time. Often, though."

"So you're, like—you're famous."

"Not as famous as Tiran."

"But you're a movie star!"

"That's what they say."

A thought crossed my mind and came out bluntly; I was still too taken aback to be concerned about offending him. "Is that why you sub for Tiran?"

"What? Why—wait, how do you know about that?"

"Oh, everyone knows." That was an exaggeration; the other kids hadn't quite figured it out yet. "Was that the deal? He said he'd make you a movie star if you let him dom you?"

Dusty seemed to find that amusing, completely unabashed. He threw his head back a little as he laughed, his fine light hair blown back by the wind, white teeth in a perfect smile. "Hardly."

"Well..." I waited impatiently for him to say more. "What then?"

He glanced at me, still smiling. "Aren't you a little young to be asking about this? You don't want to know the sordid details of adult lives."

"Is it sordid, really?" I asked, curiosity making me eager.

"Not really." He gave a little wave with his free hand, a kind of warning. "Not to me. And it's really none of your business." He focused on the road ahead, his face growing serious again. "But things don't work the way you seem to think," he said after a moment, as though compelled to set the record straight. "Tiran never promised me anything like that. He doesn't even get me work; he just gets me auditions. I mean, he has a lot of power in the industry. He probably could force directors to hire me if he wanted to, but he's a businessman, he knows it's better to let the experts make decisions."

That was a lot of information to take in. "So…wait, is he—like, your agent?"

"Oh, no. I have an agent. But I guess Tiran can open doors for me. And he—" Dusty broke off, glanced at me again, and then shrugged. "He makes the final call. I don't accept anything without his approval."

That was tacit acknowledgment of their relationship, wasn't it? I felt my eyes open wider, strangely intrigued, then quickly narrowed them so I didn't give myself away. "So…you do sub for him."

"I never said I don't."

"Well—*why*? If not that—what else does he do for you?"

For a moment I thought Dusty didn't hear me. He rested his elbow on the open window beside him with his fingers draped lightly over the steering wheel, and seemed lost in thought. When we came to a stop at a red light he turned toward me again, with a small hint of a smile.

"The world's a complicated place, Barr. You'll figure it out one day."

I never got much more out of him than that. But the incident added to a nascent fascination in the deepest part of my psyche, where Dusty's fame and Tiran's control entwined together with a kind of illicit allure I didn't fully understand.

After that, I quickly attached myself to Dusty, asking endless questions about his job, how he became so famous, and what it was like. When I pressed him to take me along on vid shoots to see his work in action, he was happy to share the experience with me. His life as a movie star instantly mesmerized me—the deferential treatment, the constant attention, the way so much revolved around him.

For the first time, I found myself craving something beyond my existing life. As much as I still loved ruling my little world on the estate, it didn't completely satisfy me anymore. Some days I wanted what Dusty had; maybe even what Tiran had.

Eventually I wheedled Dusty to find me some kind of vid job—he didn't make hiring decisions, but surely he could put in a word for me? He hesitated at first, saying he'd have to check and let me know if it was okay. I assumed he meant with Jimmy, and assured him that I'd manage my dad. Later I realized Dusty probably wanted Tiran's approval as well.

In any case, I soon landed a few small roles—not, to my disappointment, star turns like Dusty got, but walk-ons, background, extras. Hardly glamorous, and not enough to feed my growing appetite, but a start. I kept at it as I grew older, chasing that mixed up desire for fame and power.

"Don't you ever bring Pasha with you?" I asked Dusty as we waited by the craft table for a shoot to start up again. I might have been fifteen or sixteen by then. "Isn't he curious about your work?"

Dusty's usually sunny face darkened immediately. "No. He's not getting into the acting business, not ever."

"Wait, what's wrong with the acting business?"

"Plenty. You haven't seen anything yet. It can be—vicious."

I had an inkling of what he meant. Lately I'd noticed the odd glance or comment from an adult on-set that felt a little creepy, even for someone like me who enjoyed attention. "You don't have a problem with *me* getting involved in it," I said, trying to sound innocent.

"You're not Pasha," he said shortly.

In a funny way I almost understood where he was coming from. There was something about Pasha; he wasn't shy or easily frightened exactly, but he had a kind of fragility. It made you want to protect him. No one thought I needed protecting, least of all me.

Anyway, the vid business lost some of its initial charm, though I continued to take jobs whenever I could get them. Working as an extra was slow and boring and didn't seem to bring me any closer to the kind of experiences

Dusty had. No one offered me speaking roles, and auditions were a lot of work for a teenaged boy with a limited attention span and not much self-discipline. I still craved what I thought fame could bring me; there just had to be an easier way.

Chapter 3

"So what's he like?" Randall demanded.

Phillip shrugged. "It's hard to say. He's not...what I expected, exactly."

"How old is he?" Mary-Dee asked.

"What does he look like?" That was Pasha, glancing up from his homework on the table.

We were in the club house as usual; I must have been fifteen. Randall and I had been playing pool but we stopped when Phillip and Curtis came in, just back from the first visit with their new brother-to-be.

Pat and Dell were adopting again—their last, they said. This would be an older boy, one of the many so-called "lost boys", children who'd been abandoned for generations in the final remaining inner-city cores, relying on their own wits for survival. The last pockets of those wastelands were being cleared out now, and new homes had to be found for the inhabitants. Pat and Dell had gone through a long process to be matched up with one of them, and the official adoption proceedings had begun.

"He's fourteen," Phillip said, leaning against the back of the couch and frowning at the floor, like he was still trying to sort through his thoughts from the meeting.

"Same age as me," Lance said, without looking away from his game which, as usual, involved some kind of vehicle racing smash-up mayhem.

"You're not fourteen yet," Phillip said. "And he looks...well, he's a little darker than Barry, but he's got this really blond hair."

"He looks like a surfer dude!" Curtis put in, joining Steve and Lance in front of the big screen.

"Yeah," Phillip glanced up with a small bemused smile. "He kinda does. But he doesn't—*sound* like one."

"Is he as tall as me?" Lance asked. He'd overtaken me in height recently and liked to remind us of that.

"Not quite." Phillip's eyes flickered from Lance to me, then Steve. "Between Steve and Barry, I'd say. But bigger..."

"Way more muscley," Curtis piped in.

"He said he lifts weights. I'm gonna talk to mom and dad about putting in a little gym in the basement. I think he'd like that."

I leaned on my pool stick. "Why do you say he doesn't sound like a surfer, Pip?" I asked.

Phillip didn't answer right away, tracing his finger across the back of the couch, and I could see his thoughts drift away again. I gave him time. Phillip was a thinker, not a talker.

"He...doesn't say a lot. It's hard to know much about him from one meeting. And, you know—" Phillip looked up and gave a vague gesture. "He has that really dense wasteland accent. It was hard to understand him sometimes. And I'm not sure he understood us that well."

I nodded. "That makes sense. I heard it's like a different world there."

"Yeah. But I get the feeling—I don't know. I felt like he was just listening and—kind of waiting."

When we finally met Tom, a couple of months later, I understood what Phillip meant. He arrived at the estate on a day in early February, and shortly afterwards Phillip and Curtis brought him over to the club house to introduce us all. Tom was everything they'd said—well-built and striking, not exactly hostile but very reserved, with a watchful, wary quality that made you feel like you were being constantly analyzed.

I greeted him lightly and made a couple of jokes, trying to set him at ease, though I started to see that wouldn't happen for a while. Tom wasn't going to lose that coiled tension anytime soon, and to be fair, the rest of us were kind of intimidated by him as well. No one told us much about his past, but we knew he'd grown up alone, more or less on the streets, in an isolated and dangerous wasteland. We didn't know, but could imagine, what he'd gone through, and what he might be capable of.

After the introductions Lance handed Tom a spare headset and invited him to join the on-screen madness, so I went back to my pool game. Glancing over at them between turns, I almost laughed at Tom's complete lack of interest in whatever Lance was trying to show him—he obviously had no understanding of virtual games and no desire to learn.

Once I'd won my match with Randall I asked Tom if he wanted a game, and that seemed more to his liking. He must have played pool before. We were fairly evenly matched and I thought he relaxed very slightly while he focused on his shots. I took the opportunity to study him further, as he bent over the table with still guarded concentration.

I think it was the combination of his brawny build, blond hair—long and choppy, the colour of the sweet-corn that grew in the fields behind our house—and copper skin that was so arresting at first sight. Phillip was right about Tom being a bit darker than me, and less burnished; he clearly hadn't spent as much time in sunlight as I had.

I never thought much about the hue of my skin, though it was noticeably a shade or two deeper than my siblings'. Some days I wondered about the genes I might have that my brothers didn't. Mostly I liked to think of myself as exceptional.

Since my foray into acting, I'd taken a greater interest in my appearance and started to notice how changes in my hair and clothes could draw more attention. I had a somewhat athletic build, and my hair was styled now in artful tousled curls. I knew I looked good, but I didn't catch the eye like Tom did.

I kept a close eye on him at first, but Phillip firmly took the lead on helping Tom settle in. In the early days, Tom was often away—meeting with therapists, counsellors and other specialists, or getting set up with new clothes and comms—and when he was around he seemed to prefer staying close to home. Phillip said he spent a lot of time in the little gym they'd set up for him in the basement beside his bedroom. Sometimes I'd see him jogging around the estate.

We gave him space, and eventually Tom started joining us at the club house more often. He gravitated naturally to Lance—mainly, I thought, because Lance's simple-mindedness made things uncomplicated; Tom didn't seem to like answering questions, and Lance didn't ask many. The rest of us gradually stopped feeling nervous around Tom as he grew a bit more sociable, though he never lost that undercurrent of taut reserve or the hint of mystery. I sometimes got the impression he was in a kind of holding pattern, trying to get by while he figured things out in his new world.

It took me a few weeks to realize he'd expected us to see him as competition—he must have assumed we'd resent his arrival and try to freeze him out or something. I figured that was a natural reaction when you came from a place with limited resources, where you needed to fight for whatever you could get. But I hoped he'd eventually realize there was plenty here for everyone.

* * *

I finished the last page of my reading assignment and dropped my tablet onto the table beside me. Doc, my beagle—I'd talked Jimmy into him when I was twelve—napped on the floor at my feet as I surveyed the room from my chair in the corner.

We'd made a deal with our tutor that, in exchange for no actual class time, we'd use Friday afternoons to complete homework. The tutor wasn't invited to the club house so I generally monitored this with the younger kids.

Now the four littlest ones—Randall, Pasha, Curtis and Mary-Dee—milled around the big table in the middle of the room, working on some kind of group project, mercifully without squabbling. Over at the study desk, Steve stared morosely at his tablet, punching in numbers, then deleting them and trying different ones. Phillip didn't need any supervision—he'd already finished his schoolwork and gone home, probably to figure out a plan for world peace. I think we'd all given up on Lance, who never cracked a tablet even during class time, and Tom was still going through a separate "assessment" process, though he'd been here for a few months by now.

I watched Lance and Tom with their headsets in front of the big screen, Lance's movements quick and restless, while Tom's broad shoulders and arms made him seem out of proportion with the sofa. Tom still looked bored.

"Hey, Tom," I said, getting up. "Wanna go hang out at Tiran's beach? We can take Doc with us for his walk."

Tom glanced up at me, still too wary to show a reaction right away, but I was pretty sure he'd be glad to escape.

"How come *he* gets to—"

"Shut up, Curt." That was Randall, no doubt kicking Curtis under the table. We tried not to call attention to Tom's obvious academic delays, though I imagine he was well aware of them.

Tom shot a glance at Lance, as if wondering whether he'd object, but Lance just shrugged and kept playing.

"Sure," Tom said, sliding his headset off. "I guess."

I paused beside the round table for a moment to check out the kids' project. I think they were building some kind of laser-printed Eiffel Tower. "Looks good, guys," I said, tossing an arm over Pasha's shoulder as I turned the model around admiringly. "Almost done?"

"No," Mary-Dee said with a dramatic sigh. "It'll *never* be done!"

"Well, keep working on it till suppertime, then you can quit for the day," I directed. "And no fighting now, that thing looks fragile."

Tom and I changed into swim shorts and headed out. A little trail led from the club house to the main lawn, and from there we cut over to follow a path along the water. Tiran would be finished with his ocean laps by now but that was fine; I didn't need an adult anymore, and I suspected Tom didn't want any extra company.

I kept up a light stream of chatter as we walked, talking about my adventures in acting just for something to say. Tom seemed to like it when someone else did the talking so he only had to listen and nod occasionally.

"You know you don't have to go along with Lance's games all the time if you don't want to," I said, as we reached the fine sand where the beaches began.

Tom shrugged. "It's fine."

I paused to kick off my sandals and let Doc off his leash for a bit. "I feel like you don't find them too entertaining."

He smiled slightly, following my lead with his shoes. "I just never played things like that before. I'm not too good at them."

Phillip was right about Tom's heavy inflection being hard to understand at times, and I also noticed his simplified vocabulary when he spoke to us. The wastelands, as people called them, were remnants of inner-city neighbourhoods in large metropolises that had been abandoned after the coastal disasters, leaving several generations of inhabitants with almost no outside contact. Our tutor once explained that Tom's language had evolved separately from ours, so the words we had in common were limited.

"There's better games, if you want to try something else. Lance only plays those smash-up derbies cause he likes to see things explode." I rolled my eyes.

"How come...?" Tom began, after a little pause. "How come he likes it so much?"

I shrugged. "I think it started with racing games, because he used to want to be a race car driver."

"But not now?"

"I don't know what he wants anymore." I threw a stick for Doc and watched him bound over the sand toward it. Tom and I walked in silence for a bit. I got the feeling he had more questions, and maybe if I waited a while he'd ask them.

"How come Lance doesn't do homework when the other kids do?" he asked after a while. *Homework* was a word we'd taught him.

I laughed. "I mean, he's supposed to. He just doesn't."

"He says he wants to go to school."

"He means he wants to go to an actual school," I explained. "Not stay on the estate with a teacher." We'd all tacitly adopted *teacher* instead of *tutor* with Tom.

"So...why don't you?"

That was a good question. "It's a long story," I said, catching the stick Doc brought back to me and throwing it again. "You know how you have to go through security at the main gate, when you come into the estate? They didn't want all of us kids going through that every day, when we first got here. But...I don't know, it doesn't seem like that big a deal to me now."

"Lance really wants to go."

"I know." I lifted my hands in a gesture somewhere between a wave and a shrug. I didn't feel as strongly about it as Lance did, but I saw his point. "I think we all do. It gets kinda boring here after a while. I mean, I love this place but we only ever see each other. We need to meet other kids some time."

Tom didn't say anything, and I wondered how he felt about other kids. I considered asking, but he seemed to prefer not to talk about himself.

We reached Tiran's beach, and I called Doc over and clipped his lead back on. Tiran liked his beach pristine. I used the outdoor shower at the edge of the beach to fill up Doc's water bowl, then tied him to a tree while Tom went to get one of the paddleboards.

Tom didn't swim, of course—he'd never seen a body of water in his life before he joined us—and he didn't show any interest in learning. But these days the ocean was warm all year round and he'd picked up paddleboarding right after he arrived; by now he'd even moved on to sailboarding lessons. He always wore a life jacket in the ocean and when I was with him I put one on as well, to keep him company.

He paddled out toward the furthest row of buoys, the board moving swiftly under the power of his strokes, while I got started on my routine. These days I did my own laps in the ocean. I pulled myself back and forth along the line markers, tasting salt in my mouth and shaking the spray off my face until my arms grew numb from the strain.

Afterwards, lying on a deckchair on the beach, I watched the silvery water droplets ripple through the air around Tom's paddle and remembered how all of this had once been a novelty for me as well.

Later, when we'd both dried off a bit in the afternoon sun, we walked back up toward the houses, hungry and ready for dinner.

"How's the sailboarding lessons going?" I asked, when I ran out of things to chat about.

Tom shrugged. "It's fine."

"Hey, Tom." I made up my mind to find out what he wanted before I pursued anything. "Would *you* want to go to school? I mean, leave here every day and go to a real school?"

He hesitated for a moment. "I don't know when I'm going to start..."

"I mean, when you do start classes—whenever that is. Would you want to go to a school with other kids?"

"I..." He shook his head with a faint smile. "I don't care. Sure."

There were many more things I would have liked to ask but he hadn't lost his initial guardedness, and I figured the way to gain his trust was not to push too hard.

We'd taken the more direct route back to Tom's house, following a path that ran along a series of terraces at the side of Tiran's mansion. As we passed one of the outdoor sitting areas, Tom's pace changed slightly and I saw his eyes slide over in that direction. When I followed his gaze, I saw Dusty and Tiran standing near the railing with drinks in their hands.

"Hey Dusty," I called, and then, with a bit of exaggerated mockery, "Hi *Uncle Tiran*." It kind of amused me to call Tiran that after I'd started hearing all those scandalous stories about him. They didn't exactly portray him as avuncular.

If I'd been alone I might have stopped to chat with the two of them, but I suspected Tom would prefer I didn't. Dusty and Tiran waved at us, Tom gave them a small nod, and we continued on our way.

I glanced at Tom as we kept walking and saw his face had closed off again. It occurred to me for the first time that it wasn't just us kids Tom was wary of.

* * *

By the next day I'd made up my mind. I broached the subject with Jimmy first, right after breakfast.

"Hey dad, I was thinking," I said, after the others had left. "When school starts in the fall, I think we should go to the school in Whittier."

Jimmy stopped with a plate of left-overs in his hands and looked at me, then continued slowly to the fridge. "Why do you say that?"

"Well, don't you think it's time? I'll be sixteen then, Lance is fourteen—isn't it time we actually met some other kids? We need to get off the estate sometime."

"Do the others—"

"Lance is *desperate* to get out of here. But I think it'd be good for the other kids too. Tom as well."

For a moment Jimmy didn't answer me, just went on putting things into the fridge. I leaned against the counter with a dishtowel in my hands, waiting.

"Well," he said finally, "we'd have to figure out the security. You'll need to get Rick on board."

"Okay," I said, and as soon as we were finished in the kitchen I headed out to find Rick.

"Most kids aren't so keen to go to school," he drawled, when I tracked him down to his office near the main gate.

"Most kids aren't stuck inside one place for their whole lives."

"I thought you guys liked it here."

"We do! Of course we do. We just want to go to school like regular kids at some point."

"And your dad's okay with that?"

"Yeah, sure, as long as we figure it out with you."

"What about the other kids' folks? Dusty and Kat, Dell and Pat—what do they think?"

"I'll talk to them when you tell me we can do it."

Rick considered me from across the desk where he'd been sitting when I joined him. "Getting you in and out of here every day won't be that big a deal," he said, leaning back in the chair and stretching out his legs. His mild drawl still carried a hint of rural twang from the small town where we'd grown up. "We'll need a bus or van or something to carry all of you, and we can keep it here in the garage so it doesn't need a full sweep every day. The bigger problem'll be the school in Whittier. We'll have to do a complete security review and figure out some protocols with the staff there. But I guess we can work on that over the summer."

It hadn't occurred to me to think about security off-site. "I don't get it," I said. "Why do we need all that protection? I mean, I get that Tiran's rich so people might want to kidnap him or something—but *we're* not. Why would people want to bother us?"

"Lot of desperate people out there these days." Rick gave me a long look. "You think if someone told Tiran to pay up or start getting your body parts in the mail, he'd tell them to go fuck themselves?"

"Oh." I had to think about that for a moment. "No, he'd pay. Okay, I get it. But it doesn't seem fair—I mean, we don't have his money, but we still have to deal with all the hassles."

"Life ain't fair. Anyway, it's not like you don't get advantages from his money in lots of ways."

That was true enough. Our home, the club house, the private tutor—Tiran had treated us well over the years. But I remembered how Jimmy had recently sat Lance, Steve and I down for one of his infrequent paternal talks.

"You boys need to think about your future," he'd told us, as I suppose parents everywhere tell their kids at some point. It was the next part that was unique to us. "Tiran isn't going to support you indefinitely. He's not leaving you anything in his will."

"He told you that?" I asked, laughing in surprise. Never once had I thought about Tiran's will before.

"He didn't tell me he's not going to support you forever—that's just me talking. But he did tell us all about the will. He might even outlive you for that matter—all those experimental medical treatments he does. That's why he still looks twenty-two, even though he's over thirty now."

"I never expected him to leave us his money," I said. "But what if we want to go to college or acting school or something?" I had no worries about my own options—anything seemed possible to me—but I tried to think of what might be in the future for Lance or Steve. "Or, like, training or…or getting set up in a business. Is there money for that?"

"If I can't manage everything on my salary, I'm sure Tiran will help out.

Anyway, that's what I'm saying—you need to decide what you want to do with your lives so I can figure out how to help you. You can't assume that everything you want is just going to be handed to you forever."

I started to see how our connection to Tiran would create this strange sort of dance. He'd made our lives easy and comfortable in so many ways, and given me faith in a future of freedom and possibility—but we were also a kind of poor cousin, dependent on his largesse. Our association with him created a world of opportunity while also making us targets in some ways. As I got older, I saw how our proximity gave us a kind of reflected glory and in some ways increased our prestige. After Jimmy's talk, I started thinking more about how to manage this double-edged sword.

Chapter 4

Rick sorted out the logistics within a few weeks. After that, I spoke to the other parents, and everything seemed settled by the time summer rolled around. The idea of going to school outside the estate sparked a range of responses in the other kids—from Lance's anticipation of endless parties to cautious trepidation from the younger ones. But we all agreed it was time.

I was fifteen going on sixteen that summer, the prince of my little world and ready for anything. Tom still intrigued me and I kept working to gain his trust, while also spending time with the adults and chasing success in the acting business. I wasn't bored, exactly, and I didn't share Lance's impatience, but a kind of restlessness had come over me. I had a taste for more.

Lance spent the break obsessed with meeting other local kids, so that he'd know them when we started school. Since he still wasn't allowed to take any of the cars out by himself, he constantly badgered Enrico or me to drive him into town or, better yet, to the public beach just east of the estate where the kids from Whittier liked to hang out.

"Can't you walk," I said when he pestered me for the second time in one day. "The beach is so close."

"What do you want me to do, climb over the wall?" Lance demanded. He turned to Tom and added with unrepentant pride, "I did that once. Almost got shot down by one of the guards."

"Yeah, you almost got us kicked off the estate. Don't do that."

We were sprawled on the club house porch, unwilling to leave its air-cooled sanctuary on another scorching July day. The high western wall of the estate rose directly behind us, running from the ocean up to the highway. To our north lay open fields, some cultivated for gardens or crops and some left wild, with the long estate driveway winding through them to the main gate in the perimeter fence.

"Well, it takes a fucking hour to walk," Lance complained. "And we're not supposed to bike on the highway."

He exaggerated slightly, but the walk up the estate drive and along the highway to the beach did take almost forty-five minutes, which seemed absurd considering it lay just west of the club house. We couldn't even get to it by water, since Rick had set up virtual borders out into the ocean.

"Too bad they can't put a gate in the fence—right here," I said, gesturing toward the wall directly behind us. "That would solve all our problems."

"Yeah!" Lance said, brightening. "Why don't we get dad to—"

"It's not that simple though." I frowned, thinking it through. "Rick would have to put in security, maybe a checkpoint with an agent…and he'd want some kind of surveillance. Maybe even covering the beach if we're hanging out there a lot."

"So let's ask Rick," Lance said, impatient to get started. The other kids on the porch had looked up from their screens and started listening with interest as well.

"But it's a lot of work. And money. No—Rick wouldn't do it without Tiran's approval."

I could see all the faces around me cloud over. Lance looked morose. "Jimmy'll never ask Tiran," he said, half-contemptuously. "He's scared to ask for anything."

"Not scared exactly," I said, trying to be fair. "But yeah…he won't." As I spoke, an idea began formulating in the back of my brain, and I hesitated a little, considering it.

"Yeah, so forget the pipe dream," Lance griped. "I need a drive—"

I sat up straighter, anticipation creeping over me. "But I will."

Lance looked confused. "You will what?"

"I'll ask Tiran." I stood up with a sudden sense of purpose. "I'm not afraid. Might as well try right now, see if I can find him."

It's not like I never spoke to Tiran; I chatted with him whenever I saw him around, just like I did with the other adults. But this felt different. Maybe because I didn't usually negotiate with him for something I wanted.

* * *

As it turned out, Tiran was away for a few days. His houseboy, Gabe, told me when he'd be back, so I planned to try again then. Just after dinner on the day of his return, I found myself in my bedroom, changing into clean clothes. I hadn't stopped to think about it that first time when I marched over to his house, but now that I'd had chance to dwell on it I felt slightly more self-conscious.

I'd been inside Tiran's house a few times—our family occasionally had dinner with him there—but it still seemed odd to go up to his front door, ring the bell and ask for him.

This time Gabe said he was on the back terrace, so I walked through the large rooms of his inner sanctum until I found a set of open French doors that led outside. Through the doorway, I could see Tiran reclined on a lounge chair on the deck, with someone—was that Pat Van Valkenburg?—standing upright, almost at attention, beside him.

"Hey Uncle Tiran," I called out before I quite reached the threshold. For some reason I wanted to make them aware of my presence right away, just in case.

Tiran turned his head with a curious lifted eyebrow as I came outside. "Barry? You're looking for me?"

"Yeah," I said, then waved at Pat. "Hi, Pat."

Pat managed the briefest of nods in return, his whole body rigid with what I now suspected was fear.

"What an honour." Tiran glanced around, making no move to get up. "Make yourself comfortable. You want a drink? What are you having?"

I saw another chair and pulled it over. "Just a Coke would be great."

"Van," Tiran said without looking at Pat. "And another for me."

When Pat jerked to life and walked over to the outdoor bar, I kept my focus on Tiran, trying to stay nonchalant about whatever might be going on between them.

Meanwhile Tiran looked at me curiously. "Just you here?" he asked. "Where's the other kids?"

"At the club house."

"I saw you with the new boy the other day," Tiran went on. "Tom Van Mertz." Dell's last name was Mertz, and most kids took a combination of their parents' last names for their own. "How's he settling in?"

"He seems fine," I said. Tom's father was right there, but perhaps Tiran was asking more about how he was getting along with the other kids. "Did you know we're going to school in Whittier this fall?"

"Yeah, I heard." Tiran gave me a kind of congratulatory nod. "Guess it's about time you guys got to leave home. Though I thought you liked it here," he added with a kind of faux modesty.

"We do," I said, accepting my drink from Pat. "We love it." With his superpower, Tiran would know that was the truth. "But yeah, it's time for us to meet some other kids."

Tiran took his own drink and said coolly, "Pat was just leaving."

I glanced over his shoulder at Pat, who had started to return to the bar but quickly turned back toward Tiran. "Yes, si... uh," he mumbled, catching himself with a nervous look at me. I could see him hesitate, trapped between responding to Tiran's obvious order and not wanting to reveal too much in my presence. Tiran's mouth tightened and he seemed about to speak when Pat rushed in to forestall him.

"May I be excused then, s... please?" he said, his voice slightly hoarse.

I watched the little scene play out in front of me, trying to look like I didn't notice anything. Pat had always seemed kind of sweet to me, but I knew he'd had problems in the past and these days he'd become a bit of a basket case. We all knew something had happened between him and Tiran. This was the first time I'd seen their fraught relationship up close in person, and that familiar little thrill of excitement flared inside me again as I watched. How did it feel to reduce a grown man to a bundle of nerves in front of you like this?

Tiran only nodded irritably and leaned up to light a cigarette. We both waited until the French doors shut behind Pat, and then Tiran clicked his lighter closed and looked at me again. "So," he resumed. "Is something up? I assume you didn't just drop by to visit me."

Despite the way he treated Pat, Tiran had a way of tempering his self-assurance, the default expectation of getting whatever he wanted, with a kind of courteous self-deprecation, as though willing to entertain the possibility that not everyone would find him irresistible. It gave him a certain charm.

"No," I agreed, and then added playfully, "But I can always come over and keep you company if you need some."

He laughed. "That's kind of you."

"Happy to help," I returned. There was something a little thrilling about casually bantering with this rich, powerful mogul, who grown men like Pat and Dusty seemed to fear and obey. I kind of wanted to drag out the moment.

Tiran, on the other hand, still seemed slightly out of his element with me. I guess his lifestyle didn't bring him into contact with kids very often. Right now, he was looking at me like I'd just stepped out of a spaceship and he was trying his best to maintain intergalactic peace.

"But yeah," I admitted, "it's true, I wanted to ask you about something."

"Anytime," he said gamely.

I turned the glass Pat had given me around in my fingers. "You know that beach next door to us, right? The one where the locals go?"

"Yes."

"All the kids in Whittier hang out there. And we figure the best way to meet them is if we go over there and hang out too. But it's such a pain to get to."

Tiran had been nodding along, but now he looked confused again. "I thought you're allowed to take the self-driving cars out any time?"

"I am, but none of the others are. So they're always asking me to drive them, like, multiple times a day..."

"What about Enrico? Can't he give them a ride?"

"Sure, sometimes, but he has a full-time job. Dad says we're not supposed to bug him too much."

Tiran exhaled slowly, cigarette in one hand and drink in the other, and gave me a long appraising look. "So what's the idea? What do you have in mind?"

"Well, we were thinking..." I leaned forward, forearms on my knees, focused on making my pitch. "You know, the beach is right on the other side of the border wall—like, right behind the club house. What if we just—put a gate in the wall there? We'd be able to get to the beach in about five minutes."

His eyebrows lifted, but I couldn't tell if it was in surprise or objection; he kept a cool neutral expression. "A gate," he repeated. "Well, I imagine Rick would call that a security risk."

"I know," I nodded. "We'd have to work it out with him too. I know it's going to be complicated and probably expensive." I aimed for an ingratiating appeal. "That's why I wanted to get your okay first."

"Ah," he said.

His tone was non-committal, but I thought I heard a hint of amusement underneath the words. Did that mean my approach was working? "Yeah, I mean, we don't want to do anything you won't...*approve* of," I said.

Maybe the hint of deference helped; at least, Tiran smiled as he put out his cigarette in the ashtray on the table beside him. "What's wrong with the beaches here?" he asked.

"Nothing," I said more sincerely. "It's not really about the beach. It's just about meeting other kids."

He nodded and countered, "But aren't you going to meet other kids when you go to school in the fall?"

I realized then that he didn't care about the fence, the gate, the security, the cost; the whole negotiation was just a mildly novel diversion to him, like someone's pet doing an unexpected trick.

"Sure," I said. For a moment I thought about explaining Lance and how he wanted to get ahead of things, how we'd start school on a better footing if we already had some allies there. But Tiran had no interest in any of that. He was just entertaining himself. "Only we're really hoping to get that gate installed this summer…if it's okay with *you*, Uncle Tiran," I finished, half-mocking, half-appealing.

Tiran laughed again. "All right," he said, as though conceding a small battle. "It's fine. You can tell Rick it's okay with me."

He held up his glass to me in a kind of ironic toast, as I headed back to the club house to regale the others with my triumph.

* * *

I guess I created a lot of work for Rick that summer, but we had our gate within a couple of weeks. Rick held a session there to train us all on the security protocols we needed to follow, and I couldn't resist one last reminder to the other kids about who was responsible for this little quality of life improvement.

"Yeah, we all knew you'd do it," Randall said, unimpressed.

But Pasha looked at me with admiration, as he usually did. "I can't believe you just…went and asked him."

By now the other kids had also started to realize the extent of Tiran's wealth and power, not to mention the way we depended on his kindness, and the younger ones had become a bit intimidated by him.

"Yeah, well, if we ever need anything else from him again…" I smirked, always happy to remind the others of my talent for getting things out of adults.

Once the gate was completed, Lance and Steve spent most of their days at the beach; we hardly saw them in the club house except at night. I often took the younger kids over during the day, and we did meet a few of the town kids we'd be going to school with in the fall.

Tom would join us with his sailboard on these trips, and spend a couple of hours in the waves, but I noticed he didn't fall into conversation easily with the locals. I'd keep an eye on him after he got out of the water, and when I could see he'd had enough socializing I'd round everyone up and bring them back to the estate. By this time, we'd let the nanny go, so the little ones were generally in my charge.

I spent a lot of time with Tom that summer. We'd leave the kids safely at the club house or someone's house, and head off together to throw a football around—all sports were new to him, but he quickly became good at them—or go for a run, or hang out on one of the small estate beaches. I liked to join him in the little gym beside his bedroom, watching him work his already formidable muscles while I did a little cardio on another machine.

I still hadn't quite penetrated Tom's mystique. He was friendly enough with me—a little flattered by my attention, I sometimes thought—but he remained reserved and never spoke much about his past, though sometimes he'd make what I thought might be a veiled allusion to it.

"How's your dad?" I asked him, a couple of days after my meeting with Tiran, still thinking about Pat's odd behaviour.

Tom glanced at me. "Fine, I guess."

"You know I—I saw him with Tiran when I went over there," I said.

"Uh-huh."

We were sitting on one of the more secluded beaches, near the small wooded area, watching Doc dig for crabs in the sand. Tom, as usual, gave nothing away in his responses.

"He seemed..." I went on, "I don't know, like he was kind of—scared or something." I wondered what Tom knew of his dad's relationship with Tiran. "You know Tiran's a bit...I mean, he's got his—quirks."

Tom turned his head to give me a sober look, then picked up a piece of driftwood and threw it for Doc. As usual, his upper arm strength meant a casual toss sent the stick flying a few hundred metres.

"Pat told me," he said after a moment. "About his thing with Tiran."

"His thing?"

"His deal. He told me right after I got here."

"Oh." I cocked my head. "That's good."

Tom shrugged. "Yeah. He said I should know because it's kinda hard to miss."

"So...but...what *is* his deal with Tiran? I know they have something going on but..."

This was a little reckless on my part, pushing the limits of what I'd usually press Tom on, but I was intensely curious—both about Pat's arrangement with Tiran, and what Tom knew about the whole thing.

"Pat subs for Tiran." Tom spoke bluntly, but I didn't hear any disparagement or resentment. I'd been wondering if he was bothered by any of it, but evidently not. "He didn't say a lot. Just—he did something bad before, and now he owes Tiran."

That jived with my suspicions, though it didn't tell me much more. I remembered my awkward conversation with Jimmy a few years back. "Why did he…I mean, why would he tell you that?"

"It's hard to hide," Tom said, shrugging. "He turns into this…headcase whenever Tiran's around. I guess he didn't want me to worry."

I nodded, then asked, choosing my words carefully, "Does it…feel weird to think of your dad as a sub?"

He made a small face. "Not really. Just part of life, you know? It's not like I…never saw it before."

I stopped before my open mouth and raised eyebrows gave away my surprise, tucking away this little revelation to consider later.

When I thought about it, alone in my bedroom that night, I realized Tom must have seen plenty of power games in his past life. They would have been even more brutal in his previous environment. Was that why he focused so much on his physical strength? Yet he seemed completely unconcerned about his father's status, despite the stigma it carried, as though he saw no reflection of it on himself.

Despite all his brawn and muscle—Tom never used it here. I'd never seen him throw a punch or make an aggressive move; he never threatened or tried to intimidate anyone. But somehow it infused everything he did. What would it be like to have that kind of understated power? Or to control it?

My thoughts shifted to the scene with Pat on the deck. I remembered his awkwardness, the way he'd been so abashed in front of me. Not all of Tiran's subs reacted that way. Gabe, the houseboy, for example, made no effort to hide his deference; and Dusty seemed to take a kind of manly pride in it. What drew all these men to Tiran? What hold did he have over them? Was it based on fear, or wealth, or some other kind of power? Surely no one would assume that kind of debasement voluntarily.

How did it feel to control people the way Tiran did? At home, he seemed almost indifferent to his power, often barely paying attention to his subs or treating them with vague annoyance, like he did with Pat. But the other day I'd seen vid footage from a premier of one of Dusty's movies that suggested otherwise. The clip showed Tiran sauntering up the red carpet while Dusty—a leather collar around his neck and metallic cuffs on his wrists—followed a few steps behind. At the end of the walk, Tiran made a casual, imperious gesture that summoned Dusty to his side and made their relationship dynamic abundantly clear. So it seemed there were times when Tiran enjoyed showing it off.

By this time I'd started exploring my curiosity in vids, which were widely accessible and could be customized to every conceivable taste. I easily found depictions of what I knew by then was called bdsm. The ropes and chains and floggers were fascinating at first, but once the initial thrill wore off I found myself oddly dissatisfied. None of the vids answered my bigger questions; none of them told me why people did it, or what power felt like. Nothing came close to making me feel like I did when I watched Tiran run his fingers over Dusty's collar, or saw the way Dusty smiled up at him on that red carpet.

Chapter 5

Just a few weeks before school started I got called into a meeting with all the parents. Jimmy messaged my comm on a Wednesday afternoon, asking me to meet him at Dusty's place. When I got there, the blistering mid-August heat had already driven everyone into the climate-controlled interior of the house.

I found Jimmy gathered with Dusty and his partner, Kat Bellavista, as well as Pat and Dell, at the large dining table. Kat, tall and sophisticated in her trademark black suit, offered me a drink, while I glanced around at the serious faces.

"Is everything okay?" I asked.

"Thanks for joining us," Dusty said.

"Sure." I pulled up a chair and accepted my soda from Kat. "Thanks. What's up?"

Jimmy sighed, and took a long breath. "Well, I really hate to say this because I know we agreed and everything...but the truth is, I'm afraid we're all pretty worried about this whole school thing."

"What?" My hand stopped with the glass half-way to my mouth. "But it's settled! We—"

"Yes, I know. We aren't...necessarily changing our minds. We're just a bit concerned about it."

"Why?" I demanded, trying not to sound exasperated. Did Jimmy lie awake at night coming up with new things to worry about? But the others were nodding as well.

Dusty took over. "Look, Barry, none of you guys have ever been to a real school before—or even really spent time with other kids…It's all going to be brand new."

"Yeah, that's why we're doing it! And we've met plenty of kids at the beach now, we—"

"Curtis woke up with nightmares the other night," Dell cut in. "He's very stressed."

"Really?" That was news to me, but Curt had always been a little neurotic. "He seems to be okay when we're at the beach…." I paused, thinking about it a bit more. Actually, Lance and I did most of the talking with the town kids; occasionally maybe Phillip or Steve put a word in. The others tended to hang back and listen. "I'm sure he'll be okay at school," I said, with slightly less conviction this time.

"You've all been so isolated here," Kat said. "You've never been exposed to the real world."

"Especially you, Barry…" Jimmy barely got his words in amidst the others. "I'm not sure if you…"

"You'll be walking into a place where all the other kids have known each other for years." That was Dusty, cutting in; I wasn't at all surprised when he added, "I don't know how Pasha is going to handle it."

"But I'll be there," I pointed out. It felt like they were missing the most salient fact. "I'll keep an eye on everything."

The adults exchanged little smiles, as though they'd been expecting that.

"But you might find—" Jimmy began, still hesitant.

Dell leaned over to pat my forearm where it rested on the table. "We know you'll look after the others," she said. "And we really appreciate that."

"You're always kind to the little ones," Dusty agreed. "Pasha adores you. But how are you going to be in nine classrooms at once?"

"Not nine," I objected. "Curt and Dee are in the same grade. Same with Randall and Pasha. And actually, so are Steve and Lance." We'd done some placement tests over the summer, and no one was shocked to find Lance and Steve behind other kids their age.

"Okay, so, what, five classes then? And what about recesses, you're going to monitor eight different kids at the same time?" Dusty asked

"You aren't even all on the same schedule," Kat added. "You'll have lunch and recess at different times."

I looked around at the solemn faces ringing the table and figured I needed to come up with something before the whole plan blew up. "It's okay. We'll—we'll set up a buddy system."

Five sets of eyes stared into mine, and for a moment everyone was silent. Then Dell repeated, "Buddies?"

"Mentors," I corrected myself, more firmly now. "Partners. We'll match each of the little ones up with an older kid to look out for them. That way I don't have to be everywhere at once."

I watched and waited as the adults exchanged interested looks.

"You mean, like, Pasha with…" Dusty began.

"Pasha with Lance, say." Then—realizing that would hardly be reassuring—I hastily added, "or Steve. Or me. I have to figure out the details, but I'm sure I can swing something that makes sense."

"And…you think the others will go for it?" Dell asked.

"I'll get them on board," I pledged. "Don't worry about it."

There was a bit more discussion, a bunch of questions I had to wing answers to, and some perfunctory objections. But eventually they accepted my plan.

* * *

I spent the next couple of days pondering how to proceed. It's not that I had any doubts about my ability to deliver what I'd promised, but I needed to decide how to sell it. After a bit of consideration, I brought Tom into my confidence.

By this time, Tom and I were fairly…well, I wouldn't say *close*; Tom was still far too reserved for that. But closer. He hung out with me more than with Lance now, probably because I often sought him out. In some ways, Tom allowed himself to be a kind of blank canvas you could pin whatever you wanted on. If Lance and Steve saw him as a fellow gamer and partier, Tom didn't disabuse them of the idea. When he was with me, he listened to my chitchat with what at least passed for interest, and I could sometimes draw him out into actual dialogue.

But I was self-confident enough to believe he preferred being with me. In any case, he readily accepted my invitations, and I enjoyed his company. I often had to explain things and coax him into voicing his thoughts, but when that was successful, his perspective tended to be unusual and intriguing. While he wouldn't offer opinions unasked, he didn't seem to mind so much being asked these days.

We spent a lot of time walking around the estate or hanging out at one of the beaches. I think Tom liked to get away from the noise and stimulation of the other kids, while I preferred to have him to myself.

For this discussion, though, I brought him up to my bedroom, which was a large loft up in the attic—I'd naturally taken over the best space in the house. When I explained what I wanted to do and why, Tom didn't seem fazed.

"So you'll back me up?" I asked.

"Sure," he said, with his usual neutrality. "But Lance? And Phillip? You think they'll go for it?"

"I'll manage Lance," I said; my strategy centered on that. "I was kinda hoping you might help with Pip. You think you could talk to him in advance?"

He shrugged, considering it for a moment, and then said, "Sure. I can try."

To Tom's credit—or perhaps Phillip's—his efforts seemed to work. When I gathered everyone up into the club house for my pitch, I could see from the faint amusement in Phillip's grey eyes that he knew what to expect and wouldn't try to sabotage it.

"*Buddies*?" Lance said when I finished explaining. "I'm not spending my days baby-sitting little kids."

"It's not just baby-sitting," I reminded him. "They're supposed to do what you tell them, too." I hadn't told the parents that part, but I needed something to make this arrangement more palatable on both sides. Besides, if the adults got to play those little games, why couldn't we?

"So Lance and Steve are gonna boss us around even more?" Randall asked. "I don't see why—"

I glanced at my notes. "You're with Tom, Ran."

"…Oh." Randall stopped abruptly, darting a glance toward Tom.

"And Curtis is with you," I added. Randall always struck me as the most well-adjusted of us kids. He'd be good for Curt.

"Hey, buddy," Randall said, giving a little wave to Curtis, who sat frowning on the couch beside Steve, a controller in his hands.

"Who do I get?" Steve said, without looking up from his game. At least he was curious enough to ask.

I checked my list again. "Hm. You get Pasha."

At the round table in the middle of the room, Pasha lifted his head up from the screen in front of him and fixed a long, thoughtful gaze on Steve.

"What about me?" Mary-Dee demanded. "Who's my buddy?"

"You get Phillip."

She squealed a little. "Mine's the best!"

I laughed, not surprised that the little kids were an easier sell. Even with the expectation of some kind of obedience in exchange, they liked the idea of special access to an older buddy.

Curtis was still twisting the controller around in his hands. "Are people gonna be mean to us at school?" he asked.

"Oh…I don't think so," I said, honestly. "The grown-ups are just worried because we haven't been to a school before. It's going to be different, that's all."

He looked away, at the screen, for a moment, and then down at his hands. "Scary different?"

"Don't worry, Curt," Randall said, much more reassuring than me. "I'll show you around. No one's gonna be mean to you."

Tom and I exchanged quick glances. I'd told him Randall would make a solid partner.

Lance, the last hold-out, looked around the room skeptically. "I can't believe you're all going along with this. I don't aim to spend my high school days hanging out with a baby."

Time to deal with him head-on. "First of all," I said, "if we don't do this, we might not be going to school at all. Jimmy and the others were ready to call off the whole thing." A slight exaggeration, but not entirely false.

Lance lifted his chin and drew his shoulders back. "There is *no way* I'm staying in this hell-hole another year."

Hell-hole? He didn't remember where we'd come from. "You can go fight with them about it on your own if you want," I said, keeping my voice even. "But second. You get Phillip."

That stopped him. He took in a surprised breath. "Phillip's not a kid."

"Yeah," I said. That was the genius of my plan.

While we waited for Lance to adjust to this new information, Phillip caught my eye with a sardonic glint. "What about you, Barry?" he asked. "Who do you get?"

I made a show of consulting my notes, but I didn't need to. "Tom," I said. "I get Tom."

Phillip gave a knowing nod, and I shifted my gaze over his head to Tom, who still wore that neutral expression. We waited a moment in silence as Lance continued pondering.

"I guess Phillip's okay," he said finally, and the deal was done.

* * *

School started without incident. Rick arranged for an old-fashioned yellow school bus to take us there and back. We'd all meet up at the garage in the mornings and ride together. The youngest kids, Curtis and Mary-Dee, were in sixth grade, and the school in Whittier covered both middle and high school, so we were all in the same place.

As it turned out, our parents' fears were mostly unfounded. They hadn't accounted for the advantages we got from our situation. It turned out the local kids were slightly in awe of their infamous, wealthy, eccentric neighbour, and they'd been curious for years about the kids isolated behind the high perimeter walls of his estate. Meeting us in person dispelled some of the mystery but our proximity to Tiran still impressed them. We made the transition painlessly.

It was an exciting time for me, at least at first. I enjoyed meeting so many new people—the kids in my classes, the teachers, the extended school community. I'd been particularly curious about girls my own age, who were in such short supply at home and consequently somewhat mysterious to me. I joined a few clubs and sports teams, and everyone I met, from jock to theatre kid, mostly accepted me.

The only awkward incident I remember from that first year at Whittier High School happened a few months after we started. At recess I saw a group of kids I vaguely knew, standing in a circle near the football field, their voices raised in an escalating dispute. I walked toward them, wondering what it was about. A boy in a grey sweatshirt with his back toward me spoke more vociferously than the others, and I caught the tail end of his argument as I approached.

"...not fucking playing with that *ghetto trash*."

I paused, trying to process the words, and the boy stopped, apparently alerted to my presence by some of the others. He turned to face me, his skin tinging pink.

"Oh, hey, Hawkins," he said quickly, making a conciliatory gesture with one hand. "I...I didn't mean you. I was talking about...uh..."

Me? Why would I think he meant me? I held the boy's gaze, but over on the football field where a few other kids waited, I'd already caught sight of Tom, standing slightly apart, aloof as always. "Yeah?" I said encouragingly. "Who were you talking about?"

The boy's face deepened to a red so dark it almost matched his sweatshirt. He looked away, mumbling something, and one of the other kids, an older girl holding a football, stepped over to me.

"He didn't mean nothing," the girl said. "We're just starting up a game. You wanna play?"

"Sure," I said, taking the ball out of her hands. "As long as I get Tom on my team."

I headed over to the field without looking back, the other kids following behind me, and I never heard anything similar again. But I often thought about those words. I didn't exactly know what they meant, although the sentiment was obvious, and I understood they were directed at Tom. What I didn't quite get was why they might also apply to me.

There were a lot of things I didn't get in those early days of exposure to a new world. I was eager to pick up all the common knowledge I'd missed in my years on the estate—the kids' shared jokes and memes, the popular music and media, the social dynamics. At the same time, I had to remember that this was a different world from the one I'd always known. I was so used to being in charge at home that at first I assumed I'd make all final decisions here as well, instinctively correcting anyone who took a different approach from mine. It took a lot of effort to break those habits.

When the basketball coach invited me to be team captain, midway through my first year, I agreed without much thought or surprise. But later I reconsidered. At home I'd been captain of every team in every game we played, by birthright or default, and I wasn't sure I wanted to keep following the same pattern in this new environment. The next day I thanked the coach and resigned my position. I didn't tell him it felt too much like a familiar road I didn't need to travel again.

I picked up casual friendships quickly and easily, but after the initial exhilaration wore off I noticed an odd lack of connection with the other students. Their lives—centred on the small town of Whittier and filled with local gossip, school sports, the latest tech games, and weekend shenanigans at the teen hang-out spot—didn't resonate with me. Maybe I'd started too late to really integrate into this world.

I was a junior that year, close to graduating, and thinking about my future. I still figured acting was the best path to the life of fame and power I wanted, so I signed up for the theatre program at school. I liked the classes and fit in okay; learning to slightly exaggerate my gestures, voice and expressions the way the other kids did came naturally to me. But none of it seemed relevant to my actual experience in the industry.

Most of the other kids in the program had only ever worked in local musicals or plays. They struck me as earnest and passionate about their career goals, but with almost no real-life experience—the complete reverse of me.

I gravitated toward a couple of girls and one or two boys who struck me as more interesting than the others. Some became friends, and I occasionally hung out with them in Whittier or at their homes; we didn't generally bring anyone back to the estate because it was too awkward to get them through security. I went on a few dates and had a couple of minor physical experiences, trying out both girls and boys before concluding, as I'd suspected, that I much preferred boys. But I didn't end up developing any deep relationships in the couple of years I spent at Whittier High.

The rest of the gang from home seemed to be doing well at school too. Lance fit right in with the local kids and soon became their de facto leader. He didn't pay much attention in class, of course, but spent plenty of time at the Point—the local teen gathering spot—or at house parties in town, usually dragging Steve along with him. His interests had somehow evolved from gaming and race cars to the music scene, so he liked to call himself a DJ and take charge of the soundtrack at local events.

The younger kids had no trouble adapting to the more formal school setting or the social environment. The buddy system seemed to help, with the older kids showing the little ones around, helping them get to class, stepping in if trouble threatened, making sure they got safely on the bus at night. In exchange, the younger kids had no great objection to running errands, fetching and carrying, and mostly doing what they were told.

When occasional differences arose, they all turned to me to arbitrate, as usual. I didn't mind. It was entertaining to watch the way different bonds developed between the pairs. Lance and Phillip more or less ignored each other, but Phillip was always kind to Mary-Dee. I thought I could see Curtis grow a little less anxious under Randall's calm protection. And Steve and Pasha—well, Steve was no match for Pasha's trusting blue-eyed gaze. Generally well-meaning but impressionable, Steve had always tended to go along with Lance's antics. But now, being responsible for sweet, compliant Pasha seemed to make him think twice.

"It's really weird, man," he confided to me once. "When I'm with him I kind of...feel like I could be a better person."

I tried not to laugh, but I knew what he meant. Pasha reminded me of one of those boys in a really old storybook who believed in doing the right thing; or maybe a knight with a code of duty and honour. He never said anything like that out loud, of course, but being near him somehow made you start thinking that way.

The time Lance stole someone's car from a local party, disappeared for a day and eventually turned up in a hospital two towns over, I asked Steve why he hadn't gone along for the ride.

"Well, Pasha was at the party with me," he said, sounding slightly baffled. "And he said, *But how will I get home?* So…" Steve stared at me, equal parts mystified and helpless. "Well, I couldn't just leave him there alone."

As for my 'buddy', I enjoyed having a kind of special connection with Tom. I kept a close eye on him at school, especially once I realized he might be more of a target than the rest of us. He stood out in so many ways—his accent, limited vocabulary and special classes, not to mention the striking physical qualities. But he mostly seemed to hold his own.

We didn't see each other much during the day, being in different areas with different routines. I arranged my schedule so I had study hall during his lunch break, where I could check in on him regularly. The odd time I caught a gleam of trouble on the horizon—a hint of mockery, someone asking too many questions—and I'd step in to defuse any potentially awkward encounters. Tom never said anything about it.

After school he'd hang out in my bedroom with me for a couple of hours, ostensibly to look after any errands I might assign while I did my homework. In reality, I rarely asked him to do much for me; that was part of the deal I'd offered when I first asked him to back me on the buddy system. But I liked the idea of having some kind of official control over all that quiet power.

Tom also got along well with Randall, who would quietly help him with his school work at home and then hang around to watch vids with him afterward. Randall seemed to recognize that Tom appreciated low-key company and not too much conversation.

Chapter 6

Whittier, an affluent, mostly white little town that hadn't been impacted much by the climate upheavals, made a big deal out of Memorial Day. On the estate we'd never paid much attention to it, or even been aware of the town's celebrations. But this year we heard all our classmates' excited chatter and picked up their enthusiasm by osmosis. So, for the first time, we kids planned to check things out. I invited Jimmy to join us but didn't push when I saw his reluctance—he didn't really know anyone in Whittier, and he could use the time off.

We spent the day at the public beach along with pretty much the whole town. Under brilliant blue skies and an already dazzling sun, locals had set up barbeques and beer gardens, gazebos and music stages, banners and streamers. Younger kids milled around the vintage petting zoos and modern roboriders, while teens gravitated to each other, forming small clumps that merged into larger ones and then spread out again. We swam and paddled and raced, nicked unattended beer bottles from tables, dared each other into pranks, ate snacks and smoked on blankets spread over the green grass in the shade of tall trees. Some of my high school friends introduced me to their parents, and I marvelled inwardly at their wholesome nuclear families.

By mid-afternoon, everyone was spent. Little ones whined at their parents' elbows; older kids muttered cranky insults or threats at each other, too languid to be taken seriously; adults staggered across the sand, not just from the heat.

There would be fireworks and a bonfire on the beach at dusk, but we all needed some down time before we returned for the evening activities. I gathered up the younger kids and my beagle, Doc, told my classmates I'd catch them later, and led the way back to the estate. Even Lance and Steve followed me, too burnt out and wasted to continue partying for now.

Back home, we split up and headed to our own houses, agreeing to meet at the club house around seven o'clock so we could go back to the beach together. I took a short nap then showered, changed my clothes and went downstairs for dinner. Since we'd been eating all day, Jimmy just gave us a light supper, during which Mary-Dee and Randall regaled him with the day's highlights. Steve and Lance didn't show up to eat, but they met us at the club house later.

Just after seven, when everyone had gathered and I was starting to think about herding people out the door, a harsh, high-pitched siren-like blast suddenly wailed through the air.

We all stopped mid-movement, staring at each other. Before I could speak, the wail changed into words—loud, automated, warning words repeating on a loop and pouring out through loudspeakers across the estate.

Attention. Attention. Unauthorized access. Intruders on premises.

Oh. It was the first time anything like this had happened but I wasn't especially worried; Rick had spent years preparing for just such a scenario. I pulled out my comm, saw it had no service, and remembered Rick telling me that in an emergency he'd shut off all but his own communications. My training kicked in, and I went over to lock the front door of the club house, then shut and bolted all the windows and the back door.

The sound of the loudspeakers still permeated the club house walls, but the words in the incessant, robotic chant changed.

Attention intruders. Halt. You are not permitted on the premises. Halt immediately.

I could hear the noise of drones gathering around us, and glanced outside to see a small black cloud streaming across the sky, toward the ocean and the cliffs behind Tiran's house.

No one had spoken yet. I took a quick survey inside the room. Doc stood near the front door growling nervously, his ears stiff and alert. The kids were still mostly silent and frozen, but Curtis looked like he was about to lose it so I started moving toward him. Then the intercom beside the door lit up.

"You kids there?" came Rick's distinctive voice, drawling a little less than usual but still composed. "Everyone all right?"

"*Rick*!" Mary-Dee gasped, a wobbly squeak from behind me. "What's happen—?"

I jumped in quickly. "Yeah, Rick. We're here. We're fine."

"Doors locked?"

"Yes, doors and windows locked."

"Good. You all need to shelter in place. No one leave till I give the okay."

"Got it."

"Might just be nothing, but you never know. We aren't taking chances. I'll keep you posted."

The intercom light flicked off, and I turned quickly to Mary-Dee. "It's okay, Dee," I told her. "Rick's gonna take care of everything. We just need to stay here for now."

Through the locked windows, I could see a group of androids marching along the perimeter wall. On the other side of our building, a small array of mini-tanks rolled down toward the ocean, and more drones circled overhead. The discordant words filling the air across the estate grew harsher and more menacing, alternating with a screeching repeated alarm.

I looked around the room again. Lance looked more annoyed than anything; Randall had his arm around a shaking Curtis; Phillip pulled Mary-Dee into a reassuring hug...but wait, where was—

Steve appeared at my elbow. "Barr, listen—"

And at the same moment, Rick's voice came back over the intercom. "Barry, Dusty's asking about Pasha. I just want to..."

I spun around in a circle, searching, as Steve's fingers dug into my forearm. "He's at the cave," he whispered. "At the bottom of the cliffs. He told me he was going—"

"Stall them." It made no sense, but all I could think of was Dusty's inevitable panic. The deadbolt on the front door clicked open under the touch of my finger on the keypad; the doorknob turned in my hand. "Lock it behind me," I told Steve, and then I was outside.

I ducked the cameras, whose locations we all knew perfectly, so Rick's guys wouldn't see me, and headed for the back of our building. One of the tunnels actually ran under the club house but it could only be accessed from outside. I found the old, almost abandoned cellar door, praying the touchpad would still work—it did—and then I was running down the concrete steps to the tunnel entrance.

I knew exactly which cave Steve meant—a small, hollowed-out space at the base of the tallest cliff behind Tiran's house, just big enough to function as a kind of fort when we were little. Nowadays hardly anyone went there, but I immediately understood how Pasha might have sought it out as a peaceful little sanctuary after so much wearing excitement that day.

The warren of tunnels underneath the estate had mainly been used for construction. At one point Rick thought he might include them as part of his security network, but since most of the new protective technology was sky- or land-based, I guess he abandoned that idea. In any case, there were no signs of life now; these corridors probably hadn't been used since our last game of Sardines a few years back. There were no cameras or intercoms in here either—no communication channels at all. I couldn't reach Pasha or Dusty or Rick, and none of the adults would be able to find their way through these paths anyway. Rick might have an outdated map somewhere, but no one knew the routes and shortcuts like I did.

I ran where I could and crawled where I had to, using my comm for light and searching out the turn-offs and side-channels I needed. Small puddles of water splashed under my feet, and the air smelled of moss and mildew. It took a little over ten minutes before I saw a gleam of light in the distance ahead.

When I stepped out of the last tunnel into the broader expanse of the cave, Pasha was crouched against one of the side walls with his back to me, near the opening. In front of the cave, at the base of the cliffs, a small rocky ledge ran along the ocean shore. To the left, it narrowed and petered out against the cliff face, where half-way up a small cloud of ballistics drones currently hovered. On the other side, the ledge stretched westward, passing a small dock where a few watercraft were usually tied up, and widening until it merged into the sand of Tiran's beach. Now, along the grassy banks at the top of the beach, a battalion of minitanks and armed androids, weapons out, had gathered into columns and rows, slowly advancing toward the water.

Pasha didn't hear me over the blasting audio that still filled the air. When I reached him, his rigid body sprang backwards at my touch, and I had a momentary glimpse of deep, glittering eyes in a face blanched silvery white, before he collapsed against my chest. I wrapped my arms around his back to support him and felt the dampness of his tears on my shirt. Pasha was twelve by then and no coward, but I could imagine how it must have felt, alone and isolated, surrounded by the cacophony of alarms and watching an automated army descend around him.

I tugged him gently backwards, into the cover of the cave. Rick's team had no idea we were out here and I didn't want to inadvertently set off any nearby sensors or trip some kind of alarm.

"Barry, what's going on? Is it because of them?" Pasha pulled away from me and pointed out toward the ocean. I didn't understand him at first, until I spied the silhouette of a small boat, and then another, and perhaps one more, a few hundred meters from the shore. Then I looked over at the dock and realized it was empty.

"Wait, is that—the intruders, did they take the boats out?"

We were hissing into each other's ears to be heard over the racket.

"Intruders?" Pasha gripped my arm. "It's just a bunch of guys from town—I recognized one of them, it's my friend Cody's dad."

"You saw them? What—how many..."

"There's like, five or six of them, I think they're drunk or something."

"Do they have any weapons?"

"I don't know but—no, I'm sure they just came from next door. Barry, the robots aren't gonna, like—attack them, are they?"

I hesitated, then crept up to the front of the cave again. To the left I saw a small cambot, maybe one of the original group Rick had set up all those years ago, still toddling along the narrow ledge beside the ocean. As it made its way back toward the cave entrance I dropped to the ground and slithered forward, hooking a fist around its wheels and pulling it closer to us. Once I had it inside the cave, I waved into the screen until one of the guards monitoring the cams caught sight of me.

"*Barry*? Is that the—what are you doing?" Her voice crackled through the cambot's small speaker.

"I need to speak to Rick, can you patch him in for me?"

"Hang on." The guard was a pro; she didn't argue with me. As we waited, I put an arm around Pasha's still trembling shoulder.

"Barry, what's going on?" Rick's voice came over the speaker, brusque and alert now.

"I'm at the cave under the cliffs, I can see the—"

"I told you to *stay put*."

"I came to get Pasha. Listen, the intruders are just a bunch of drunken locals out for a joy-ride. Pasha saw them getting in the boats, he says they're unarmed, one of them is his friend's father. Can you call off your army, or at least notch them down a couple levels? Or maybe get an actual human down here to communicate?" The tension and adrenaline, not to mention the still-blaring alarm system, made me crankier than usual.

I could hear Rick speak sharply in the background, issuing orders and directions. Then he came back on the speaker. "We're on it, Barry. Now—how did you get there?"

"I came through the tunnels. I can bring Pasha back the same way. Then we'll wait at the club house with the others, okay?"

Rick gave a little sigh, of exasperation or relief. "Okay. But this time stay put. And...thanks."

We made it back without incident, Pasha never letting go of my hand though he knew the tunnels almost as well as I did. By the time we reached the club house his skin had returned to its normal level of paleness, and he answered all the other kids' excited questions calmly.

We found out afterward that Rick and his team did go down to the beach in person, de-commissioning some of the bots and keeping just enough to restrain the intruders when they eventually steered the boats back to shore. Of course they turned out to be harmless—just curious, overheated, and intoxicated townsfolk, a combination that not surprisingly led to some unwise decisions.

Once the all-clear came, we kids didn't even make it out of the club house before we were beset by our parents, teary and frantic, trying to hug all of us at once. Dusty, in particular, not convinced by whatever Steve had told him, was desperate to find Pasha.

Our story came out shortly, when Rick filled everyone in on Pasha's misadventure and mine. I braced myself for lectures about not following Rick's directions but I was kind of treated like a hero instead. I tried to point out that Pasha was the real hero—he hadn't broken any instructions, he'd been alone, scared and unprotected, and yet he still paid enough attention to provide the information that defused the whole situation. But the adults seemed convinced that I'd risked life and limb on some kind of daring top-secret rescue mission, and couldn't stop talking about my *courage* and *fortitude*.

That night Tiran invited the whole estate to a big gathering on his terrace, where we could all hash out the events of the day, exchange stories, and decompress. There was a lot of fussing over me. Rick, back to his usual unruffled self, made a speech praising everyone for following protocols and thanking me and Pasha in particular. When Dusty saw me, he threw his arms around my neck and could barely speak through his tears. Jimmy walked around beaming like he'd personally raised the next messiah or something.

It was all a bit odd, but I've never really minded attention so I rolled with it. Pasha might have been a bit overwhelmed, but Dusty and Kat kept him close to their sides all night and shielded him from the worst of it.

* * *

The next day when I showed up at the club house around noon, Lance glanced away from his game and said sardonically, "Well, if it isn't the hero of the hour."

I rolled my eyes. "Cut it out, Lance. I can't help it if—"

My comm buzzed, and I looked down to see a message from Rick, asking me to meet him at his office. Intrigued, I headed over there directly. They must have found something out about yesterday's incident.

The security office was located near the main estate gate. I walked through the building to Rick's office and was surprised to find Jimmy in a chair in front of the desk, with Rick behind it as usual.

"Hey, dad. Hey, Rick. What's up?"

"Thanks for coming," Rick said. They both looked more serious than they had last night. "Take a seat. We wanted to talk to you. Not sure if you know, we identified the location of yesterday's breach."

It took me a moment to parse his words. "Oh, you mean you figured out where they got in? Where was it?"

Rick kept his gaze on my face. "It was at the side gate, the one behind the club house."

"Ohhh." A rush of thoughts tumbled through my mind. That gate had been my idea—hadn't I promised we'd keep it safe? How could this have happened? "I'm sorry," I began, my mind still running through the previous day's events. "I know I promised to make sure everyone followed protocols. But..."

We'd gone through the gate on our way back from the daytime activities at the beach, just a couple of hours before the intrusion—someone must have left it open then. Who'd been the last one through, though? I remembered Lance and Steve following behind the rest of us, and winced. It made sense, but I didn't want to rat them out. My voice trailed off as I wondered what to say.

Rick leaned forward, folding his arms on the desk. "We've reviewed the cambot footage. Barry, it seems you were the last one to go through the gate."

Huh? No I wasn't. I squinted at him, not understanding.

"The footage shows you went in last, and left the gate open behind you."

"Well—" Confusion made me say more than I meant to. "That's because Lance and Steve were there. They were right behind me. I assume...I mean, I guess, maybe they—"

"They weren't there. We can see it on the recording—Lance stops to talk to someone, and then the two of them go back to the beach. They got dropped off here at the main gate later by one of Steve's friends."

I sat motionless, staring at Rick with my mouth slightly agape. It seemed impossible to make sense of what I was hearing. "No," I said finally, my voice fainter this time. "They were right there..."

"They were behind you at first, but not when you got to the gate. No one followed you in." Rick leaned back in his chair and watched as I tried to absorb this information.

"But...I..." I said finally, and then stopped.

"You know that door has to be shut for the security systems to activate," Rick went on after a moment. "That's why we have the protocols."

Of course I knew that. What was happening?

"Barry, you know how much we rely on you," Jimmy said from his chair in the corner. "We all count on you to keep everyone safe."

When he stopped, there was a silence in the room. I looked around, not seeing anything.

"I know," I said finally.

"I guess mistakes happen," Rick said, not sounding very convinced. "But aren't you sixteen now? We need to know if we can depend on you or not."

Beside me I heard Jimmy sigh. "I've always had so much faith in you, Barry. What if something had happened?"

For one bizarre, blinding moment I thought they were going to expel me, tell me I had to leave the estate. I had my mouth open to ask where I would go before I realized they weren't saying that.

"What—" My voice came out hoarsely. "What do you want to do?"

Rick shook his head. "I don't know, I'll have to speak to my team. And the other parents. We were lucky this time, nothing really came of your mistake. But they might not want the risk of something like this happening again. We may have to close that gate up permanently."

When they finally let me go, I didn't return to the club house. I left Jimmy with Rick and walked alone to my empty house, up all the stairs to my bedroom in the loft. Then I lay down on my bed and stared out the window across the room, where green tree tops swayed slightly under another brilliant blue sky, and saw nothing.

After a long time, Tom came in, wondering what had happened to me. I didn't feel like talking much but eventually it all came out. I looked at Tom's muscular arms as I spoke, wondering how it might feel to be wrapped up in them. Tom listened without expression as usual, and at the end he shrugged his shoulders.

"Well," he said, "nothing happened."

That kind of missed the point, but I wasn't up to arguing with him.

"If you don't need anything, I'll go back," he added. "You comin'?"

The last thing I really wanted to do was face the other kids. But it had to happen sooner or later. After a moment I pushed myself up from the bed and said I'd go with him.

Everyone was at the club house when we arrived, and they all turned to look at me. I guess they'd seen or heard about my abrupt departure and figured, like I had, that it must have been related to yesterday's events.

"Hey guys." I didn't really need to get their attention; I already had it. I stood with my back against the door, my hands twisting the doorknob behind me, and took in a breath. "Might as well tell you," I began. On my way over, I'd had some idea of brazening it out, of making my confession without embarrassment or apology. But now I found it hard to keep my voice steady. "I just met with Rick and dad. They checked the cambot footage to find out where those idiots came in. It was through our gate. Turns out I left it open when we came back from the Memorial Day thing yesterday."

The faces around me showed surprise, shock, and in some cases, an odd kind of sadness. No one looked angry.

"Yeah..." I went on. "I thought Lance and Steve were right behind me but they weren't. So...the whole mess was my fault. I'm sorry I fucked everything up. And the worst thing is, they might close the gate up for good."

Lance had resumed his game after I started speaking, but now he threw his controller down onto the couch beside him. "If they shut that thing up, I am done with this place."

I looked at him without understanding.

Randall piped up before I could respond. "Who cares about the stupid gate. It's not like we're locked up in here. Don't worry about it, Barr, it could've been any of us."

The others mostly seemed to be nodding in agreement, but even so, I couldn't bring myself to stick around the club house with them. It was a while before I felt like hanging out with the kids again.

In the end, Rick left the gate as it was, and we never had another incident. But that turned out to be the least of my concerns. The bigger impact was how the adults treated me after everything came out, and I don't mean just Jimmy and Rick. They all had the same way of looking at me, like I'd let them down or betrayed them. The first time I saw Dell she made a wistful little comment about how she'd always trusted me with her kids. I couldn't even argue when Dusty said something like, "He wouldn't have needed rescuing if you'd just shut the gate in the first place." It was weeks before I stopped feeling like an imposter.

* * *

The kids at school didn't know much about my drama at home, which helped me forget about it while I was there. By now I was planning for the summer; I didn't like the idea of just hanging around at home, or in Whittier or the local beach, as I had every previous summer. I didn't want a regular job—I was still picking up occasional acting work—but there had to be something I could do to better prepare for the future, the world outside the estate.

Some of the kids in my theatre program took acting classes in the summer, and when I looked into it I found one that appealed to me—a highly regarded course at a prestigious industry school in downtown New Ellay. The only problem was the price tag it came with.

I considered asking Jimmy if we could afford it but, somehow, the idea of appealing to him for help made me hesitate. It wasn't that I thought he was angry or upset with me, exactly; I knew Jimmy loved me despite my flaws. It was more because I had a vague sense that my plans, my ambitions, were on a different kind of scale than he would understand. It was going to be up to me to figure out how to make them work.

Early on a late June evening I walked up the stairs that led from the ocean to the top of the cliffs, then followed a path skirting along the terraces outside Tiran's house. I was alone, wrapped up in my thoughts, pondering my options for the summer, my career, and the rest of my life.

"Hey, Barry."

Tiran's voice startled me; I'd just been thinking about him as a potential funding option. I hadn't noticed him on the deck beside me, leaning on the railing with a drink in one hand and a cigarette in the other.

"Hi, Tiran," I said.

Maybe he thought I sounded a bit more subdued than usual, because he gave me a curious look and, after a short pause, added, "You okay? Wanna come up for a drink?"

The unusual invitation took me by surprise, then seemed fortuitous. I recovered quickly and nodded. "Yeah, okay."

Tiran called to Gabe while I found some stairs leading up through the terraces to the deck Tiran occupied. I took my usual Coke, and parked myself against the railing opposite him.

"So what are you doing at home on a Friday evening?" I asked, trying to rally. "Shouldn't you be out...debauching virgins or something?"

Tiran laughed. "Rocky's coming this weekend. Wanted to be around when he gets here."

Rocky Van Valkenburg, Pat's older brother and Tiran's best friend, lived further up the coast with his wife and two children, but occasionally came to the estate for weekend visits.

"Is he bringing the kids?" I asked. They were a little older than me; I'd met them a few times.

"No, just him."

I nodded and tried to think of something else to banter about, but Tiran kept looking at me with that odd curious expression.

"Are they all still being mean to you?" he asked.

"What? Who?"

"The adults. You know, about the gate thing."

The abrupt change of topic took me aback, and I didn't know how to respond.

"I mean, they were pretty fast to put all the blame on you, weren't they?"

"I—" I opened my mouth and hesitated uneasily. "I mean, I did leave it open. It was my fault."

Tiran waved his cigarette dismissively. "You're a kid, you made one mistake. I think you're allowed one mistake, aren't you? Without being treated like the anti-Christ."

I thought I'd recovered some equilibrium by now, but somehow his words brought everything back, a rush of emotion that threatened to overwhelm me. "I'm old enough," I began, and then had to stop, blinking.

"Yeah, I've noticed they treat you like you're in charge of everyone. But you're what, sixteen?" He shook his head. "That's just a kid."

I couldn't understand the tears that suddenly drenched my cheeks. Or why, when Tiran saw my face and put an arm briefly around my shoulders to give me a reassuring squeeze, I had to choke back sobs.

He didn't say anything else, just let go and leaned back against the railing across from me, smoking, till I managed to calm down.

"Sorry," I said finally, with a little gasp. "I don't know what—"

He gave that dismissive wave again. "Forget about it. You want another drink? Maybe a real one this time?"

That made me laugh between gulps for air. "You just said I'm still a kid."

"Oh yeah," he said with a smile. "Another Coke then?"

I shook my head. "I'm good." I swallowed again, and abruptly decided to take the leap. "Hey Tiran. I wanted to ask you. There's this acting class I'd like to sign up for this summer, but it's really expensive. Do you think you could...help me out with it?"

He didn't seem surprised at this change of subject. Afterwards I realized he probably got asked for money every day. "The one at the Mountebank

Institute?" he said. "I've heard it's good. Lots of pros go there."

"Yeah, that's the one," I said. "It's just a lot for Jimmy to cover, I think."

Tiran nodded. "Sure," he said. "I'll let the accountant know."

"You mean Paul?"

"Paul Armstrong? No, he manages the Foundation—you know, the do-gooder stuff. Not my personal bills."

After that, I never asked Jimmy for anything again. Whenever expenses came up—new head shots, coaching, skill training to build my resume—I went straight to Tiran. It never seemed to occur to him to say no to me, and what Jimmy didn't know wouldn't hurt him.

Meanwhile, that unexpected sympathy from such an unlikely source must have been just what I needed to start getting my mojo back. By the end of the summer, I'd pretty much fully recovered. The funny thing was that the person I recovered into always felt slightly different from the person I'd been before. My confidence returned with a kind of edge, more insular and self-reliant now. And while I eventually regained my usual assurance with the other kids and adults at home, my connection to the estate seemed to have shifted in some indefinable way.

Part II: Chapter 7

The Mountebank summer course marked a kind of turning point for me. Based in downtown New Ellay, the Institute prided itself on its close relationship with the vid production industry, offering programs that focused as much on networking, connections, and working the system as they did on skills development. The facilitator of my course, a veteran actor and director herself, often brought friends and colleagues from the industry to class, ostensibly to teach but really to provide us with insider access. The whole thing catered mainly to people already deep in the business, mostly older than me and only nominally there for the acting lessons. I fit right in.

Unsurprisingly, my connections to Dusty and Tiran gave me instant credibility. Not that I mentioned anything myself, but word got out fast and the other students seemed almost awestruck at first. In this crowd, Dusty had a reputation as a hard-working, highly respected, A-list star, while Tiran was a figure of mystery and reverence—not for his personal shenanigans but for the immense power and influence his money wielded in the industry.

Even the facilitator treated me with a kind of deference. At her suggestion, I asked Dusty to come in for a session one day, and he cheerfully obliged, cementing my reputation with the rest of the class. But when the facilitator hinted that a similar visit from Tiran would be welcome, I gently passed.

I'd spent a lot of time, by now, thinking about Tiran's power and how he got it; the way he attracted people to him. Watching his casual domination over other men always sent a little frisson of electricity shivering down my back. If I wanted a taste of what he had, I figured I needed a similar quality that would draw people to me. Without the kind of money or influence Tiran had, I would need a different currency, and fame had always seemed like the obvious choice. I couldn't understand Dusty; if I had as much celebrity power as he did, I wouldn't throw it away subbing for someone else. I would know how to use it.

But the more time I spent with the Mountebank crowd, where connections, status, and appearance counted for everything, the more I caught glimpses of other possibilities. Fame had universal value, of course, but I saw how people treated me when they knew where I lived and who I knew. Could *access* be a kind of currency as well? I also recognized the particular power of youth and beauty, especially in this older crowd. I'd always noticed how people responded to Tom's striking presence, and now I thought about cultivating my own advantages. Perhaps I had a few tools to work with.

I was familiar with New Ellay because of my acting work, but this was my first chance to spend time in the big city socially. While the class field trips to vid production studios didn't do anything for me, I liked hanging out with my classmates afterwards, at restaurants or coffee shops, or bars when I could get away with it. I'd be turning seventeen in September and could make myself look considerably older when I wanted to. Once in a while we'd get invited to industry parties or events, and I especially enjoyed mixing with the movers and shakers of the world where I intended to find fame.

I had my driver's licence now, and took one of Tiran's cars into the city each day. In mid-August, Tom—who had somehow started bonding with Dell over cooking and baking—signed up for a short culinary course downtown. He'd just turned sixteen but didn't drive yet so he caught a ride with me every day. When I wanted to stay in town for an afternoon or evening event, I'd invite him along. As always, Tom turned heads wherever we went. Sometimes when I was with him, I almost felt like Tiran on the red carpet with Dusty.

Toward the end of the summer, as the course wrapped up, our facilitator threw a party to celebrate. This was a lavish soirée at a hip club with a guest list of mid-level actors, industry insiders and even production moguls—

none close to Tiran's level, but influential enough. I hired a professional stylist for the event, invited Tom along, and oversaw his styling as well. The night before, I asked Tiran if I could borrow his gorgeous Alfa Romeo convertible and, somewhat to my surprise, with a little coaxing, he agreed.

I knew how to make an entrance. Tom and I pulled up in the convertible when the party was in full swing. As a valet came over to take the car, I directed Tom to follow my lead, then put my arm around his waist and led him through the throngs on the sidewalk into the club.

Inside, I kept Tom close to me, only partly because he didn't know many of the other guests. Once in a while I'd send him off to get us drinks or a snack, then amuse myself by watching the gazes that followed him. The two of us spent the night entertaining a constant stream of people looking to make or renew our acquaintance. And every conversation inevitably came around to the same general questions.

"Is it true what they say about Dusty and Tiran?"

"How do I get Tiran to look at my project?"

"What's the deal with Dusty and Kat? Are they open?"

"Is Tiran really a Dom? What clubs does he go to? Where can I meet him?"

By this time, I knew exactly how to smile mysteriously and say nothing. Without a doubt, Tom and I were the shining stars of that event. And at the end of the night, as we cruised away from the club in Tiran's convertible, with the top down and music blasting, the breeze in our hair and the eyes of everyone around on us, I really thought that he and I would someday rule the world.

* * *

"Hey, Ti." This time I skipped up the terrace steps without waiting for an invitation. Since that odd conversation last spring, and my summer course, I'd developed a kind of camaraderie with Tiran. Whether he took me seriously or simply tolerated me with his usual courtesy, I didn't question too deeply. These days I relished any opportunity to trade work stories, gossip and advice with him and Dusty.

"Hi, Barry," Tiran said, flicking the ash from his cigarette with a faint smile. "How was the audition?"

"I guess it was okay," I said, heading over to the bar to pour a soda. "At least I remembered my lines."

"What did the director say?"

I made a little moue. "*Thanks for coming in.* The usual."

He gave a sage nod, and I took the deck chair beside him.

"Did you find out who's producing?" he asked.

"Yeah, an outfit called Red Sun." I glanced over and saw Tiran's blank look. "I know, you never heard of them. They're way too small potatoes for you."

"I work with up-and-comers occasionally," he said, a bit defensive. "But you're right, I don't know those guys."

I shrugged, unsurprised. Despite my efforts so far, I knew I was starting pretty much at the bottom tier of the industry. It was still a long way to Tiran's league, and I'd need a big break to get there. "Did you hear about LaDivinia getting busted by her boyfriend?" I asked.

"Oh, did that come out? Yeah, she told me a couple weeks ago. She knew he'd find out when the bank statements came in."

It was always fun to share industry gossip with Tiran. The names I heard in the media were often people he knew personally, and he could usually add a few juicy details. I especially enjoyed being able to casually share his stories with the Mountebank crowd.

"So it's true?"

"Oh yeah. She claims it was revenge for him firing her when they broke up. Sounds like him to me."

We were still discussing the latest scandal when Gabe stepped out onto the terrace. As usual, Tiran ignored his presence at first, before finally glancing at him with a half lifted eyebrow.

"Excuse me, sir," Gabe said quickly. "Pat's here to start his shift."

Tiran lit a new cigarette. "He can wait outside."

"Yes, sir."

I watched the door shut behind Gabe with that little tingle of excitement I always got from these exchanges. Tiran's face gave away nothing. I'd hung out with him enough to pick up scraps of information about his subs—I knew they took turns serving him in shifts, for example, and that Pat needed specific permission to enter his house. There was still so much I didn't get, but I thought it would make me look naïve to ask.

"So how was Indra's party last night?" I asked, moving on to more potential gossip. "They're supposed to be legendary."

That cheered Tiran up. I couldn't see his eyes behind the sunglasses but the small, reminiscent smile gave him away. "Oh…it was fun."

"What did you do there? Or should I say, who did you do there?"

He gave an offhand wave with the inevitable cocktail glass, which I noticed was almost empty. "I can't give away all my secrets, now, can I?" he demurred.

"When are you going to bring me to one of those parties?" I asked, not really serious.

Tiran looked incredulous. "Are you kidding? Your dad would kill me if I let you go to something like that."

"I know." I was only seventeen, after all. But I didn't want to be thought of as a kid forever. "Maybe in a few years."

"In a few years, Indra will be long gone and someone else'll be throwing the legendary parties."

I eyed Tiran's glass, wondering if he'd call Gabe or Pat to refill it. He always had at least one sub available at any time, but he didn't always keep them nearby. He seemed to like some more than others.

As I considered offering to do it myself, I saw Tiran's gaze shift over my shoulder and soften slightly. I turned my head just as Dusty bounded onto the terrace.

"Hi Dusty," I said.

"Hey, Barr. Hey, Ti." Dusty strolled over to peck Tiran's cheek in greeting, then glanced around the deck with a playful frown. "What's this, no drink? Who's on duty and slacking off like this?"

"Pat's here," Tiran said languidly. "I just haven't let him in yet." He watched with a small smile as Dusty bent over to take the empty glass, his fingers brushing against Tiran's like a subject bowing over a benevolent king's hand.

I never tired of watching Tiran and Dusty together. They chatted, bantered and even squabbled with an easy intimacy, like close friends or colleagues, and yet their personal arrangement was unmistakable. Unlike his apparent disdain for Gabe and Pat, Tiran showed an obvious fondness and even appreciation for Dusty, while accepting his service with tranquil entitlement. On his part, Dusty seemed completely comfortable in his position. He had a way of looking up with laughing eyes that showed his deference even while arguing with Tiran, and he'd often make himself comfortable on the floor, leaning against Tiran's legs or his chair as they talked. Why someone as famous and influential in his own right as Dusty would so willingly submit to Tiran was still a mystery to me, but I could see why Tiran enjoyed it.

Dusty and his partner Kat—who had her own subs, mostly women from what I understood—were tight, but not exclusive. A few days ago I'd arrived on the terrace and found Tiran just passing through the French doors from inside the house, looking a little distracted, and followed by Dusty, his hair tousled and eyes slightly glazed. I didn't need to see the look that passed between them to get the idea.

It made me wonder, not for the first time, about Tiran's love life, which he managed to keep surprisingly private despite endless public speculation and gossip. Were all his subs also lovers? Were all his lovers subs? I knew he rarely brought people back to the estate—probably for the same reason we avoided it, the security hassles—but what about all those nights he spent away from home, returning late or not at all? Did he have any long-term relationships?

The media constantly ran stories linking Tiran to every conceivable celebrity in every possible industry or walk of life. I had stopped paying attention to those reports years ago. Once I came down for breakfast to find my siblings all agog about a story that claimed Tiran was dating a famous astronaut who'd recently returned from a major space mission.

"Maybe she'll give us a ride on her rocket ship!" Mary-Dee was saying.

"What? Who?" I asked, reaching for the cereal.

"The lady astronaut Tiran's dating."

"*What*?" I laughed. "Where did you hear that?"

"It's just some nonsense in the news this morning." Jimmy shook his head at Mary-Dee. "Don't get your hopes up."

"Yeah," I agreed. "Tiran doesn't date women."

To my surprise Jimmy demurred. "Oh…I don't know about that."

"Really?" That surprised me more than the astronaut. "Since when?"

"Well, not lately. But years ago…there was someone."

"Huh," I marvelled. "What happened to them?"

"They just drifted apart, I think. No big drama."

"Did she break his heart?"

"I don't think so." Jimmy reached down to offer Doc a piece of bacon. "That was Rocky."

I stopped with the spoon halfway to my mouth. "*What* was Rocky?"

"Oh…" Jimmy hesitated, looking a little embarrassed, like he thought he'd said too much. "I meant it was Rocky who broke his heart. I don't know, that's just what I've heard."

The kids had moved on to discuss a possible new home on Mars, so I leaned in toward Jimmy. "What's the deal with Rocky anyway? If he's supposed to be Tiran's best friend, how come he doesn't live here with us?"

I'd never quite understood this. From what I gathered over the years, Rocky and Tiran had been best friends since birth, having been born on the same day in the same hospital to mothers who were already friends.

"Yeah, I don't really get it either," Jimmy said. He shooed Doc away and turned his focus to me. "I know they had some kind of falling out, way back, around when Tiran was making all the money. But then Rocky spent years kinda making it up to him, and by the time Tiran started building the estate they seemed to be tight again. So we all assumed Rocky would have one of the houses here but…next thing we know he's adopting the kids with Celeste. And from what I hear, that's just a child-raising arrangement; there's nothing romantic between them. I really don't know what the deal is with him."

Rocky was a big, exuberant, physical man, full of joy and energy, who had a way of enlivening whatever scene he was part of. The Van Mertz kids, in particular, adored their uncle, and would often climb all over him like he was some kind of playground equipment. He worked as a high school football coach, which always struck me as a somewhat prosaic job for the best friend of one of the most powerful men on earth, but otherwise suited him well. When he visited, generally on weekends or in the summer when he wasn't working, he'd stay at Tiran's house, since he didn't have his own on the estate. The two of them would round us all up for football and basketball games on the big lawn, like in those early days when we'd first arrived. Most of us had outgrown those activities by now, but something about Rocky made him hard to resist.

Once in a blue moon I'd see clips in the media of Rocky and Tiran at a club or party downtown, but they usually hung out together on the estate. Tiran would send his hovercraft to pick Rocky up, which only took an hour or so, and as Rocky's children grew older, he came over more often. Tiran would generally stay home during Rocky's visits, seeming to give up the night life circuit in favour of his company.

I'd noticed that despite the whole best friend thing, Rocky also had a way of occasionally deferring to Tiran, as though ultimately conceding to his authority. It was hard to imagine Rocky as anyone's sub, but what Jimmy said about him trying to make up for some long-ago fight kind of checked out. And once or twice, I'd seen them share that same tell-tale, intimate glance that confirmed my suspicions about Dusty. It occurred to me that if Tiran had a long-term relationship with anyone, it might be with Rocky.

* * *

I'd started my final year of high school in Whittier that fall, but it didn't interest me much. By now my life centred mostly around auditions, shoots, casting calls and industry events; I spent more time downtown than at school or with the other kids on the estate. The more I hung out in New Ellay with the Mountebank crowd, or talked shop with Tiran and Dusty, the younger the other seniors seemed to me. That year I didn't join any clubs or teams, and I missed a few classes, though I did eventually graduate.

By this time, Lance had also made a few contacts in the big city. He was almost sixteen and had learned how to parlay his estate cachet into a bit of profile in the music scene. Occasionally he'd score a paying gig, or a "sponsorship" to appear at some exclusive event, and talk Jimmy into letting him go under the guise of career development.

Sometimes I'd join him at one of these shows, or at a downtown house party, which he'd started to swap for the teen hangouts in Whittier. Jimmy found it reassuring when I went along with Lance, but in truth it was mostly out of curiosity. These events had a kind of carnal energy I found exciting at first—dark rooms lit by pulses of light and saturated with driving, robotic beats; bodies pressed against other bodies; screens playing explicit blue-lit scenes on endless loops; murky corners where anything might be happening; free-flowing substances, fleeting encounters, a constant undercurrent of sex and desire.

I'd had a few wholesome teenage experiences with kids at school, but this was something different. All kinds of acts were on offer and display in these spaces; activities I had only heard of or imagined. I'd get any number of proposals there, and while I declined most of them, I had my first anonymous encounter at one of Lance's events, which had a certain appeal.

Still, I grew bored with the scene pretty fast. Its stars and celebrities were too niche for my tastes, people didn't converse much at events, and none of it aligned with the kind of future I wanted. I preferred the old-fashioned glamour, powerbroking, and fame promised by the vid production world.

Chapter 8

"On your way out already?" Randall asked, as I stood surveying the room.

"In a few minutes. How'd that math test go today?"

He shrugged. "It was fine. You got a date?"

I smiled and elbowed him lightly. "Yeah, but you're not getting any details."

It was a Friday evening, in the spring of my senior year. One of my friends from the summer program had snagged us invites to a small wrap party, and I'd invited a good-looking young actor from a recent shoot to go with me. We planned to have dinner first at one of the downtown joints, and with luck there'd be paparazzi waiting outside when we left.

But before heading out, I liked to check in at the club house to make sure no crises were underway. The younger kids still mostly hung out at home in the evenings, and tonight even Lance sat working on his portable audio system; his night would no doubt start much later.

Randall exchanged rolled eyes with Curtis and they went back to their pool game, mumbling about how some people thought everything they did was such a big deal.

I checked myself in the mirror one more time. My closely fitted outfit showed off a solid physique—nothing like Tom's, but my workouts and laps had made a difference. I'd added a sweeping floor-length duster for drama and style and to emphasize my height, which surpassed Lance's now. My face had changed too; the jaw and cheeks had lost their roundness and grown firmer and more defined. And if I still wasn't quite as striking as Tom, the combination of my auburn curls and warm amber skin, with brown eyes lined in a dark kohl, looked good enough to me. I'd even picked up a few modelling gigs lately.

From another corner, Pasha said shyly, "You look nice, Barry."

"Thanks, man." I couldn't help shooting a quick glance at Tom, whose admiration I particularly enjoyed. I caught him watching me and smiled a little. "You got plans tonight, Tommy?"

He shook his head. "Think I'll just stay in."

"Hey Tom, how's your *friends* doing?" Lance asked out of the blue, sliding his headset half off so he could hear over the music.

Tom and I both turned toward him. I didn't understand his question, or where the pointed tone came from.

"What do you mean," Tom asked with his usual wariness.

"You know, the ones that got mugged," Lance said. "I heard it was pretty vicious."

I knew what he was talking about now; everyone at school had heard of the apparently random knife attack on two local boys in Whittier a couple of days ago. But his question didn't make sense.

"What's that got to do with Tom?" I asked, baffled.

"That's what I'd like to know," Lance smirked.

I stared at him, then switched my gaze to Tom, who was watching Lance without expression.

"I didn't know you were friends with those guys," I said to Tom. "Are they—"

"I'm not."

"Then why is—"

"I don't know what Lance is talking about."

Lance gave a kind of knowing laugh. "That's not what I hear," he said, and then slid the headset back on and returned to his work.

Tom didn't say anything else, and I couldn't figure it out that night. But later I asked around, and when I found out the names of the two boys, I had a sudden, sick inkling of what Lance was getting at. I knew who the kids were; I'd caught them harassing Tom in a school hallway a week ago, mocking him, perhaps not for the first time, for being so many grades behind. As usual, I'd stepped in to defuse the situation. The boys had scuttled away, Tom carried on with his usual stoic indifference, and I hadn't thought about it since.

And now, one week later, the same two boys were victims of a brutal mugging in which, it turned out, no actual money had been taken. In the hospital, where they'd been in life-threatening condition for a couple of days, both claimed not to have seen their attacker and refused to provide any details. Rumour said they were both too terrified to speak.

There were other rumours too, as I discovered once I started paying attention. Lance hadn't invented them; they were all over the school. Not just about this incident—the halls practically exploded with speculation about Tom, and his past.

I didn't know what to think. It hit me with a kind of shock that Tom was still pretty much a blank slate to me. What did I actually know of his background, or how he'd spent the first fourteen years of his life? How could I be sure of what he might or might not be capable of? Every time I turned my mind to it, a creeping nausea spread through my stomach.

Sure, Tom and I were friends, of a kind, but didn't our relationship mostly consist of me leading him around, making conversation and enjoying the attention we got? He was agreeable enough with me, but then, his reserve gave him a certain chameleon-like quality that let him fit in almost anywhere. Had I been lulled into assuming the best of him because I liked having access to his particular blend of strength and charisma?

A couple of days later, I bumped into Paul Armstrong on one of the walking paths near the ocean. I hadn't spent much time with Paul since I'd stopped joining him for his daily walks a few years back. I knew about him, of course—he ran Tiran's charitable Foundation, worked out of an office in Whittier, and occasionally took trips overseas. He was single, rumoured to have been a Dom once, and still considered a bit of a player. He often spent his evenings clubbing around New Ellay, occasionally even with Tiran, which was kind of funny since Paul made his dislike for Tiran clear. In fact, he generally seemed a bit dour for a supposedly swinging single. It was hard to figure him out.

This time, to my surprise, he stopped me. "Barry, hey…hang on a moment."

I paused, and he glanced around, then led me down to the water, presumably so the crash of the ocean waves would eliminate any possibility of being overheard.

When I waited for him, Paul seemed unsure how to begin. "I just thought I'd ask you—" he started, finally. "Because you seem to…to know everything that goes on around here."

"What do you mean," I said, laughing a little since I knew exactly what he meant.

"At least with all the kids, right? So I was just wondering…you heard about those boys in Whittier, the ones who got mugged?"

The question caught me off-guard. I answered uncertainly. "Well, yeah, sure, I guess we've all heard about that."

"Do you know…I mean…" He floundered a bit, frowning uncomfortably. "I keep hearing these rumours."

"You do?" How had he picked up on them? I thought they'd only circulated around school. "Where?"

He dismissed my question with a quick wave of his hand and went on, "So you've heard them too? You know what I mean?"

I hesitated. "You mean the rumours about…Tom."

"Yes."

We stood facing each other for a moment. I didn't know what else to say.

At last Paul asked, with a kind of reluctant guardedness, "So…are they true?"

"How would I know?" My words came out sharply. "He says he doesn't know anything about it."

"And do you believe him?"

"I…don't know." The conversation made me almost as queasy as the rumours did. Tom was my friend; no matter what I wondered privately, I didn't like the idea of sharing my uncertainties with an adult, especially ones based on unsettling gossip that might or might not be true. "Shouldn't you…I don't know, talk to his parents or something?" I said finally.

Paul sighed and looked away, out over the ocean. "Yeah," he said, after a moment. "I guess I should."

"I mean, they should know him better than I do," I added.

He nodded. "Okay," he said. "You're right. I'll talk to them."

That was the end of our conversation, and Paul never spoke to me about it again. Afterwards, though, the nausea in my stomach kind of faded away; the idea that his parents, or the adults, would take care of things made me feel easier. When time passed, and nothing else came of it, I let myself forget the whole incident.

* * *

Toward the end of spring, with my graduation on the horizon, Jimmy started asking about my post-high school plans. I told him I wanted to attend Mountebank full-time in the fall and start working toward an acting degree, though internally I fully expected a big break to launch my career anytime, eliminating the need for credentials.

Jimmy seemed satisfied with my response, but then seemed alarmingly close to launching into some kind of birds-and-bees talk. "You know, Barry," he began, trying to broach the new topic with his typical hesitancy. "When you leave here, you might find that some things..."

I cringed inwardly and hunted for a way to forestall what must be coming. "Look," I rushed in, "I know the tuition's going to cost a lot, and I likely won't get a scholarship—I'm not good at school like Ran or Dee..."

He ignored me and continued his train of thought stubbornly, as though he'd braced himself for this and didn't want to lose his nerve. "I mean, there's things that might set you apart—"

"But do you think we can afford it?" I asked, more loudly. "Even with what I've saved from working I know I don't have enough money to cover all the tuition, even if I live at home..."

After a moment Jimmy gave in, dropping his topic and explaining that Tiran had agreed to support all of us kids through post-secondary school if we wanted to go. I wasn't surprised about that. I'd already arranged with him to cover my summer course again this year.

Meanwhile, my life on-set hadn't improved much. Most of my work still involved a lot of standing around waiting, and very little of the kind of adulation Dusty got. On the few occasions I managed to land speaking parts I struggled to fully remember my lines or deliver them with conviction. Once, after I'd missed the mark a few too many times, the director lashed out at me in frustration; I remember the shock of thinking *This must be what it's like for other people.*

Occasionally I'd land a job on a project with Dusty and watch him work. Everything he did looked so effortless and natural, and the people around us treated him with so much reverence, that I found myself almost resenting him. How could he be such a big deal in the industry when in reality I knew he was just a guy? Why him, and not me?

Standing around waiting for my walk-on or background roles, I often thought about how Tiran put up the funding for so many of these productions. Dusty had told me he didn't get involved in creative decisions, but surely he could if he wanted to. All I needed was one good break. I considered asking Tiran outright for help, like I did when I needed financial support, but somehow I knew this was different.

By now I understood exactly what Dusty meant about the industry's seamy side. I'd had my share of those experiences: I'd submitted head shots and been asked for full-body frontals; I'd been to auditions and invited to the casting couch; I'd taken a few modelling jobs that started out as one thing and turned into another.

I hadn't yet turned eighteen but some of my colleagues were starting to make their interest in me obvious, and not just because of my proximity to Tiran. I recognized the lingering gazes, the pointed comments and half-serious invitations. It didn't bother me; I liked attention, and I'd always enjoyed flirting with others on the crew, boys and young men around my age. Only now the attention was coming from much older, more influential people—directors, casting agents, backers and studio execs; powerbrokers who could make a difference in my career.

I found the implied offers somewhat gratifying. They meant I had power—not enough to control people directly, the way Tiran controlled his subs, but enough to bargain with. Perhaps I could exchange this currency for opportunities, for the big break that would lead to success and fame. The idea tempted me at first, but the more I thought about it, the more I held off. Why squander what I had on people at this level, when the most powerful man in the industry was within my reach?

* * *

"Who is *that*?" I asked.

Dusty followed my gaze, then gave a knowing chuckle. "That," he said, "is Severin."

Tall and lithe and regal, the young man had sailed onto the set a moment earlier and swanned straight up to Frank, our director. All activity had crashed to an immediate halt as the entire crew stopped what they were doing to stare, and not only because an interruption like this on a live set was unheard of. We were riveted by the striking figure, wrapped in flowing silk fabric, with lustrous black tresses, a delicate face and large, dramatic eyes.

"But what is he doing here?" I asked. "And why is Frank standing there talking to him instead of calling security?"

Dusty looked at me like he wanted to see my reaction when he answered. "Because he's Tiran's boyfriend," he said.

I sucked in a breath and then held it, the "*Ohhh*" on my lips not quite coming out.

"At least," Dusty added, "for this week."

"Is that—" I forced out my exhale and tried to gather my thoughts. "Is that how long they last? Is that what Tiran likes? How *old* is that kid?"

"Probably older than you think." Dusty squinted at Severin thoughtfully. "Late twenties, I'd guess. Close to thirty. And yeah—that's exactly his type."

"Huh..." I said, letting out another breath. For a moment we stood in silence, watching the ongoing scene, where a few studio types had now gathered around, clearly trying to placate and humour Severin, as his words rose in pitch, accompanied by florid hand gestures.

As I continued to study him, I realized that what I'd first thought of as exotic or flamboyant was actually more like a kind of camp. The same camp I saw in the theatre kids at school and the students at Mountebank, and shared myself, in some degree, as well.

"A week, you say?" I asked.

"Couple of weeks, maybe." Dusty seemed amused by the whole thing. "Tiran meets these guys, falls head over heels, tries to sign over half his fortune to them while he's high, and then a few days later he's bored and barely remembers their name."

"Huh," I said again. "He...gives them money?"

"He tries to, but that's why we have all those complicated accounting processes. Nothing goes out now without one of us co-signing, and we keep an eye on things." Dusty elbowed me playfully. "I've signed off on a few of your tuition payments."

Whatever it was Severin wanted, it seemed like he got it. His voice dropped to a more languid, satisfied tone, and he allowed himself to be steered off, toward the edge of the set and away from Frank. A few minutes later production started back up, and I lost sight of him.

On the drive back home with Dusty, I kept thinking about how carefully Severin had been managed during his brief and dramatic appearance; how he'd been able to take over the whole shoot, at least for a while. I'd always figured my association with Tiran gave me some kind of advantage in the industry, but apparently it was nowhere near the kind of treatment a closer connection would yield.

* * *

As my eighteenth birthday approached at the end of the summer, it became a major topic of conversation on the estate. I'd be the first of us kids to reach adulthood, and the whole place wanted to celebrate this milestone. It seemed to be taken as some kind of vindication, proof that our community could successfully produce an adult human. I had no immediate plans to move out or anything, and Jimmy assured me I could stay as long as I wanted, but I did like the idea of officially leaving childhood behind. I hadn't felt like a child in a long time.

The day itself was one long party, with games and festivities, big communal outdoor meals, speeches, and a long succession of gifts. I opened a bunch of gag gifts from my brothers, and some very kind offerings from the other families, mostly either sentimental or acting related; everything from photos from my childhood, to antique Hollywood stars. Jimmy had obviously put a lot of thought into his presents: he gave me a lovely gold chain with a theatre mask pendant, along with a few pieces of high-end clothing and accessories that exactly matched my style, and must have required some sacrificing on his part.

I spent the whole day being fussed over, accepting hugs and kisses, and admiring each new item I received. By the end of the night I felt more beloved than I had in a while.

The next morning, when I came down for breakfast wearing the new gold chain, Jimmy and the others seemed to be waiting for me. I couldn't miss the current of anticipation in the air, but when I glanced curiously at Jimmy, as he leaned against the counter with his coffee, he only gestured at the toast and eggs waiting for me.

"What's up?" I asked, filling my plate.

The others exchanged looks. Most of them had finished eating but for some reason still sat around the table.

"Finish your breakfast," Jimmy said, handing me a cup of coffee. "Then we'll go outside."

I ate dutifully, still wondering what the deal was.

"How does it feel?" Randall asked, half-mocking. "To be an adult now."

"Not so different." I shrugged, and kept eating. "But uh...like maybe there's things I can do now that I couldn't before."

"Like *what*?" said Mary-Dee.

"I dunno." I smirked at her. "*Adult* things. You're too little to get it."

Lance and Steve rolled their eyes at each other. "C'mon, move it Barry," Lance said, uncharacteristically interested in whatever was going on. "We want to go try it—"

"Try *what*?" I stared at Jimmy, finishing up my plate as quickly as I could.

"What's going on?"

Jimmy sighed with a kind of resignation. "Tiran's gift is waiting for you outside. He wanted to hold off till today…" He paused for a moment, then went on, "so he wouldn't upstage anyone else."

My eyebrows shot up at that, and my mind spun in a dozen different directions. I swallowed and pushed my plate away. "I'm done. Let's go."

We all headed outside, Jimmy and I in front and the others following behind us.

"This way," Jimmy said, and led us across the big lawn toward the main estate drive and the garage. As we approached, Enrico opened one of the garage doors to reveal a brand new, cherry-coloured Alfa Romeo convertible, with a big red bow covering the front grill.

I halted in my tracks, and at that moment Tiran appeared, walking over from his house with a set of keys in his hand. Which he handed to me, once he got near enough.

At first I was too frozen to put out my hand, but in a second I'd thrown my arms around him, my fist curled over the keys.

The rest of that day was spent with my new baby, inspecting and admiring every inch of her, and then taking all of the kids out for a spin, each in turn so they could ride in the front seat beside me. It honestly felt like the best day I'd ever had, and I'd already had plenty of amazing days.

"Man, this is so wild," Lance said, when it was his turn to ride with me, and after I'd flat-out rejected his proposal to take the wheel. "Can't wait till it's my turn. Just a year and a half to go. I want a vintage Hummer."

"What?" I pushed the hair out of my eyes, making a mental note to wear it back next time.

"When I turn eighteen. Tell Tiran I want a Hummer."

I could only spare him a shooting glance. "You think Tiran's going to buy everyone a car when they turn eighteen?" I wasn't sure Tiran even knew Lance's name.

"He has to now," Lance said, smirking. "He can't treat you special. Unless there's some reason he likes you more," he added with what I suspected was a leer.

"I wouldn't count on it," I said.

That night, after Enrico and I had polished up my baby and put her to bed, and I'd listened to his long lecture about how to take care of her, I left the garage and looked toward Tiran's house. By now, I'd learned to read the light patterns in his windows to know whether he was home; the main living areas tended to be dark when he wasn't. Tonight I saw a tell-tale golden glow from the great room.

I went round the back, walked up the terrace steps and tapped lightly on the French doors, before opening one and letting myself in.

Tiran stood by the fireplace in the great room with a drink in his hand, lost in thought, but he glanced up when he heard me come in. He was an inch or two taller than me and very fit, with dark, slightly curly hair and a Mediterranean complexion. I sometimes thought he looked like an old-fashioned leading man from the Hollywood era; even his most casual outfits were custom tailored to give him a kind a suave sophistication. Those medical treatments Jimmy mentioned kept his face looking a perpetual mid-twenties, though he had to be almost ten years older than that by now.

No question, he was an attractive man. It would be no hardship.

"I know I already thanked you," I said to him, smiling. "But I wanted to do it again…" As I drew near, I slid both arms over his shoulders and added, in his ear, "…*privately*."

He'd been laughing as I reached out to him, patting my back sort of mechanically in response to my hug. But he stopped and pulled back a little just as I moved toward him. When he turned his head as though to offer his cheek, I ignored the suggestion and kissed him full on the mouth instead.

His head jerked back. "Barry—*no*."

Somehow, in that split second between hearing the words and reacting to them, I recognized the choice I was forced to make: I could accept the rejection and humiliation of failure and slink off into the night; or I could brazen it out, dig in, and hold out for the long game.

"What?" I said in a playful murmur, leaning in to chase his receding mouth. "You don't like this?"

"No, I...please *stop*, Barry." His words were firm; he broke away from me and took a couple of steps back.

We stood a foot or two apart. He watched me, wary and troubled, his weight on his back foot. Once again, I faced the prospect of that black cloud of mortification and refused to accept it, grasping at the ropes of my confidence and forcing myself to pull through.

"Don't you...find me attractive?" I asked, managing a small pout.

He fell into the trap. "Of course I do." Then he realized his mistake, took another couple of steps backward, and added more coolly, "You're a very attractive young man, Barry. I'm flattered. But you know you're way too young for me."

"But I'm an adult now," I coaxed, though I already knew the battle was lost for today. "I'm completely legal."

Tiran laughed, relieved, I guess, that I hadn't followed him. "Legal isn't the only factor. Your dad would kill me."

Jimmy? He was worried about Jimmy? I opened my mouth, but he added quickly, "And the others too. I'm not going down that path."

"You care what your subs think?"

"Of course I do."

"What? Really?"

"Just because they're subs doesn't mean they won't call me out when they have to," Tiran said. He'd moved far enough away to lean against the back of a couch now, his hands folded loosely in front of him. "And not everyone here belongs to me anyway. I don't need this kind of flack."

Did that mean he would have accepted my advances if not for his fears about what people would say? Or was he just covering rejection with his usual courtesy, a polite sop to my pride? I couldn't tell, but I didn't have to figure it all out tonight. What was that line about retreat being the better part of valor?

I put a bit of defiant swagger into my steps as I headed over to the French doors, then halted before opening them. "Thank you, though," I said, dropping the bravado for now. "For the gift. Really."

He deflected my words with a small wave and a smile. "Good night, Barry."

I walked back over the familiar paths to my house, stymied but not ceding defeat.

Chapter 9

The fall session at Mountebank started a couple of days later. Unlike the summer classes, which were mainly excuses for networking, the full-time degree program was a serious combination of theory, skills development and training. I had resolved to make a genuine effort this year; to focus on my work and learn more about the actual craft of acting, which had never been of great interest to me.

Even so, nothing beat arriving at school on the first morning in my new convertible, and then, when my fellow students expressed admiration, casually mentioning it was a gift from Tiran Marx.

I kept my resolve for the first few months, driving to school on time every day, attending all the classes and putting effort into my assignments. Just like in high school, the students and teachers seemed to assume we'd start off working on small-scale projects—local theatre, corporate events and the like—which didn't reflect my experience. I remembered the earnest Whittier theatre kids, and had the same sense of being in a different world.

One day in the late fall or early winter of that year I came home from school to find construction vehicles and crews milling around the top of the cliffs behind Tiran's mansion. As I walked over, I saw mounds of dirt piled up and a large, squarish pit in the process of being dug out.

I glanced around, and after a moment saw Tiran standing on the back deck of his house, watching the proceedings. He waved at me, so I went over to find out what was going on.

The first awkwardness of that night after my birthday had quickly dissipated. We'd bumped into each other on the big lawn a couple of days later, and made a bit of public small talk as though mutually determined to pretend nothing had changed. After that, I'd deliberately resumed my old pattern of dropping by his place or Dusty's whenever they were around, to talk shop and gossip. Tiran seemed to have no objection to that, treating me more or less as he had before.

But that wasn't good enough for me. The more Tiran politely pretended nothing had happened, the more I liked to remind him it had—and that I declined to accept defeat. Why would I? He still had what I wanted, and now my pride was at stake as well. In that infinitesimal, monumental moment, I'd made my choice and committed to it.

"Hey, Ti," I said, sashaying over to him. "What's going on?"

"Well, they started work today," he said, his gaze still on the machinery and activity behind the house.

"I can see that," I said. "But work on what? What are they building?"

"Oh." He glanced at me as though surprised I hadn't heard. "It's a new house. Well, a small house. A chalet, really. For Rocky."

"Rocky?" I recalled Jimmy talking about heartbreakers that time, and a vague unease crept over me. "Is he moving in here?"

"I think so," Tiran said "I mean...maybe not full-time."

Something in his voice told me discussions with Rocky were still ongoing. Was this some type of wish fulfillment? Build it and he'll come?

"What about his family?"

"He can..." Tiran waved his cigarette vaguely. "He can go back and forth."

I glanced around; there was no bar on this deck, so I stood beside Tiran as he leaned against the railing. These days he generally tried to avoid being alone with me, often keeping one of his subs around or gently leading me to more populated locations when I showed up. Maybe this time he figured the construction crew gave him enough cover.

He continued watching the workers with his usual impassive expression, but I thought I glimpsed a slight forlornness in the set of his mouth, and felt a momentary twinge of sympathy.

Not for long, though. I liked to take advantage of our small moments together to remind him the game wasn't over. "I thought Rocky sleeps at your place when he's here," I said, giving him a little nudge with my elbow. "Won't you miss him when he's way over there?"

Tiran shot me a cautious glance. "He needs his own space."

At that moment Gabe came outside with a tray of drinks and small plates. Two drinks, I saw; one for me. Had he been watching from inside?

"Well," I drawled, irritation driving my vindictiveness, "if you ever need company, you know where to find me."

If I was mildly flirtatious in private, I didn't hold back in public. The more he tried to protect himself with other people, the more I wanted to provoke him. I got away with it because Tiran was too chivalrous to let me lose face. He'd smile politely at any brazen comment, as though vaguely flattered, even when we were met with obvious disapproval from whoever else was around. It amused me to think of him being lectured by the other adults.

Not that I didn't get some of that myself. Jimmy had taken me aside shortly after my birthday, asking if anything happened with Tiran and sternly telling me I should stick to friends my own age. I listened patiently, not making promises, and not letting on that I'd been the one rebuffed.

A few weeks later, as we drove to a job together, Dusty had been even more blunt.

"You know you're barking up the wrong tree, Barr," he'd said, more harshly than I was used to from him.

"Don't know what you're talking about," I said with a deliberate smirk.

"Yes, you do." He made no effort to hide his antipathy. "And I'm telling you it's not going to work. You won't get what you want, and you're way too young to try."

Of course, they both just made me more determined than ever.

* * *

Tom wanted to talk to me. It had been obvious for a couple of days, from the way his quiet gaze followed me when I dropped by the club house or passed him playing soccer with the other kids on the big lawn. I'd been too wrapped up in my world of school and work and social events to follow up at first, but finally, on a Sunday afternoon early in the new year, I had some time and meant to get to the bottom of it.

"Wanna help me run my lines, Tommy?" I asked, after checking up on the scene in the club house, where everything seemed fine.

He gave me a thoughtful look, probably recognizing the ploy. Since he still hadn't really mastered reading—he generally relied on speech apps for written material—Tom wasn't likely to be my first choice for line practice, on the rare occasions when I actually wanted to prep.

"Sure," he said, getting up.

I called to Doc, and we walked the short distance over to my house together, grabbing snacks in the kitchen before heading up to my room.

"So, what's up, man?" I threw myself onto the bed, invited Doc up to join me, and unwrapped an energy bar. "I can see there's something on your mind."

"Oh." Tom glanced around the room, as though wondering if he should sit, and then nodded. "Yeah, I…kinda wanted to tell you something."

"I'm all ears. There's a chair—make yourself comfy."

But he didn't; he just continued standing in the middle of the room, watching me. "The thing is…" he began. "Well…you know how my dad's been so stressed lately? I mean, because of his deal with Tiran."

I nodded sympathetically. We'd all seen that; something had happened between them a few years back and Tiran had been particularly harsh with Pat ever since. As I understood it, Pat was now required to follow a set of onerous rules on threat of being expelled from the estate if he broke them, which obviously put him under a lot of pressure.

"Well, I've been getting really worried about him," Tom went on, twisting his energy bar around and around in his hands. "Every time he sees Tiran I think he's going to have a heart attack or something."

"It can't be that bad, can it?" I wanted to reassure Tom, but I'd seen Pat with Tiran and I knew what he meant.

"I don't know, but I don't like it. Anyway, so, I…I just started working for Tiran."

I didn't understand. "You…what?" When he didn't answer right away, I sat up straighter on the bed and narrowed my eyes at him. "Working on what?"

"I mean I'm taking shifts with him. For my dad."

"What do you mean? What shifts?" I choked on the bite I'd just swallowed. "You mean like a—*sub?*"

"For my dad," he repeated, his hands motionless now. "I'm taking some of his shifts so he can take less."

For a moment I couldn't speak, and somewhere in my belly an angry knot began to form. "You're subbing for Tiran," I said finally.

"I don't know what you call it. I'm just helping my dad."

"That's…that is quite the move," I said, the words coming out icily as I tried to make sense of the jumble of thoughts spinning around my brain. "I didn't realize you were playing *that* game."

"It's not a game." He spoke with more force than usual. "I thought he was gonna keel over the other day. I don't want to—"

I couldn't listen to him. The knot grew harder and more painful, making it impossible to sit still. I jumped off the bed and paced across the floor, arms folded over my stomach. "I didn't figure you for a—a—" *double-crosser,* I wanted to say, but that didn't sound right. "A *sub,*" I finished instead, with disdain. "Why would you do this? What are you trying to get out of him? And why is he even…letting you?" I wheeled around and stared in disbelief. "Jesus, you're only seventeen. How could he agree? Why didn't your parents stop it?"

"They tried." Tom looked down, then took a tentative step towards me. "Look, it's no big deal. It's nothing new to me. I just wanted to give my dad a break, that's all. I don't want to lose him."

I backed away, toward the window, as he approached. "You wanna give your dad a break, you take him to a ballgame or something. You don't make a pass at a—an old man." *Mine,* I thought. Tiran had always been my territory; Tom barely knew him.

"Barry." He stopped advancing on me. "It's not like that. There's not going to be anything physical. My folks would never go along with that. We agreed…"

I turned around, staring out the window at the deep August green of the trees and lawn, and the whitecaps in the ocean beyond. "It's not even going to work," I added after a moment, with a little flick of my hand. "Tiran doesn't respect his subs, you know."

"I don't care about Tiran. I'm not trying to…cut in on anyone or—or anything. I'm just worried about my dad."

I needed to put an end to this conversation. I'd find out more directly from Tiran. "Well," I said finally. "Good luck, I guess."

Tom came up beside me and put a tentative hand on my arm. "I know I should've talked to you first. You're, like, my buddy, right?"

Of course he didn't talk to me first; he knew what I would have said. "I guess you didn't want my advice."

"I mean, I wasn't even sure it would work. I had to talk Tiran into it and then my folks and then Tiran again…they only just agreed."

"How could your dad *let* you?"

"I told him I needed him," Tom said. "He's the one who brought me here. I need him alive."

I wanted to scoff and call him melodramatic, but it was unusual for Tom to speak with so much conviction. "If you say so," I said, turning back to face him with slightly exaggerated injured dignity. "Look, I have to get some things done."

"Oh…you don't want to work on your line readings?"

"Maybe later." He knew that was only a ruse anyway. I walked away from the window to the bedroom door, opened it, and stood there, waiting.

Tom followed me obediently, but stopped just before going out. "Are we…okay?" he asked.

The cold smile I gave him took all my effort. When he left the room, I went back to the window. After a few moments Tom came into view outside, walking slowly toward the little grove of trees beside the water. Even from here, three stories up, his striking physique and coiled strength were unmistakable.

I remembered that end of summer party last year; the way he'd turned all the heads in the room; the eyes that were on us as we drove away in the open convertible. I'd always taken a kind of pride in his mysterious allure, as though his value enhanced mine. Why did he throw it away so easily? Did he not realize that when he gave himself away for free, he devalued my currency as well?

Something in the way I thought about Tom had changed. After three years, I still had no idea what went on beneath that enigmatic exterior. I didn't understand him and now I wasn't sure I trusted him.

* * *

Of course Tiran wasn't home. It made sense that he spent a lot of time away, especially in the evenings, though often during the day as well. His estate was just a sanctuary that he came back to when he'd had enough of the wider world.

That didn't make it any less frustrating for me when I wanted to see him. Like right after I watched Tom disappear into the little woods and then marched downstairs and straight over to Tiran's mansion.

When I heard he wasn't home, I considered heading over to Pat and Adele's house and giving them a piece of my mind instead. But in the end I didn't bother. I could imagine Dell's soothing justifications and Pat's anxious uncertainty only too well. It was Tiran I wanted to talk to.

A couple of days later, I found him out on the terrace after I got back from school. He looked up from a meeting on his comm as I walked onto the deck, and his eyebrows lifted slightly when he saw my face.

"Hey," he said into his device. "Something's come up. I'll call you back in a bit."

When he closed his screen I didn't speak at first, just looked pointedly at Gabe, who was working behind the bar with his head bowed.

"Oh, uh—" Tiran began, getting my point. "Gabe, maybe..."

"No, never mind," I said. The terrace was too public anyway. I went to the French doors that led inside the house, pulled one open and posed there, one hand on the door and the other on my hip, while I stared down at Tiran.

He glanced into the empty room, then warily at me. "I'm not sure we should…"

"Oh, get over yourself," I snapped. "We just need to talk in private."

After a moment he stubbed out his cigarette and pushed himself up from the deck chair. "Fine," he said. "Let's chat inside."

I followed him into the great room, a luxurious space full of plush armchairs, deep sofas and an old-fashioned fireplace dominating one wall.

"Drink?" Tiran asked, heading behind the bar. "Pretty sure *I'm* gonna need one."

"What are you doing with Tom?" I asked, parking myself in front of the fireplace with my arms folded over my chest.

He didn't seem surprised or look up from the cocktail mixer, though I thought I saw a small half-smile, or grimace, as though he'd been expecting this. "Nothing," he said, without any emphasis. "I'm not doing anything with him."

"He just told me you—"

Tiran lifted one hand to forestall me gently. "Yes, okay, I let him take on a few shifts. It seemed like the only way to satisfy him. But that doesn't mean he's going to do anything while he's here."

"So he is, he's subbing for you."

"Come on, Barry." This time Tiran glanced over at me, almost skeptically, like he couldn't believe I was taking this seriously. "He's going to show up here for a couple hours, once or twice a week, and maybe I'll let him bring me a drink or something. It's just so he can feel like he's doing something."

"It's completely inappropriate."

"Of course it is." Tiran picked up his glass and went over to the sofa, stretching his feet onto the coffee table in front of him. "Come on, sit down," he added, waving at a chair across from him.

"So why did you agree?" I demanded without moving.

He sighed. "Tom is very persuasive when he wants to be. I tried everything I could think of to avoid it."

I frowned a little, my arms lowering as though of their own accord. "You did?"

"Of course I did," he said with dignity, spreading out his hands in a kind of shrug. "I get how he's worried about his dad. I mean, he's wrong—Pat needs rules, he's doing better now than he has for years. But I can see how it looks to Tom."

A small part of my outrage had drained away, replaced with a smidgen of confusion, or perhaps curiosity. I took a few steps forward and sank into an armchair. "So why didn't you tell him that?"

"I tried, of course, but he wouldn't listen. So then I told him I'd take it easier on Pat, but that didn't satisfy him either. He kept saying he wants his dad to spend less time with me. So fine, I offered to cut Pat's hours on the schedule. But no, he said that wouldn't be fair to the other su—the others, if they had to pick up more shifts instead."

Tiran paused to take a drink, and I rallied a little. "Couldn't your primadonna ass just manage without a sub for a few hours a week?"

He laughed. "I suggested that too! But he has some kind of—manly idea that he can't ask for favours. He'd only accept a trade." Tiran swirled the drink around in his hand, looking down at it with eyebrows drawn low over his eyes. "I don't know, he seems to treat everything like a negotiation with me. Like he thinks that's all I understand."

"Still," I said, after he'd been silent for a moment. "You could have—"

"I told him he was too young, he didn't need to, his parents would never agree, all of that. He wouldn't let up. Finally I said if he got his folks' permission I'd consider it. I mean—" Tiran looked up and lifted his free hand in a disbelieving gesture. "I was just trying to get rid of him. I assumed they'd kill the whole thing. Who knew he'd be back a few weeks later, telling me they were on board?"

A few weeks? How long had Tom been working on this, and not telling me about it?

"Yeah, why the fuck did *they* let him do this?" I asked, venting.

Tiran shook his head. "I had a long talk with them both," he said. "They seem to think it's good for Tom, it's supposed to make him feel more in control or something. I don't really get it, but what do I know about parenting?" He half-shrugged and finished off his drink.

I got up to pour myself a soda at the bar, suddenly realizing how thirsty I was. "Did he come on to you?" I asked, without looking up. "Is that what he was doing?"

"Come on to me?" Tiran sounded disbelieving. "He's seventeen. Why would he?"

I could think of a couple reasons, but I let it go. "Yeah, well, now you've got a seventeen-year-old sub."

"I told you," he said, and for the first time his voice held a mild impatience. "He's not going to do anything. I'll just—"

"Your subs do more than make you drinks, Tiran."

He paused in the act of setting down his glass, then turned a long, level look on me. "Some of them do. What are you getting at?"

"You know what I mean. I've seen you with the others, those looks, we all know what—"

"I am not interested in children," he interrupted, definitely testy now. "If that's what you're insinuating."

His voice held a kind of warning that a contrary part of me wanted to challenge. I held his gaze for a moment, then picked up my drink. "If you say so. I still think it's not appropriate."

"I still agree with you," he said, more playfully now, as though he recognized the battle was over. "If you can talk him out of it, please be my guest. But let's drop that for now." He got to his feet and headed toward the terrace door. "Come on outside and tell me about your new gig."

This time he stood holding the door and waiting for me. After a moment I shrugged and followed him outside.

Chapter 10

By the spring of that year, I'd lost patience with school and given up the pretense of taking it seriously. I showed up to classes less often, socialized more, and took as much work as I could get, still convinced I just needed one big break to find the fame I sought.

Though my parts were still minor, I got offers frequently and my earnings swelled, giving me new freedom. I could afford to go out often, and even to stay downtown overnight. The legal drinking age had dropped to eighteen, since smart cars and advanced infrastructure had more or less eliminated the possibility of traffic accidents, so I no longer needed to fake my age.

The kids at home didn't need me anymore; I was no longer the centre of their world. They had other friends now, and mostly did well at school—better than I ever had. Something was going on with Tom again, but I didn't care to find out what. And Doc mostly followed Randall around these days. The kingdom I used to rule had faded away; wasn't I free to pursue new ambitions?

At first I went out with my usual friends, the Mountebank crowd and other actors. I followed where they went, to restaurants, bars, clubs, after-hours parties. Soon I was sleeping through the days, getting up only for work or to go out in the evening. For a while life felt exhilarating, dissolute, decadent. I wanted to taste a bit of everything.

Sometimes, in the loud, dark night-time spaces, mixed in with the drinking, drugs and dancing, I'd catch a fleeting glimpse of the kind of interactions I used to witness between Tiran and his subs. I tried to hide my reaction—the shiver of excitement, the almost painful throb tugging at my stomach—

but my companions picked up on it and began introducing me to more specialized clubs.

There, once again, I found the visible trappings of my secret desires, the power games that always enthralled me, on full display, this time live and in person. Intrigued and inexperienced, but emboldened by alcohol or chemicals, I let myself be talked into joining a few public scenes, where I dispensed punishment ineptly, tied cumbersome knots, or awkwardly accepted elaborate acts of worship. None of it was very satisfying. My partners mostly seemed distant, unmoved, or disappointed. I never felt powerful, only incompetent and vaguely fraudulent.

Thinking physical contact might be the missing ingredient, I tried experimenting with more personal encounters. It wasn't hard to find other club-goers with preferences that aligned with mine, men who wanted someone else to take charge of them for a time. We could get each other off easily enough, but when I tried to imitate what I'd seen in vids or at the club, my clumsy, amateur efforts satisfied no one. The brief liaisons would always end as soon as they were consummated.

It was frustrating. I lacked skill in the role I wanted to play, and hated the sense of letting people down. The scenes felt acted out, my encounters were impersonal, and nothing involved any kind of emotional investment. Where was the mystery, the connection, the flash of intimacy I'd sometimes witnessed at home? What most appealed to me—the glazed eye, the head bent over the hand, the willing service and casual imperiousness—I sought here in vain.

But why should I expect any of that? Everything I did made me feel more like an imposter, like I was claiming an authority I had no right to. Why should anyone look at me the way Tiran's subs looked at him? What could I offer them? People called this dynamic a *power exchange*, but how could I exchange what I didn't possess?

Just as with Lance's parties last year, I eventually gave up on the scene. What I needed seemed to live elsewhere—in the world where Tiran and Dusty moved, the world of money, fame, exclusivity, and the power that still eluded me.

I grew more critical and selective in my socializing. By now I knew which industry media were legit, and I followed them more closely to figure out who the powerhouses actually were and where they congregated. At work, I began to identify the players with the most influence, and cultivate those relationships–the ones who could help me access that other world. And once in a very exceptional while, when someone at the top, someone with real power, dropped a hint about what they could do in exchange for certain favours, I took them up on it.

Gradually, my social world shifted. While the best opportunities were still out of reach to me, a few doors opened, and the people around me changed. I could show up at a private event on the arm of someone of minor importance, and be introduced to people I only recognized from the media or gossip reports, people who worked on bigger and more celebrated projects than the ones employing me—sometimes even on projects that Tiran funded.

And occasionally, on a good night, I'd bump into Dusty, or Tiran himself, at a particularly upscale club or after-party. Dusty never seemed thrilled to see me; when I went over to say hello, he'd ask me when I last spoke to Jimmy, disapproval pulsing away from him like electron waves. But I particularly enjoyed swanning up to Tiran in a crowded room and greeting him with little cheek kisses. Gallant as ever, he'd humour me, returning the pecks and chatting gamely, until I figured I'd been seen by enough people.

Afterwards I'd outwardly ignore Tiran for the rest of the night, as though his presence was immaterial to me. But in reality, I saw it all—the assurance he moved with, knowing crowds would fall back to make way for him; the way his briefest glance would instantly secure a drink or cigarette; his look of bland boredom while being courted by the most important people in the room; the endless string of beautiful men on his arm—Severin was long gone, by now, but his successors followed regularly. At the height of the evening, Tiran always seemed to disappear, no doubt led into some deep, ultra-exclusive inner sanctum open only to him, and I'd find myself wondering, yet again, what I needed to do to gain access to all the privileges he had.

* * *

"A party?" Tiran said, squinting at me through a small plume of cigarette smoke. "I'm not much of a party planner."

"You don't have to do the planning; I'll take care of that. I just need you for the guest list. And, uh…to pay the bills."

"But here? Why not do it somewhere in the city?"

"No, it has to be here. In your house."

Tiran studied me from his lounge chair, skeptical. Across from him, I sat sideways on another chair, leaning forward earnestly to make my pitch. It reminded me of that long-ago negotiation, when I won the new gate. Only this time, Dell stood quietly in the background, behind the bar, apparently acting as our 'chaperone' today.

Around us, small coolingbots worked their miracles, humming faintly in the background to keep us comfortable in this early July heat. With school over for the summer, I'd come home for a little respite from the big-city life, arriving in time for Tom's eighteenth birthday a few days earlier. It was a very different affair from mine. His parents held a small dinner in their home, with his brothers and the other kids, but no one else around. Tiran had sent over a modest gift, some kind of fancy cooking gadget, which no doubt Gabe picked out.

I'd had my brainwave that night, as I thought about the differences between Tom's celebration and mine. It was the perfect plan. But I took a couple of days to mull it over, working out the details and making sure I had answers to the obvious objections, before I approached Tiran.

"What's Rick going to say about it?" Tiran asked. "How's everyone going to get through—"

"It's not going to be, like, some kind of keg fest at the Point. We'll have a very strict guest list—invite only, and limited numbers. It'll be *exclusive*." I was prepared for this one, and spoke frankly, with no attempt at flirtation. While I didn't believe Tiran was completely immune to my charm, I wasn't looking to provoke him just now. "I can get all the biometrics cleared with Rick's team in advance."

"So what do I have to do, exactly?"

"Just help me figure out the right people. The invites will go out in your name."

"I'm going to be inviting people you don't know to a party for your nineteenth birthday."

"A party you're hosting for my birthday. You know they'll all show up."

"What about the house?"

"I'll only need access to it a day or two in advance. You likely won't even be around."

I knew I'd won when he gave that familiar careless shrug, the one that meant it was easier to agree than to keep arguing. "As long as I don't have to do the work," he said.

"Only the guest list. You have a business secretary or PA or something, right? They can send the invites."

"Yes, but Aisha's not going to organize a party for you. That's a big job. Who's going to help you with that?"

I'd been wondering the same thing. My eye fell on Adele as I tried to come up with a response. I paused, looking at her deliberately, and then at Tiran "Maybe...you have someone who could help me."

He got the idea. "Dell," he said, very civilly, looking over at the bar, "I imagine you know how to plan a party. Can you help Barry?" For some reason, he always gave her orders in the form of a question.

She'd been watching the exchange, so she wasn't surprised. "Of course."

"I imagine you'll hire caterers, but you can borrow my subs if you need extra help on the day," Tiran added. He'd already picked up his comm and started scrolling, a sure sign he'd lost interest in the conversation.

"All of them?" I raised my eyebrows at him.

He glanced up. "You've already got Dell. You can have Pat. Gabe." He offered people up with such casual authority; it never ceased to fascinate me. "I guess Tom if you want. Not..."

"Dusty?"

"Uh...yeah, not Dusty."

But he hadn't meant Dusty. After a second, I realized who he'd been thinking of. Did Rocky belong to him that way?

The chalet was complete by now, and from what I understood, Rocky lived there for a few days or a week at a time, then returned to his family for a similar period.

"Is it working out with Rocky like you wanted it to?" I asked, but he only shrugged and lit another cigarette.

Over the next few weeks, as I worked on the guest list with Tiran, planned the party with Dell, and tried to avoid Jimmy's endless attempts at heart-to-hearts, I also started to notice some new dynamics in our little community.

Rocky had a more visible presence now, even if he still only lived here part-time. I often saw him outside, rounding up kids and adults for a game of football or soccer, which even I occasionally joined. He hung out with his brother Pat, Pat's kids, and many of the others as well; everyone seemed to love Rocky.

Of course, he also spent time with Tiran, if they were both around. But when I saw them together, I thought I could see hints of tension. Their old easy camaraderie remained on the surface but something simmered underneath, occasionally erupting in a caustic comment from Tiran or defensive rejoinder from Rocky.

And then there was Tom. By now I couldn't avoid the confused rumours that swirled around about him. People said there was a girl; that she died mysteriously; that it might have been self-inflicted. Others claimed he was involved with Paul Armstrong, which I dismissed at first; it made no sense. Paul was almost Tiran's age, and had a better idea of Tom's potential dark side than anyone—any of the adults, at least. What could possibly bring the two of them together?

I couldn't get any details about the girl, and when I asked Tom if there was anything he wanted to talk about he declined with his usual stoic reserve. In public, he and Paul never spoke to each other, as far as I could see, and Paul seemed to actively avoid any interaction with him. But when I watched Tom while Paul was nearby, I thought I saw something different in him—a kind of nervous consciousness combined with deliberate restraint. That's when I wondered if some of the rumours might be true.

CHAPTER 10

Towards the end of July, Tom asked me to go and look at an apartment with him.

"What? Why?" I asked. "You're moving out?"

"I…think so," he said cautiously. "In September."

"But—why?"

"I just think it might be time. Will you come with me to check it out? It's in Whittier."

As we passed behind Dusty's house on our way to the garage, I glanced up and saw Dusty, Kat, Rocky and Tiran on the back deck. They stood around with drinks, probably about to have dinner, but as we came into view, all of them stopped talking for a moment and watched us. I'd almost forgotten Tom's effect on people, and how much I enjoyed it. I couldn't resist sliding an arm around his waist, putting on a bit of a swagger, and giving Tiran a sly smile as we passed by.

We took my convertible into Whittier. The apartment was a modest but pleasant one-bedroom located downtown, near the school. I gave Tom my approval and he went downstairs to sign the papers.

When he came back up, he wanted to take some measurements of the vacant space and plan what to bring with him. I leaned against a wall with my take-out coffee while he explored his new home in more detail.

"I'm not going to high school this fall," he explained, pacing out dimensions in the main room. "I'll take a culinary program at the college instead. And night courses at the adult school till I can graduate."

"How are you going to afford all of this?" I asked; and then, as it occurred to me, "Is Tiran helping?"

"He's paying the college tuition but that's it," Tom said. "I've been working at that Italian restaurant down the street. I figure I can keep a few shifts once school starts. My folks said they'll keep giving me my allowance while I'm in school so between all of that I think I can make it work."

His vocabulary was so much better now. "What do your folks think of you moving out?"

"They don't really get it."

"Well—neither do I. What's the point of knocking yourself out to live so close to home anyway?"

He was in the kitchen at this point, so I couldn't see his face as he answered. "I just need a bit more independence."

"From your parents?" I couldn't imagine Pat or Adele being overly intrusive. "Are they giving you a hard time?"

"Not...exactly." As always, he didn't want to reveal too much. "Hey, do you think I could fit a four-seater table in here?"

I looked down at the coffee I was swirling around in my cup and thought of the strange tales I'd heard lately. "Does it have something to do with Paul Armstrong?" I asked, keeping my voice neutral.

"What? No. Come and look at—"

"Look, I don't get it, but you're eighteen now. An adult. They can't stop you."

Tom appeared in the kitchen doorway, looking unhappy. "Barry, don't. Please. Just—"

"There's obviously something going on. Everyone's talking about it." When he didn't answer me I said, more bluntly, "Are you involved with him or not? Just tell me."

"I'm sorry," he said, not meeting my eyes. "I can't."

A sudden suspicion came over me, and for a moment I couldn't breathe. "Is he—are you in trouble, Tom? Is he *blackmailing* you?"

"*No*. It's nothing like that. He's...helping me."

He spoke firmly at first, but the last words came out with more uncertainty, almost humility. I remembered those other rumours, about Paul once being a Dom, and my thoughts switched direction. The idea seemed absurd at first, too far-fetched to contemplate. But hadn't he also made that offer to Tiran? I heard myself asking: "Are you—subbing for him?"

He turned away from me without speaking, but not before I saw his face.

"*Why*?" I demanded, disbelieving. "Why would you do that? What does he have on you?"

"It's not like that. It's not—"

"I'll help you," I said. But even as I said them, I knew the words were futile. "If you need a way out."

"I don't," he said quietly. "I don't want out."

"You're telling me it's voluntary? Tom—" I grabbed his arm and tried to pull him toward me, though my strength was obviously no match for his. "Look at you! You have so much—people are so drawn to you, you have so much power. Why would you just...give that away?"

He turned toward me with his old, blank expression. "Let's just drop it," he said. "Please. I have what I need now. Let's get out of here."

We hardly spoke in the car, or in the days that followed. The conversation left me baffled and incredulous, and I couldn't shake the bitter taste of betrayal.

Chapter 11

A week before my birthday, everything was set. Tiran had helped me identify the hundred most influential people in the vid industry, and his invitations had been met with an almost perfect acceptance rate. I'd worked relentlessly through assistants and staff to gather biometric data for these guests and pass it on to Rick, so that none of them would have a hard time getting into the estate that night.

After some further negotiation with Tiran, we'd opened up the guest list somewhat. While we both agreed that adults and kids from the estate should be allowed to attend, Tiran had also insisted on including some locals and regular friends so that everyone would have someone to talk to. I didn't like the idea of watering down my exclusive guest list but eventually realized that additional invites would create more buzz, and raw numbers would add to the excitement during the event. I made Tiran promise not to include any of his own *inamoratos* though.

Dell and I had made every plan, checked every list, and confirmed every booking. The party was on Sunday, and we wouldn't have full access to the house till Friday, but we used Gabe's inside knowledge and some blueprints to map everything out. The party would start outside, on the terraces and lawns around the mansion, where we'd have gazebos, bars, food, light shows, and music from a couple of live bands fronted by famous actors. That would keep most of the regular guests happy.

Tiran's great room would act as an inner sanctum for the more exclusive attendees. I knew enough about how these affairs worked, by now, not to plan any gaudy entertainment indoors. This room, along with a couple of small reserved terraces directly outside of it, would feature much more sophisticated food and alcohol, dimmer lighting, a lone piano player, and what Tom always called "product" discreetly placed in multiple locations.

Finally, one or two smaller rooms off the great room, well stocked and very private, would be available to a small handful of the most select guests, to be determined, of course, only by Tiran or me.

It all appealed to my appreciation for hierarchy, while also ensuring I'd have plenty of opportunity to network with my chosen targets.

Dell and Tom consulted closely with the caterers on the food planning, paying special attention to the inside menu, and I deferred to their expertise; they both took food very seriously. There was a small prep kitchen off the great room that the caterers would use as their base, and Tom offered to work there with them during the event, but I declined. Pat, Dell and Gabe had been assigned to help the servingbots inside, so they'd be available quickly if any issue came up.

For the last few days before Tiran gave us full access to his house, I floated around in a state of perpetual nervous exhilaration. When I wasn't directly working on the party, I'd go for long aimless rambles with Doc, completely absorbed in the whirlwind of my thoughts and plans.

On Thursday evening, during one of those walks, I meandered into the small wooded area between Paul's house and the ocean. It was almost dusk, and clouds filled the sky, blocking the sun's low rays from penetrating the deep August tree cover. Narrow dirt paths wound through the grove, and I could see well enough to follow them, but the vegetation formed shapeless masses on either side of me.

Doc trotted slightly ahead, and I guess he gave away our presence a couple of seconds in advance. When I followed him into a small clearing in the middle of the woods, Tom climbed awkwardly to his feet just as a tall, thin figure slipped away along a path on the opposite side of the opening.

I startled, then recovered in time to pull Doc back to my side and face Tom as he stood up. "Hey, Mertz," I said. "Wasn't expecting to find you here. Or Paul. I guess he was just *helping* you."

Tom moved stiffly, and his eyes followed the figure disappearing into the gloom across from us. "Yes," he said.

The opaque response, the endless reserve, the way his attention seemed focused only on Paul…all of it infuriated me. "Don't you have any—*self-respect*?" I hissed.

Tom's gaze switched to me, and I saw the same analytical eyes he'd watched me with when he first arrived on the estate four years ago. Who was this man? Had I ever known him at all?

I remembered the way he could dominate a room, draw every eye; the vicarious thrill of pride I used to take in his presence. I'd always considered him an ally in my ambitions. I thought our goals were aligned, and that together we'd be unstoppable. But we both traded in the same currency, and he betrayed me every time he gave his away for free.

"You don't understand," Tom said after a moment.

"You're right," I said, my voice flat to cover the rage flaring behind my eyes. "I don't." I turned to leave the way I came, pulling Doc with me, then paused and glanced back at him. "Oh, I changed my mind. I want you working in the prep kitchen at my party."

* * *

Everything peaked around three a.m. All the guests I cared about had arrived, and hardly anyone had left. Outside, a band played and the crowd milled, still too dense to navigate, while projector screens and laser beams punctuated the darkness, and human servers threaded through with round trays lifted over their heads. Amplified music, multiple voices, laughter and shouts merged into a blanket of noise surrounding Tiran's house like a bank of clouds.

I stood on the highest terrace, near the French doors, taking a survey of the scene before heading back inside. This segment of the party would likely end first, but so far it was still going strong.

Lance stumbled up the steps toward me. "Jus' a few more months to go," he slurred, "till my Hummer…"

I pushed my glass against his chest to keep him a few paces back. "Hey, you're up next," I said. I'd agreed to let him run one of his sound mixes between bands. "Will you be okay?"

He waved a bottle vaguely. "Fine. Am fine. Stevie'll..."

Yes, there was Steve, standing by the sound board and looking to be in relatively good shape. "Okay," I said, and turned Lance around to steer him back into the crowd.

As I moved toward the doors, Jimmy appeared at my side. "It's been amazing," he said, "but I don't think I can stay up much longer. This is way past my bedtime."

"Glad you could join us." I took another look at the hordes clustered around the gazebos and stage on the route to our house, then seized Jimmy by the elbow and began to lead him through the chaos.

"Congratulations on the shindig, what an incredible job you've done," Jimmy rambled as I forced a path between the throngs. Crowds didn't part for me like they did for Tiran, though people sometimes stepped back when they recognized me. "But can we chat tomorrow or sometime soon?" Jimmy asked, as though he'd forgotten all the other times he'd asked the same thing. "There's things I really need to tell you. And I'm worried about Lance."

"Sure," I said, thinking *too little too late*. On the far side of the last gazebo the crowds thinned, and when we reached the path leading to our place I let go of his arm and gave him a quick hug.

Jimmy had to look up at me now. He gripped my upper arms and said unexpectedly, "Be careful."

"Good night, dad."

On my way back to the mansion, I passed Pasha, Randall and Curtis, standing in a circle with a few of their friends. I waved at them and continued on, but Pasha broke away and came over to me.

"Hey Barry," he said, reaching into his satchel. "Happy birthday. I made this for you."

He handed me a piece of thick folded cardstock, rough with the texture of paint and ink. My mouth dropped open a little as I took it; handmade art was almost unheard of these days. The cover showed a painted lion with a flowing tawny mane; inside, a handful of small lion cubs circled a slogan,

Never change, with *Happy birthday* and his signature hand-written in the bottom corner.

I threw my arm around his shoulder and squeezed. "It's gorgeous. Thank you, sweetie."

While he headed back to his friends, I made my way quickly through the terraces to the French doors and the inner party. I hadn't meant to be gone so long; I'd only wanted to take in a breath of fresh air and, hopefully, allow my absence to make hearts grow fonder.

Inside, I slid Pasha's card behind a vase on the nearest sideboard, and paused to adjust to the change in light and atmosphere. With the doors shut, the outside noise became a dull background rumble, a small reminder of what we escaped in this more serene, tasteful sanctuary.

Dim lighting illuminated small clusters of expensively dressed adults with high-end cocktails or canapés in their hands, sultry jazz piano providing a mellow counterpoint to the conversational buzz. Most guests stood in small groups, regaling each other with amusing anecdotes or escapades, although a few had paired off at the side of the room, probably negotiating new vid deals. Others sprawled comfortably in armchairs like they'd settled in for the night, or perched on the edge of sofas looking for better options. Virtually everyone in this room had been a stranger to me a few hours previously, but I knew them all by name and profession now.

A few familiar faces stood out, interspersed among the newcomers. There was Dusty over by the window, holding court with a handful of famous directors and actors. Rocky and Paul shared a sofa at the far end of the room, surrounded by a mix of new and old friends. I hardly recognized Dell and Gabe in their formalwear as they circulated among the guests, managing the catering company's servingbots. In the small prep kitchen, Tom heated appetizers and arranged them on trays. And where…oh yes, there was Tiran out on a small balcony, smoking and laughing with one of the many producers I'd met earlier. From his loose gestures and slightly louder than usual voice, I knew he'd begun indulging. He wouldn't be of much use to me now, but that was okay—he'd already played his part to perfection.

CHAPTER 11

I'd made my entrance a few hours back, once the party was well underway and most of the invitees had arrived. I captured most of the company's attention as soon as I appeared, but Tiran sealed the effect by immediately abandoning his conversational group and coming over to greet me with an affectionate embrace and double cheek kisses. Then he'd put his arm around my waist and led me around the room, introducing me to each guest with a pride that implied I could be anything from a beloved godson to the latest, hottest ingenue.

I saw the curious interest in each eye as I accepted handshakes and birthday greetings, trying to project grace and charm and just enough reserve to suggest further acquaintance with me was a favour that would have to be earned. I'd chat amiably for a minute or two, mentioning nothing about the industry and silently memorizing names, faces and professions, until we moved on.

Once we'd finished our rounds, Tiran set me up in a conversation with one of the most legendary directors in the country before making a graceful exit, his duty complete. Meanwhile, I opened by innocently asking the director what he did for a living, as if I didn't know, and finished up by allowing that I might possibly be open to hearing more about a potential role in his latest project, if my schedule allowed.

By the time that conversation ended, a big-name producer was waiting to talk to me, and after that, another. For the next couple of hours, I'd been approached by one intrigued powerbroker after another, until I finally took that break, to check on the scene outside and give people time to wonder if they'd missed their opportunity with me.

Now, as I lingered just inside the door, idly adjusting the gold theatre mask at my throat, heads had already turned my way, and a few new acquaintances started making their way toward me. Time to get back to work.

* * *

By around five o'clock, things had started to wind down. The outdoor sound system was off, and the crowds gone. Most of the inside guests had left, with the few who remained either nodding over the last of the product or curled up intimately in small groups in one of the more private spaces. Servingbots moved around the room picking up empty glasses and napkins, while the piano player spun out desultory arpeggios in the background. I didn't see Dusty anymore, but Tiran had joined Rocky and Paul on the sofa, and now seemed to be chatting with Rocky, while Paul glanced around like he was sizing up the end of the party.

I said good-night to a well-known director after yielding with feigned reluctance to her request for a lunch date to discuss her latest project. Though I'd had a few drinks, enough for a pleasant buzz by now, I still knew how to play the game.

Over on the couch, Tiran's voice grew louder as his conversation with Rocky escalated to a spirited squabble, though I couldn't make out the words in his erratic speech or Rocky's placating responses. Paul stood up, looking mildly annoyed.

"Hey, Barry..."

I turned around to see Tom, a dishtowel in his hands, standing beside me.

"Hey. How's it going in the kitchen?"

"I haven't had chance to talk to you all night," Tom said, drying his hands on the towel. "I wanted to say happy birthday and, um...you look really nice."

"Thanks."

He paused beside me, but I didn't offer any encouragement. The little drama continued to play out over on the sofa, where Rocky stroked Tiran's arm soothingly until Tiran wrenched it away and said something I couldn't make out, sharp and bitter. I glanced at Tom and saw his eyes follow Paul, who seemed to be approaching us.

"Listen..." Tom said in a low voice. "We finished up in the kitchen. Do you think it'd be okay if I left now?"

I smiled slightly, and turned to face Paul as he came up.

"Happy nineteenth, Barr." Paul gave me a quick hug and a peck on the cheek. "Great party, but I think I'm gonna take off now."

"Sure," I said, watching with amusement as he carefully avoided Tom's eyes. "Thanks for coming. Hey, Tom, weren't you just about to help Gabe pack up the servingbots?"

There was an almost imperceptible pause, and then Paul said, "Good night, Barry," and went out through the French doors into the night. Tom watched him go, gave a tiny sigh, and headed over to Gabe without saying anything else.

I picked up another drink from the bar and downed it before moving a little closer to the scene on the sofa. Leaning against the wall in a shadowed corner, I tried to catch the words flying between Tiran and Rocky.

Tiran had staggered to his feet by this time, and was pacing unsteadily back and forth in front of Rocky, who kept putting out a hand, trying to catch him as he passed. I'd never before heard Tiran speak so stridently; he usually got anything he wanted with a word or a gesture. Now his pitch kept rising, as though he'd lost control of his voice, but his words were too incoherent for me to decipher.

All around the room, people had started to watch the scene, discreetly or from the corner of their eyes—the few remaining guests roused by the noise; Dell, Pat and Gabe exchanging concerned glances; the last of the catering staff pretending not to notice.

On the sofa, Rocky pulled ineffectually at Tiran's arm, coaxing him to sit back down. It sounded like he was trying to reason calmly, but his voice kept rising to match Tiran's and also seemed to slur. I couldn't make out everything he said but caught a few words. *Still too young*. His kids? Or were they arguing about me?

"What do you care?" Tiran snarled suddenly, pushing Rocky's hands away, and this time the words rang out in the quiet room. *"You're—never—here!"*

They were both in sad shape, consumed with the energy of ancient unresolved battles. Rocky started to stand and Tiran shoved him, clumsily, but with enough force that Rocky lost his balance and fell backward onto the sofa. When Tiran turned and reeled away, Rocky called after him once, then gave up and covered his face with his hands.

A sympathetic chord thrummed inside my chest as Tiran's shaky steps brought him towards me, his face a jumble of bitter frustration and betrayal.

I stepped out from the wall to stop him, sliding my hands over his ribs, up to his shoulders and around his neck. "It's okay," I whispered, and held him for a long moment, until I felt his body slump against mine. Then I reached up to cup his jaw, lifted my face, and kissed his mouth. For a second he didn't respond, but I held the kiss until, finally, his lips pressed back against mine. I reached down to take his hand and led him away, to the private door I knew from the blueprints, through the rest of his house, and upstairs to his bedroom.

Chapter 12

It was a disaster, of course. Not that night, not immediately, but in very short order. We dragged it out for almost six months, though for most of them I already knew the truth.

We both woke up heavily hung over after the party. I found water, medication, and fresh fruit waiting on the bedside table, and recovered quickly enough to distract Tiran before he could try to take back the previous night's events. After that he never made any protests.

For the first few days we barely left his bed, and those days were better than any that followed. With my limited experience, I had a lot to learn. I'd only ever topped before, and since Tiran naturally assumed that role—as I'd expected—I started out in unfamiliar territory. But I was game for anything and adapted quickly, surprised at how much I enjoyed it all. Tiran seemed amused at my uncharacteristic artlessness and soon taught me what he liked, starting with the basics and moving on to more advanced techniques. I soaked it all up, exhilarated by the novelty, proud of learning new skills, and eager to develop a more sophisticated palette.

Tiran wasn't exactly a selfish lover; more just a competent one. He knew precisely what he liked and expected to get it, but was willing to accommodate me as long as it didn't take too much effort. He had a way of simply moving me around, positioning my body where he wanted it without any discussion, and then proceeding. If I tried to initiate or propose something new, he'd accept my awkward efforts patiently, then return to his own preferences. To my surprise, he wasn't particularly rigid about roles; he went down on me regularly, and once or twice wanted me to top, as though to sample my skill in that area, which I'm sure he found lacking.

"Shouldn't you be, like...tying me up or something?" I asked as he pulled me toward him at some point, early on. "I mean, isn't that what you guys do?"

He paused, and looked at me with mild interest. "Why? Do you want me to?"

I didn't, especially. But he was a Dom, and I'd always assumed that to be with him I'd have to play the role that complimented his. I'd made my peace with that before the first pass. On the other hand, there was no point feigning enthusiasm I didn't feel, since his lie detection superpower would recognize the deception immediately. "I mean...I don't mind. If you want to."

He half-shrugged, then got out of bed and rummaged around in a closet. "I think I have some rope here somewhere..."

I'd expected to be nervous or excited or something the first time we did this, but I found myself not feeling much of anything when he eventually produced a bundle of coiled rope. He positioned me on the bed and tied my wrists and ankles to the bed posts, the synthetic cord sliding smoothly against my skin. I was already used to him manhandling me into place and expecting me to stay there, so the physical restraints didn't change much for me. As far as I could tell, he didn't enjoy it any more than usual either.

"So what do you think?" he asked afterwards, as he untied the knots. "Did you like it?"

"Not especially," I admitted, scratching my wrist. "But don't you? I thought Doms got off on bondage and whatnot."

"I like to be in charge." Tiran tossed the rope back into the closet and returned to bed. "But I don't need to tie someone up to be in charge."

It was a relief to know I didn't have to play that part with him. But I still wondered about his life as a Dom outside the estate. Did he go to private clubs of the kind I once tried? Did he parade around in black leather and moto boots like the Doms I'd seen there? If restraints didn't appeal to him, did he enjoy inflicting pain or public humiliation? I remembered the frustration of my experiences, how the small, intimate moments always seemed to be missing at the clubs. The vulnerability, the private surrender, the palm kiss—surely Tiran knew where to find those.

* * *

My confidence remained intact, at first, despite my naïveté. Those early days were heady and exciting. I took a smug satisfaction in having finally won the game and gained the access I wanted. On his part, Tiran lost some of his cool reserve, and became more open and familiar with me. We laughed, talked and shared stories between escapades, and while I always assumed my main draw was physical, I believed he was fond of me.

"Have you called Jimmy?" Tiran asked after a couple of days.

"No." I lay by his side, running my fingers through the dark curls on his chest.

"Don't you think he might be worried?"

I scoffed. "Plenty of people saw us leave. He knows where I am." But I did turn around to grab my comm and send a brief message to Randall, asking him to look after Doc for me, before turning it off completely so I wouldn't be bothered.

I had no desire to join the rest of the world just yet, and no need to leave Tiran's bedroom. It was spacious and comfortable, with a large jacuzzi in one corner, a sitting area, bar, private balcony, luxurious ensuite, and a door that led to an adjoining room, which I soon discovered was Gabe's.

Gabe looked after everything. He had a way of slipping into the room, discreet and almost invisible, to stock the bar, deliver food trays, and look after our clothes. Any time we took a joint shower or otherwise both left the bed, we'd return to find it neatly re-made with fresh sheets and our side-tables equipped with water, fresh flowers and all the supplies we might need.

It was probably the fourth or fifth day when I woke up alone. I stretched, reached out and realized Tiran wasn't in the bed, then turned over and went back to sleep. A few hours later I woke again to find he still hadn't returned. I spent the day nosing around his room and scrolling through vids on the big screen.

"Where'd you go?" I asked, when Tiran came into the bedroom late that afternoon.

He sat on the bed and began unbuttoning the cuffs of his Italian-designed, custom-made shirt. "Had to go make up with Rocky."

I laughed, leaning over his shoulder to help with the front buttons. "You mean that fight at my party? I thought it was all his fault."

"Of course it wasn't." Tiran spoke with a dry matter-of-factness, like he'd been through this all many times before. "I was an asshole. Didn't I, like, hit him or something?"

My own memory was a bit hazy. "I think you shoved him."

Tiran stood up to finish undressing, then slid under the covers. "Well, whichever…I had to fly to his place, so that's why it took a while. But everything's fine now." He stretched out next to me in the bed. "Hope I didn't ruin your party, by the way."

That made me laugh again. "Not at all. Just gave people something to talk about. Anyway, it was pretty much over by then."

He turned his head to look at me. "So how was the party? A success? Did you get what you wanted from it?"

"Yes," I said, kissing him. "Thank you." I didn't tell him the party no longer mattered to me. Why would I need all those industry connections when I had him? Tiran's power dominated that world, and now I had direct access to it. If I played my cards right, I could get anything I wanted.

But not quite yet; I needed to fully secure my position first. In the meantime, I reveled in our new familiarity and intimacy, testing out my freedom to ask all the naïve or intrusive questions I'd avoided in the past.

"What were you guys fighting about anyway?" I asked the next morning, over our usual breakfast of yogurt and coffee.

"Me and Rocky?" Tiran shrugged. "The usual."

He'd always brushed off my personal questions like this, and before I would have let it go. But now I boldly pushed on. "So what's the deal with him? If he's your best friend, how come he didn't move to the estate when everyone else did?"

Tiran took a spoonful of yogurt. I might have liked a heartier breakfast, but Gabe's trays reflected Tiran's preferences, not mine. "He was going to, at first."

"So...?" I coaxed. "What happened?"

"He said he didn't want to be...too close. He said living here wouldn't give him enough distance from me."

"Why would he need distance?"

"To protect me."

"What?" I paused over my coffee. "Isn't that Rick's job?"

"Not like that." Tiran pushed the tray aside, then turned away from me and put his feet on the floor. He wore silk pyjama pants in bed, saying he didn't like the cold, but I preferred to stay undressed. After a moment, he asked, "Do you remember Jack?"

I scrunched up my eyes, searching my memory. "I think I've heard people mention him."

Tiran nodded. "Pat and Rocky's brother, the one in the middle. You might have met him once or twice, when you were very little."

"Didn't he—I think I heard he died?"

"He did, just before we moved here. He was twenty-two. It changed everything."

"I'm sorry," I said, still not understanding, but gratified to be getting so much information. "What happened to him?"

Tiran went over to the bar and reached for the whiskey bottle, though it was early even for him. "Jack was kind of a kid genius," he said, adding a shot to his coffee. "He invented these, like, special effects, some new technology for making explosion effects in vids. Made him famous almost overnight, at least in the industry. He moved out here for work, got a ton of jobs, made all kinds of money. But he was barely twenty, and all alone." Tiran paused, and lifted one of his hands slightly, palm up. "That's mainly why I got involved in the industry. I figured we'd come out here and join him, me and Dusty. I just needed a couple more years to wrap up my business."

It wasn't hard to see where this story was going, but what did it have to do with Rocky not living on the estate?

Tiran gulped half of his coffee before resuming. "Well, we were too late. Jack was out here alone, with no one who really cared about him. He crashed his car one night while he was wasted. This was in the old days, when accidents still happened. Anyway...that's how he died."

I waited a moment, then said, "That's a sad story. But what does it have to do with you and Rocky?"

"It's not complicated. If you can indulge your worst excesses with no one around to call you out, you're going to end up like Jack."

I recognized his words. "That's why you keep all your subs around?"

"Some of them happen to be subs," he said, a bit sharply. "But that's beside the point. I just need people willing to stand up to me."

"So you built the estate to keep all those people close to you. But that doesn't explain why Rocky didn't come. Doesn't he stand up to you?"

"Of course he does, more than anyone else. But after Jack died...well, he kept saying, if he lived with me, he'd be doing all the same things I did, indulging alongside me, and he wouldn't have any perspective. He said he wouldn't be able to keep me safe."

I could hear the old resentment in his voice. "You didn't agree?" I asked.

Tiran shrugged, and came back to sit on the edge of the bed. "He talked me into it."

"What's changed now?" I asked, moving my hand over the silk that covered his thigh. "Why build the chalet and expect him to spend more time here?"

This time he didn't respond. I coaxed a little more but he stayed silent, and I eventually gave up on words and just pulled him back into bed. He'd never shared as much with me as he had in the last ten minutes, so I took it as a win.

A couple of days later, when he went out on the balcony to smoke, I tried a different test. I didn't usually join him there, not wanting to risk being seen, but this time I grabbed the spare robe I'd appropriated and joined him, figuring I could manage an insouciant wave if anyone happened to be around.

"Can I have one?" I asked, indicating the pack of cigarettes on the table beside him.

“No,” he said, as I expected; Tiran never allowed anyone else to smoke on the estate.

“Why not?” I cozied up to him on the loveseat, not at all interested in cigarettes but ready for a challenge.

He exhaled without looking at me. “Because they’re bad for your health.”

“What about you, then?”

“You know I get treatments.”

“So why can’t I get the same treatments?”

“Because they’re experimental.” He spoke briefly, like the conversation bored him.

“Come on, Tiry,” I wheedled. “One smoke isn’t going to kill me.” I stroked his chest and nuzzled into his neck, then reached for the cigarette in his fingers.

“No.” He pushed my hand away. “Stop it.”

I pouted as prettily as I could. “I just want one taste. Why can’t you…”

He stood up so abruptly I almost fell off the loveseat. By the time I recovered, he’d disappeared inside. The cigarette package remained on the table and I was provoked enough to consider defying him, but knew that would only end badly.

I took a couple of deep breaths before following him inside. He was already dressed and fastening a gold watch around his wrist.

“You’re going out?” I asked, stopping mid-stride.

“Yes.” He gave himself a brief once-over in the mirror.

“When will you—”

But he was gone before I could finish the question. I went to the balcony door and watched him stroll down the path to the garage; a minute later a car pulled out and disappeared through the main gate.

That would soon become a familiar pattern. When I provoked him or pushed too far, he never bothered to argue with me; he didn’t chide or remonstrate; he just left. If I failed to amuse him, he found amusement elsewhere.

* * *

The next time Tiran got ready to go out, I begged him to take me with him. I didn't mind being left alone but I dreaded the idea of people seeing him come and go without me. Hadn't they all tried to warn me away? I wanted to flaunt my success, not look like some kind of helpless kept boy.

"You'll be bored," Tiran said coolly, as we stepped out of the shower.

"No I won't." I pressed up to him, running my hands over his stomach.

"It's just a business lunch."

"I'll be good, I promise. I won't say anything."

He started dressing, and shot a brief glance at my naked figure. "I'm leaving in ten minutes. You'd better be fast."

I searched around hastily for something to put on. I hadn't worn anything but a robe since the night of my party, and the only clothes I had here were the ones I'd been wearing that night. A fleeting thought of the lovely sweater and hand-crafted boots Jimmy gave me for my eighteenth birthday crossed my mind. But even if I'd had time to run over and get them, the last thing I wanted was Jimmy's inevitable lecture.

Fortunately, Tiran and I were close enough in size that I could make do with some of his pieces; a long designer wrap and silky draped shirt worked, along with the jacket I'd worn to my party. I gave my hair a quick tousle and followed him out of the room.

As we made our way over to the garage, I took his hand, and my smile was genuine, but we didn't run into anyone from the estate that day.

The lunch was with a celebrated director named Skylar. I listened to the two of them discuss details of an upcoming project Tiran was co-financing, and noticed how Skylar made a point of telling him the names of all the lead actors. He didn't ask Tiran for approval, exactly, but clearly gave him chance to express any objection. Surely if Tiran could veto project details, he could also propose them.

A few days later, when Tiran had another appointment in town, I drove in with him and then went clothes shopping, running up a tab in his name. After his meeting, Tiran took me to his personal tailor and ordered a few pieces he said would suit me. When they were delivered a few days later, I tried them on for him, amazed at how right he was.

CHAPTER 12

* * *

A couple of weeks after the party, Gabe brought us lunch and then returned a moment later with an apologetic knock.

"Jimmy's downstairs," he said to me in his quiet, neutral voice. "He'd really like to see you."

"Not now," I said shortly, reaching for my plate. Greens and egg-white omelette for lunch again; Tiran liked light lunches too.

Gabe hesitated. "What should I tell him?"

I put down my fork and reached for the theatre mask chain at my neck, feeling Tiran's eyes on me. "Tell him I'll see him when I'm ready. I know where he lives."

As Gabe slipped out, Tiran said, "You can't avoid him forever. He just wants to know you're okay."

"I know." I unhooked the chain and tossed it onto the nightstand beside me. It didn't really go with my new clothes anyway. "What about you?" I asked. "Are they all giving you a hard time about me, like you said they would?"

Tiran drizzled dressing over his salad and made a little face. "I've heard what they have to say."

He'd already stopped spending all his time with me in the bedroom. He didn't generally go out at night yet, but he hung out in other parts of his house during the day, where I'd so far declined to join him. Seeing other people didn't worry me, exactly—I wasn't embarrassed about my obvious success—I just wanted to avoid any lectures or scenes for as long as I could.

Tiran was right though; I had to face the rest of the world eventually. So I started to get dressed and go with him to the more public areas of his house—the great room or out on the terrace, where his subs brought drinks for both of us and visitors frequently dropped by.

No one looked surprised to see me there, or made any direct comments. I sensed obvious disapproval from some of the adults, like Rocky and Dusty, but put it down to jealousy. I was young and inexperienced, so no doubt they thought I wanted to serve him like they did. They didn't realize that my real desire was to sit beside him on his throne.

While the honeymoon might have ended, Tiran didn't seem to be over me just yet. He still treated me like a lover or a boyfriend, and I sometimes tested my hold on him. When other people took up too much of his time or attention, I'd whisper a sultry suggestion in his ear and could easily lead him back to the bedroom.

Chapter 13

I *could get used to this,* I thought, stretching out against the cushions beside Tiran. We'd just finished dinner on the terrace, cooked by his private chef and served by Pat, who was now bringing us nightcaps. Upstairs, the king bed awaited us, freshly made with pristine linens, and one of Tiran's closets contained a whole wardrobe of fine clothes custom-made for me. All I had to do was keep Tiran happy, which didn't even require the more disagreeable activities I'd been expecting; I just had to let him be in charge, and avoid the kind of scene that drove him away. Even his subs deferred to me as well as him now, and I enjoyed being waited on.

I understood the appeal of being a Dom all right. It was the other side that left me mystified.

"So let me get this straight," I said, once Tiran had dismissed Pat and we were alone again. "You're a Dom, but you're not into bondage. What about the other parts—hurting people or whatever—isn't that what the S stands for?"

He looked amused. "Did you want to try that too?"

"No," I said quickly; no need to go through it if I didn't need to. "But do you like it?"

"I don't get off on causing pain," he said, shrugging. "I like the idea that I *could* hurt someone if I wanted to. But I've tried it once or twice and it doesn't really do anything for me."

"What about your subs? Do they like it?"

He frowned a little, looking down at me. "There's not really one *they*. Everyone's different. Most of mine aren't into it though."

I tapped my fingers against the drink in my hand, thinking of everything I'd been wondering about over the years. It felt good to finally be able to ask all my questions. "So...what's in it for them? Why did they agree to sub for you?"

"*Agree*?" He pulled away from me, offended. "Do you think I forced them? They came to me."

"Really? Why?"

"Different reasons. You should ask them if you want to know their stories."

I already knew they wouldn't tell me anything; hadn't I tried with Dusty? None of the other adults here took me seriously enough to answer my questions.

I changed tactics. "So you didn't actually want subs? You just got stuck with them or something?"

He laughed. "No, I'm not saying that. I like having them around. I like being looked after." He paused and seemed to consider. "I mean, I guess I could just pay people to look after me, but...there's something satisfying about knowing they do it because they want to."

"Don't they, like...want something back, though?"

"Not really," he said. "You know, I used to go to the clubs or play parties and I'd meet these subs who wanted me to take them on permanently. But they always wanted me to teach them a bunch of rules or do specific things or whatever...and I just don't have the time or interest for that." He waved his cigarette dismissively. "That's why I like my guys. They figure all that stuff out by themselves. They set up their shifts and decide who does what; I don't have to deal with any of it. If I don't like something, I let them know and they fix it. It's their problem, not mine."

He spoke with such imperious authority. How could he treat the people who chose to serve him so cavalierly? I was fascinated but almost disconcerted.

"What about me, then?" I asked, rattled enough to sound abashed for once. "Why are you with me, when I don't do any of that?"

He laughed again, pulling me into his arms with enough force to dispel my sudden uncertainty. "You don't have to. I like subs but I like plenty of people who aren't." He lifted my chin with his fingers and leaned down to kiss me. "Like you."

* * *

The next time Jimmy came by looking for me, I went outside to meet him. As I stepped through the door, Doc almost bowled me over in his joy at our reunion. I had to give Jimmy credit for bringing him; it instantly put me in a much more receptive mood.

When I'd finished hugging Doc, I took his lead and Jimmy asked if we could go for a walk. I steered him away from the houses, toward the cliff behind Rocky's chalet, where we were less likely to bump into anyone else. As we walked, I asked about Doc's health—he was middle-aged by now—and whether Randall took good care of him. Jimmy told me Lance was away from home too much, drinking too much, using too much product, dragging Steve along with him too often. He said Randall and Dee were fine and doing well at school, but they missed me. For a moment, I wondered if I missed them too.

We reached a small sitting area at the top of the cliff and Jimmy pulled me onto the bench beside him, as Doc flopped on the ground at our feet

"Look, Barry, I know you don't want to talk about it," Jimmy said, putting a tentative hand on my knee, "and I can't stop you, but...are you really sure this is all a good idea?"

I patted his hand. "It's fine. I know what I'm doing."

"He's so much older than you. It can't be—"

"Please stop worrying about me, dad," I said, trying to hide my impatience. "I can take care of myself."

"But what kind of—of relationship can you have..."

"Come on." I interrupted him, laughing. "We're just having fun. I'm not looking to marry the man."

Jimmy studied me for a moment, and then gripped my hand in both of his. "Well, maybe that's all it is. Maybe it'll all turn out fine. But just remember, if things don't work out...you can always come home. Whenever you want."

"I know." I looked at the creases in his brow, the lines I'd spent so much effort trying to erase, and wanted to tell him I'd never live in his house again. I had confidence, I had plans, I had a future, even if he had no faith in me. "I'll be okay. Thanks for offering, though."

It took a while to satisfy him; he was probably never fully convinced. When we eventually walked back toward the mansion, I almost considered asking Tiran if I could keep Doc with us. Then I remembered my new life and realized Doc would be better off getting regular walks and attention from Randall.

I hugged and kissed them both goodbye, and went back inside the house to Tiran.

* * *

From the beginning, I'd told Tiran I didn't want Tom on duty when I was around. In the early days, when I kept to the bedroom and private parts of the house, he probably still took some shifts and I just didn't see him. But since I'd been making more public appearances, Tiran had banned him, as I asked.

When Gabe told me Tom wanted to see me, a couple of months after I'd moved in, I flatly declined. I didn't know what he wanted and didn't care; I had no interest in seeing him.

"Did you two have some kind of falling out?" Tiran asked me, after Gabe disappeared. "I thought you were buddies."

I shrugged, standing by the bar and watching the cocktail mixer work. Had we ever really been friends? "Sometimes I think there's something—wrong with Tom."

"Wrong?" Tiran looked up from his comm, where he no doubt had multiple deals underway, and leaned back against the sofa. "What makes you say that?"

"I don't know. He doesn't seem to act like other people."

"He seems normal to—"

"You've always had a thing for him." I tried to keep the resentment out of my voice, though it probably didn't work.

"Don't be ridiculous. I just feel responsible for him."

The mixer finished its work. I picked up both drinks and brought them over to the couch. "Why would you be responsible for him? He's Pat and Dell's kid."

"Yes, but..." Tiran accepted his Manhattan as he always did, like it was his birthright. "I vetted him."

"What? You what?"

"I mean, the consultants did the main vetting, like always. You know, they checked his background, did the medicals, all that. But Pat and Dell always asked me to give the final okay on their kids."

I looked at him, baffled. "Why you? Did they need your approval?"

He laughed. "No, nothing like that. Because of my superpower, you know. To make sure there were no big lies, no major red flags in the background that we didn't know about."

"Oh." I thought about that for a moment. "I guess it makes sense. But weren't Phillip and Curt too young for you to grill them?"

"Yes, for them I mostly just doublechecked the consultants, to make sure they were honest about what they knew. But Tom was fourteen, so I interviewed him directly."

When Tiran paused, I looked at him with growing curiosity. "Well? I guess he passed?"

Tiran tilted his head a little, holding his glass without drinking. "Technically, he didn't. I knew he was lying about something, but...well, I used my judgement. I thought they could take a chance on him. I've always wondered if I was right."[1]

I took a long breath, then a long sip of my drink. Tiran's interest made more sense now, but would I say he'd been right? And if he wasn't... what did that mean, for any of us? When I looked back at him, Tiran had returned to his screen, as composed as ever.

"Do you...think he's involved with Paul?" I asked, after a moment.

---

[1] For Tom's full story, see *Judgement, Part 1* by Mex Tate, on Kindle and Kindle Unlimited.

"Yeah, that's what they say, isn't it?" Tiran half-shrugged. "I don't know, Paul doesn't tell me anything. It's hard to believe. Paul's the most moralistic person I know."

I finished my drink, as Tiran returned to his endless messages and briefs. Tom and Paul still seemed like an odd combination to me, but they weren't my problem.

By this time, Tiran had started going out in the evenings again. The first few times he told me it was something he couldn't get out of—a work-related event, a commitment he'd made weeks ago—and I pretended to believe him.

Soon it became apparent this would be the new normal. I tried once or twice to stop him, using whatever arts I had and then sulking when they weren't enough. On those occasions, he left anyway, and stayed out all night. When he returned, I realized I had to change my strategy.

I'd been monitoring the media and saw a bit of speculation about me after the lunch with Skylar. A couple of sources had figured out my identity as one of the kids from the estate, but most referred to me as Tiran's "mystery date". Perhaps it was time to end the mystery. Didn't I want the world to know who I was and what I was to Tiran?

He had no objection to bringing me with him when he went out at night. Soon we were making appearances together all over town. I'd arrive on Tiran's arm, and he'd introduce me to the host without elaboration, letting our appearance speak for itself. Then we'd separate and circulate on our own; I'd be treated with courteous curiosity and deference, while he had his freedom.

Everywhere we went, young men who looked a lot like Severin hovered around, and at first I watched Tiran covertly to see what he did. He generally gravitated to friends and business partners first, but he clearly enjoyed other attention as well, accepting and returning it more openly as the night wore on and he drank and otherwise indulged himself. Still, I never saw him slip away with anyone, and when I went to collect him at the end of an evening, sliding my arm around his waist with a smile and a whisper in his ear, he readily headed home with me.

In the meantime, I didn't mind spending time with new acquaintances and people I'd met at my party. I drank and flirted and picked up news and gossip; I didn't have to show off my connection with Tiran since I'd arrived with him. And I stopped keeping an eye on him once I realized I'd get him back at the end of the night.

But somewhere in the recesses of my mind, I remembered Dusty laughing about how Severin would last a week or two before Tiran grew bored. No matter how much confidence I had in myself and my ability to hold Tiran's interest, I was well aware this affair wouldn't last forever. I'd secured my position as best I could; now it was time to put my plan into action.

I knew exactly what I wanted: what Tiran had. All of it; the power, the loyal subs, the casual assumption that anything I desired was mine.

The question had always been how to get it. Power had to come from somewhere. Tiran's came partly from his character, but mostly from his money. My association with him would never net me that kind of wealth. I smiled to myself when I thought of Jimmy's warning about not being in the will. For one moment I wondered if I could use my influence to change that; then I remembered what Dusty had said about the checks and controls on Tiran's finances. I had a mental image of Rocky being asked to sign off on a revised will or transfer to me, and shuddered. No, that wasn't the answer.

I thought about Tom's stunning presence and the charisma that attracted attention wherever he went. That was a kind of power, even if he threw it away. I could work out at the gym and build up muscles like his, I could dye my hair blond and stand out in a crowd, but nothing I did would ever give me his aura of mystery and danger. That came from the life he'd lived before we met him—a life that might also have warped and corrupted him. I would never have that, and I didn't think I wanted it.

The only power I'd been able to use myself came from my physical appearance—youth and beauty and charm; qualities that had obsessed older men for millennia. Qualities that, by definition, didn't last forever.

It all came back to fame. How many times had I thought that with Dusty's level of celebrity, I could write my own ticket? His kind of fame gave you power just as surely as money or looks did. And it had to be within my grasp.

I'd tried the hard way; I'd worked, gone to school, networked and played the game. None of it got me far enough. What I needed was a break, and Tiran could give it to me. Up till now, I'd never asked him directly to help me with my career; since we got together, I hadn't even mentioned it. But it was time to make my move. Now or never, I had to cash in.

So every time we went out, I listened. I talked and joked and drank and flirted but all the while I listened and waited for the opportunity I needed.

The first one came up after an opening gala for a vid Tiran had financed. I knew everyone in the room by now, and always gravitated to the players with the most clout. In this case, I spent much of the night with a group of producers discussing their new project.

"So..." I said to Tiran over breakfast the next morning, "Devlin says they're casting the new human-scripted prestige superhero vehicle."

"Uh huh?" He didn't look up from his comm.

"And they're looking for an 'unknown male' for the lead."

"Uh huh."

I pulled the comm out of his hand, and kissed him when he looked up. "Tiry," I said, "are you listening to me?"

"Um, sure, new vehicle, superhero, unknown lead. Oh." He laughed and squeezed my thigh under the covers. "Sure, you should audition."

I pouted a little. "I'm not great at auditions."

"I can help you," he said cheerily, and reached for his comm. "But give it back. I need to finish this note first."

"Help me how?"

"With the audition. We can practice if you want." He retrieved the comm and went back to his work.

After a minute I nudged him. "Thanks," I said when he looked up. "I appreciate that. But you know what would really help?"

I saw the mildness start to leave his eyes. "You know I don't do that, Barry."

"What? You don't do what?"

"What you want me to do."

"What do I want you to do?" I tried to keep my tone arch and playful, like this was a game.

"You want me to talk to Devlin," he said bluntly, pushing the breakfast tray away. "And you know I'm not going to."

"But why not?"

"Because I don't get involved in decisions that aren't mine." He was already out of the bed.

"Well, you *could,* if you wanted to."

He went into the ensuite without answering me. I considered going after him, joining him in the shower, turning on my charm to try and keep him from leaving. But I didn't, and when he came back out he dressed and left the room without looking at me.

He was gone for three days that time. When he finally returned I'd lost all my defiance, and made no recriminations. He offered again, perhaps kindly, to help with an audition, but I declined. The last thing I wanted was for Devlin to see that I didn't have enough pull to bypass the process.

A couple of weeks later a similar opportunity came up, and I tried again, this time with more active physical persuasion. But his reaction was the same, and this time, when I sulked in response, he left for almost a week.

From then on, the pattern was set. Projects came up, and I'd beg him to get me the break I needed. When calm discussions didn't work, I tried wheedling and cajoling, telling him his influence would make all the difference in my life. He barely listened, wouldn't engage with me. I tried to reason, to coax, to tease or flatter him into compliance. The harder I tried, the more bored he grew.

We kept up the fiction in public, at least for a while, going out together and generally returning as a couple. At home, we'd stop squabbling whenever someone joined us, and he'd make a show of treating me gallantly in front of anyone else. I could see in the looks I got from Rick and Rocky and the other adults that they recognized the pattern and saw the writing on the wall.

At one party, I spent the entire night flirting and sharing product with Devlin, a producer who almost rivalled Tiran in influence and power. He was older, distinguished, well-respected, and seemed to enjoy my company very much. After several hours, I just happened to see Tiran when he was apparently on his way out the door.

"Oh, are you coming home with me?" Tiran said casually, when I caught up with him. "I thought you might want to stay. Didn't want to disturb you."

Not knowing what else to do, refusing to concede defeat, I kept fighting. I'd sulk, pout, make demands or threaten until I drove him away, then throw myself at him when he returned—yielding, submissive, seductive, desperate to regain my hold.

The idea of giving up, of ending things with nothing to show for the whole affair, terrified me. Everyone knew exactly what was going on; my failure and humiliation would be visible to the whole estate. The faintest thought of returning to Jimmy's house sent a stabbing pain to my stomach that took my breath away. I drank far too much, and in despair I'd turn to Tiran again, trying one more time for something, anything, one break, one public triumph that would allow me to claim success. And every day he grew more distant and disinterested, more icily polite in public, and more immune to my persuasions in private.

It all came to a head about six months after it started, at a dinner party at Rocky's chalet. Rocky called it a housewarming, had Tom cater it, and invited Tiran, Paul, Dusty and a couple from New Ellay who'd never been to the estate before. Tiran drank too much and bickered with Rocky all evening. I alternated between trying to provoke Tom and seduce Tiran, culminating in a drunken proposal for a three-way with the two of them. Tom left with Paul, the new couple made an appalled escape, and Tiran said a few terrible things to Rocky before finally staggering home with me.

In the morning I awoke to find Tiran gone, probably on his way to make up with Rocky once again. I took the pain meds Gabe left out for me, got out of bed, and found an empty overnight bag. When I'd filled it with as many of my clothes as I could fit, I grabbed a handful of the loose bills Tiran always left on his dresser and headed downstairs. In the great room I paused to call Devlin, and reached behind the vase to retrieve the card Pasha made for my birthday. Then I headed to the garage, got into my little convertible and drove away from the estate for the last time.

Part III: Chapter 14

A few spindly weeds pushed up through cracks in the paving stones, and slabs of concrete ringed a crumbling, overgrown structure that might have been a small fountain once. It was only April, but already the blistering sun rendered most of the small parkette uninhabitable. As usual, I'd arrived early enough to claim the only usable seating, a faded blue bench under the shade of an ancient white oak tree.

From here I could see both the coffee shop across the street, where I'd picked up my daily iced coffee a couple of hours earlier, and the dilapidated motel on the opposite corner, where I paid for sleep by the hour. I nursed my coffee slowly, fending off the creepy old men who approached me periodically, and waiting for the sun to start its downward journey so I could return to the coffee shop for the single pastry I allowed myself each day.

Three years after I'd left the estate, the world seemed like a different place.

I'd lasted almost a year with Devlin. He probably did like me at first, although I often thought he liked the idea of possessing something Tiran valued even more. The two of them occupied the same space in high-end vid production and had a kind of semi-friendly rivalry. Of course I didn't let on to Devlin that Tiran had lost interest in me long before I left him.

I was clear from the start that I wouldn't sub to Devlin, and to my relief he had no problem with that. But as charming as he initially appeared, I soon discovered how much Devlin enjoyed using his immense power in the industry to control the people around him. Watching him dominate so openly was intriguing at first, until I saw how others reacted to him. These weren't people he had a private arrangement with, like Tiran did with his subs; they were simply employees trying to do their jobs while trapped in an unequal relationship with a man who relished his ability to force others to his will. No one loved Devlin, they only feared and hated him, but in an industry where everyone wanted something from him, he could get away with it.

For a while we made public appearances together, whenever I could be sure neither Tiran nor Dusty would be around; I had no desire to see either of them. I'd trail around the room on Devlin's arm a couple of times and then retreat to a corner where I could drink quietly and pretend to be indifferent. At private events, dinners or cocktail parties in his home, I dolled myself up and assumed the role of trophy partner, taking my place at one end of the long dining table and making bland conversation with the nearest guests.

I had free access to Devlin's tabs at the high-end stores, services and suppliers he used. That was probably intended to keep me occupied while he worked, which was most of the time. In the early days, I used them to update my appearance and furnish myself with a full new wardrobe. Later I shopped desultorily to keep myself presentable, and killed the rest of my time with alcohol and product. I'd deliberately left my own comm behind at Tiran's house but Devlin gave me a new one. I disabled all incoming signals, then used it once, to message Jimmy. *I'm fine, don't worry. Ask Ran to look after Doc.* After that I couldn't think of anything else I needed it for.

Devlin didn't really think of himself as a Dom, and had no regular subs. But when I let something slip about the clubs I'd been to, he immediately suggested setting up a private session and promised I could top alongside him. I had a few misgivings, but liked the idea of being treated as Devlin's equal, and thought I might finally satisfy my curiosity about what real power felt like.

We met our hired partner in a private room at a high-end club. Devlin approached the scene with a transactional brutality, no doubt justified in his mind by the amount the man charged to put up with him. The sub showed no interest or enjoyment as Devlin cuffed his hands together, gagged and blindfolded him, threw him into different positions and assaulted him with various implements. When Devlin paused to offer me a turn with the whip, I could only deliver one stroke before handing it back with a queasy shake of my head and the familiar sense of alienation.

"Suit yourself," Devlin said, "but I'm finishing." He seized the sub by the hair, removed the gag, and pushed him down to his knees. While the sub worked indifferently, with Devlin controlling his movements, I sat in a chair and waited for it to be over. Afterward Devlin suggested I take a turn, and I refused. This might be power, of a cold and scarifying kind, but it was nothing I had any desire for. I never joined Devlin in a scene again.

At home, in bed with me, Devlin didn't have Tiran's casual dominance, just the typical entitlement of older white men that I was becoming familiar with. He took what he wanted, rarely involving anything complicated or imaginative, and sometimes remembered to look after me before falling asleep. Once the initial euphoria wore off, he treated me with the same kind of surface courtesy Tiran did, which I started to recognize as the rich man's tool for avoiding scenes and keeping unpleasant emotions at bay.

When I first brought up the idea of a lead part in one of his productions, he responded benevolently, assuring me he'd find just the right project to guarantee my future. For the first six months or so I believed him. For the next three months we fought about it, and for the last three months I drank.

By the time we finally gave it up, I was in no shape to drive. Devlin loaded me and a couple of bags into my convertible and dropped me at a residential rehab facility somewhere in the suburbs. To his credit, those programs are expensive and he paid for a full two-month stay. I checked myself out after seven days.

That was just long enough to dry out. As soon as the worst was over, I searched my room until I found the phone Devlin gave me, and called Skylar, then gathered up my things and headed out of the facility.

As I crossed the parking lot toward my car, I saw a familiar figure emerge from the restaurant across the street and head my way. How had he known where to find me?

"Barry—" Tom said, trying to intercept me before I reached the car.

I stepped around him without breaking stride, my sunglasses hiding the small shock of surprise in my eyes. "What are you doing," I asked coolly. "Stalking me, now?"

"I just wanted to see you." He fell into step beside me, reaching for my arm. "Is everything okay?"

I shook his hand away. "How did you find me? Hire someone?" Reaching the car, I tossed my bags into the back seat and opened the driver's side door.

"Can we just talk for a minute? Please—we could go to—"

But I was already sliding behind the wheel. "Did Tiran pay for your private eye?" I slammed the door and started the engine, then put my elbow on the open window and looked up at Tom with my most sardonic expression. "Tell him not to worry about me. And for Christ's sake—stop stalking me."

I drove away before he could say anything else, and watched him grow smaller in the rear-view mirror.

* * *

Skylar was a director, a kind of *auteur*. He took his work very seriously, considering himself an artist and story teller. He used old-fashioned techniques and only worked with human-drafted scripts, refusing all modern artificial assistance and tools. Not surprisingly he had a reputation for being demanding, difficult, and brilliant.

When I came along he treated me like a muse, with a kind of exaggerated reverence. He talked endlessly about how I inspired him to new heights, how I created a fever of desire in him that could only be expressed through cinema and allegory. His vaguely European accent gave the words a chic sophistication that was hard to resist at first.

Skylar took a more creative and inventive approach to sex than my previous lovers. He often invited others to join us, and would shift roles and activities with enthusiasm. Sometimes he'd tell me he was putting me in charge of a scene, and the old spark of excitement would return—until I realized he never actually relinquished control. He had a way of manipulating the action, expertly leading and directing everything, from beside or below me or wherever he chose to be.

His approach was more creeping and insidious than Devlin's, but those encounters were just as devoid of whatever it was I'd been looking for. By this time I could hardly remember what I once found so appealing about power.

I lived with Skylar for about nine months in total, a bohemian life full of fellow *artistes*, strange followers, and an endless stream of houseguests. The media loved him and there were sometimes stories about us, about the great man and his beautiful young protégé. I finally achieved a tiny measure of that fame, or at least celebrity, I'd been seeking.

Unlike Tiran or Devlin, Skylar actually did find a part for me early on, in one of his more experimental projects. I didn't understand the piece at all and could not fathom what he wanted me to do in the role. To no one's surprise, the vid bombed when it released six months later, with my performance being particularly savaged. After that, Skylar would shrug his shoulders, exhale delicately, and say in his usual melodic accent, "But I tried, darling, is it not enough that you inspire me?"

Sometime after this debacle, between the drinking and the product, I had one brief moment of clarity—a fleeting recognition that if I didn't do something to change my trajectory it would soon be too late. But when I made a vague suggestion about going back to school or taking classes, Skylar only laughed gently and asked why I'd want to put myself through that.

In September I turned twenty-one, which was marked with a brief toast from Skylar over dinner and nothing else. I still had the comm Devlin gave me, with incoming signals disabled, and shortly after my birthday I sent Jimmy another message telling him I was fine.

Soon afterward, Skylar managed to pass me off to one of his friends while I was blissfully unaware of anything going on around me.

From then on, my memories are hazy. I know I moved frequently and spent less and less time lucid. The men I lived with varied—some older, some younger; some kinder, some crueler; a few genuinely appreciative of me, and many more callous and indifferent. Most of them, as far as I can recollect, were involved in the industry one way or another.

I remember glancing in a mirror now and again and noticing the change in my looks. *I'm losing all my bargaining power*, I'd think, and then try to recall what I was bargaining for.

I lost track of dates, but it would have been more than a year later when I spoke to Jimmy for the first time since leaving home. I'm not sure where I was, whose comm I used—I'd long since lost Devlin's—or what my thought process was. Perhaps I had some vague idea of going home, but if so it didn't last long. Jimmy gasped when he heard my voice, and peppered me with quick anxious questions that I fended off as well as I could. Then his voice changed.

"Did you hear about Lance?" he asked, and went on without waiting. "I guess you couldn't have, we didn't know how to reach you. Barry, Lance is gone." This time he paused, as though waiting for me to respond, but I only stared blankly at the comm, swaying a little. "He OD'd. I'm sorry. We wanted to tell you but I didn't know where to find you."

"What—what…when…?"

"It happened this past summer. Jul. He was living downtown with Steve." Jimmy's voice cracked a little, and when it resumed he sounded tired and old. "He was only twenty."

"But…what about the funeral or—or…wasn't there anything?"

"We had a service right afterwards, and then a memorial last month. I'm really sorry, Barry, if I'd known I was going to hear from you I would have waited."

I could hardly blame him for not expecting my phone call. Even when I signed off so I could go and drink myself to sleep, I made no promises about when he might get another one.

* * *

Toward the end of that year, I grew dimly aware of being back in the vid industry. *Oh look*, I'd think; *I'm on a set. I'm working again.* But the sets were so small, they were rife with alcohol and product, and working had become oddly entwined with having sex—sex that grew more unpleasant, mechanical, and brutal in strange and numbing ways. When I eventually woke up to where I was, I could only focus on a single horrified thought: *I can't do this, what if the kids see me?*

That's when everything changed in my mind. Once—it seemed like long ago—I'd believed in acting as the path to fame and power and something that would send warm currents through my body, make my stomach twist with desire. I'd found power easily enough—the whole industry seemed to be built on it, inextricably tied to it. But not the power I wanted; something uglier and more debasing. Something I no longer wanted anything to do with.

Suddenly I'd had enough. I wanted to halt everything, go back, find a way out. Only it was like getting up in the middle of a spinning carrousel and saying *Stop I need to get off*: it's hard to find the exit when you're too dizzy to stand upright. I didn't know where I was, I had no resources, and I was kept more or less continually in a daze. In my short moments of lucidity I'd try to formulate a plan, but it took a long time to execute one.

Sometime in January or February I managed to get hold of a comm. I think I shut myself in a bathroom when I made my first call, which was to the rehab centre Devlin dropped me off at two years ago. I probably had some vague idea that, since my stay had already been paid for, I could go back. When they declined to accept me, I started making random calls to anything that looked or sounded like a similar facility. Whenever I reached one, they'd quote me prices beyond anything I could imagine, and say I needed to pay half of it upfront. I had no idea where to start.

I was sitting on the bathroom floor with my head in my hands, thinking queasily that someone must owe me something for the work I'd been doing, when the comm beside me buzzed. I picked it up, and a woman told me she was calling from Harmony Recovery.

"I just spoke to you," she said, her voice warmer now than it had been earlier. "A few moments ago. You indicated you wouldn't have the funds to be able to complete our program…But I've just been advised that we do have one spot available in our sponsored stream."

My brain spun too erratically for me to decipher her meaning. "I don't get it."

"We have a free spot. Can you get here this afternoon?"

"I—I..." I had a car once, didn't I? But I hadn't seen it in a long time. "I don't..."

"Take a taxi, and we'll pay for it when you get here. I look forward to meeting you, Mr. Hawkins."

And so I'd entered the residential recovery program at Harmony, and this time I completed the full sixty days.

It wasn't easy, and there were times I didn't think I'd make it, but after the initial detox it mostly got better. A nihilistic recognition that I'd already lost everything I'd ever wanted in life brought me a strange kind of peace, and I had no desire to get back on the carrousel I'd just escaped. I even borrowed a comm with the idea of calling Jimmy, though when I remembered our last conversation I sent him a message instead. He probably wouldn't believe my usual assurances, but at least he'd know I was still alive.

Consistent sleep, food, exercise and medical treatment went a long way, but of course the program also involved counselling and therapy. While I didn't mind discussing mental health strategies, therapy was a different story. I faked my way through most of it, flat-out refusing any discussion of my background or history. I'm not sure if the staff ever figured out who I was or where I grew up, but it was impossible for me to talk about any of it. The past was a no-go zone in my mind; any time I tried to call up a memory from the estate or the rest of my past, my brain would combust, like a spark igniting a flame. Everything inside was a toxic jumble I couldn't begin to sort through.

Aside from that, I completed the program more or less successfully, and they released me in mid-March with a follow-up plan I vaguely committed to.

I left the facility with a backpack holding a couple changes of clean clothes and nothing else. The convertible was long gone; I faintly recalled selling it for quick cash somewhere along the way, probably at a fraction of its value. Anything I'd gained or been given over the last couple of years was lost.

But I knew I had earnings from before then, from all the small acting and modelling jobs I'd taken during those pre-Tiran years. That was the basis of my follow-up plan. Without a comm I couldn't access those funds directly, but they had to still be in whatever bank held them.

My first mission when I got out of rehab was to find the right banking access portal, which took a while since only a few physical portals remained in the city, and I didn't know or couldn't remember any details about my account. I eventually found the closest place that accepted my biometric data, just around the corner from the coffee shop here in this seedy little corner of New Ellay.

That was when reality hit. I'd expected to find a tidy little savings stockpile that would tide me over till I got re-settled, only to discover almost nothing left. I'd spent far more than I realized on hotel rooms, parties and general decadence in those last few months, after I'd left school and before the affair started. The limited funds remaining would keep me going for a few weeks at best.

Once I recovered from the shock, I tried to adjust my plan and keep following it. I cashed out everything I had, paid for three weeks in advance at the nearby motel, and started looking for work—anywhere but in the vid industry. Of course, that didn't go well either. Most low-skilled jobs had been long lost to robot technology and AI, which meant few options and fierce competition. With no experience, no skills, no education and now, for the first time, no connections and no looks to lean on, I didn't have much of a chance.

So here I was, pretty much where I started, near the banking portal. When my advance payment at the motel ran out, I began paying for sleep by the hour. I limited myself to one coffee and one pastry a day. The coffee shop manager would ask me to leave after a couple of hours, so I spent most of my life in this little parkette, staking out my bench in the morning and not wanting to leave it.

The options ahead of me shrank daily. Sometimes I wondered why I didn't just go home, but when I tried to imagine asking Jimmy to pick me up somewhere my brain simply shut down. The tangled knot filling my mind repulsed any attempt to explore it.

I dug through my backpack, searching for lost bills. The bunched-up clothes stuffed inside were damp because I'd washed them in the motel room sink and had to take them with me before they dried. Under the clothes I found a few torn and sodden pages, and smoothed them out. There was my "release plan" from Harmony; I crumpled it up and tossed it into the trash can beside me. I spread out the other, slightly heavier sheet and could just barely make out the image of a yellow lion on the cover. Had I really dragged that birthday card around with me for the last three years? I looked at it for a moment, folded and unfolded it a couple of times, then threw it into the trash with the release plan, and continued my search for cash.

With everything I scraped up from my pockets and the backpack, I had just enough for today's pastry. Nothing for the motel, so I'd have to sleep on the small patch of weeds behind the bench tonight. Tomorrow I'd head over to the rent boy district and see if I could make a living there.

Chapter 15

I noticed the man while I lingered over my last pastry at a table in the coffee shop. He gave me a searching look from the lineup, which I met with the haughty expression I reserved to rebuff advances.

After he finished his purchase he made his way over to me, a lean, fit, very dark-skinned man with close-cropped hair and gold-rimmed eyeglasses. You didn't see many people with glasses anymore; it gave him a slightly old-fashioned air.

"Barry…Hawkins, isn't it?" he said, standing in front of my table with a coffee in his hand.

No one had said my name since I left the rehab centre. "Uh. Yes?"

He put out his hand. "Jonah Demille. I guess you don't remember me, but we've met a couple times at industry events."

"Oh." I froze for a moment, caught between conflicting instincts to fend off a potential proposition and to meet civility with civility. Old habits won out, and I reached up to shake his hand.

"I think I've seen you here before," he went on. "My studio's just a few blocks away, so I'm in here a lot." He gestured out the window with his coffee cup, and then at the chair across from me. "May I?"

I didn't exactly want company but somehow this had turned into a social exchange, which I'd almost forgotten how to navigate. After a moment I gave a slight nod.

"How are you doing?" He pulled out the chair and sat down.

"Fine, thanks," I said mechanically; then, "I don't remember where I met you."

"Pretty sure the first time was at the opening for *December Rain,*" he said. "At the Century Theatre."

I nodded; that checked out. It was a war vid I'd had a bit part in, just before I turned nineteen. "Yeah, I would've been there."

"You still doing vids?" he asked.

"No."

He sipped his coffee for a moment, and there was a brief lull. Then he put down his cup and said, "Listen, I could be out of line but I'm just wondering if by any chance you might be looking for work?"

I hesitated. "Why? You have some?"

"Well, to tell the truth, I'm looking for a house—" He stopped, catching himself. "A housekeeper."

I knew what he'd been about to say. "Not interested."

My flat refusal made him pause and weigh his words. When he spoke again, it was with a kind of reluctance, as though revealing more than he wanted to. "I had a houseboy once," he said, looking down and pushing his coffee cup around in a small circle. "But he left, and I don't want another one. I just need someone to keep house for me, nothing else. I work long hours, and I can't afford all the new robot tech. It's a paying position."

I broke off a small piece of the pastry and put it in my mouth. There wasn't much left. "What do you mean by keep house?"

"The regular things. Cleaning. Cooking. Laundry."

Somehow that made me laugh. "I don't know how to do any of those things."

"I can teach you."

There was another pause, while I studied my plate and wondered if I could get two more bites out of the pastry.

After a moment he said, "I'm not looking for company, but the job comes with a room in my house if you happen to need a place to stay."

I took another long look at Jonah. He had to be at least ten or fifteen years older than me, maybe more. And I was mighty tired of older men. "I don't know," I said. "I'm not really interested in providing personal services." As I said it, I thought of my plans for the next day, and the services I'd be providing then.

His coffee cup was empty now. He nodded and pushed back his chair slightly, as though to leave, then seemed to re-consider and leaned across the table toward me. "Look, I get how you might be cautious. I'll tell you what we can do. Come on over to my place now and let me show you around. I'll give you a week's pay in advance. If you don't like the looks of things, you can just let yourself out."

I considered my options and didn't really like any of them. But I'd finished off the pastry and would have to leave the coffee shop regardless. "I'll go with you," I said, keeping my voice neutral, "but no guarantees."

Jonah didn't talk much on the walk to his car, an older model that he drove manually, or during the ride to his house, which was in a modest neighbourhood about twenty minutes away. Dusk had set in by the time we arrived, and he pulled his car against the curb under a glowing streetlight.

"Bus stop is just over there," he said, pointing. "In case you're wanting to leave."

His house was a small, neat box, one storey, with a peaked roof and yellow shutters. He led the way up a path made of concrete pavers crossing a tiny green lawn. Inside, I stood with my back against the front door.

He turned on the foyer light, which illuminated a living room in front of us, then disappeared through an opening to the left and turned on another light. "Come on," he said, returning. "I'll show you around."

When I followed him, he gestured to the left. "Kitchen in there. This is the living room." He crossed to a short hall on the other side of the room, and started down it. "This one's my room, on the right. First on the left is the guest room, the second would be yours. Bathroom at the end."

He stepped aside as I walked around him and opened the second door on the left. It revealed a simple, clean room with a single bed, dresser, chair, and curtained window. I stood in the middle of the floor, still holding my backpack.

"Feel free to check things out," he said from the hall. "I'm gonna get started on dinner. You prefer an omelette or steak?"

"Steak." My heart leapt at the question, and I made up my mind to stay long enough to eat, anyway.

His footsteps retreated, and I circled around the room. The window looked out on the back of the house, and the only door opened into a narrow closet. No bathroom, I noted; we'd be sharing the one at the end of the hall. Then I noticed the bedroom door had a small lock on the inside, and tried it out. It seemed to work.

I put my backpack on the chair and went into the bathroom to clean myself up a little. When I came back out to the kitchen, Jonah was standing over an old gas stove, two steaks sizzling in a pan in front of him.

"I'll just get these started on top," he said. "Then they'll go in the oven. Maybe you could scrub a couple of those potatoes, you can find a brush there by the sink. I'll try to find something green in the fridge."

As odd as it was to be cooking companionably with a man I'd only met—or only remembered meeting—an hour or so earlier, the smell of the steak made me ravenous. It was a long time since I'd eaten more than a single daily pastry.

Just like in the car, Jonah didn't say much over dinner. When I couldn't finish my plate, he told me to put it in the fridge and heat it up again later if I wanted. Afterwards I helped him load the dishwasher and scrub a few pots.

Then he led me through a door at the back of the kitchen into a compact utility room with laundry machines and cleaning supplies. In one corner, three stairs led down to a landing with a back door, before turning and continuing on to a basement or crawlspace.

Jonah opened the door to reveal a small bare yard, more dirt than grass, with a shed and a path leading along the side of the house. "If you want to leave while I'm not around, you can go out this way and leave the door unlocked behind you." He picked up a ceramic jar from a ledge beside the door and added, "Hold on now."

He disappeared up the steps, and I sat on the back stoop, feeling faintly ill from eating too much too quickly. In a couple of minutes Jonah returned, with a roll of bills in one hand and the jar in the other.

"I'm thinking cash might be your best option for now," he explained. "That's one week's wages." He slid the roll inside the ceramic jar, put the lid back on, and returned it to the ledge beside the back door. "You can help yourself any time if you decide to vacate."

He went back up the stairs and I followed slowly behind him, still thinking about the cash in the jar. In the kitchen, Jonah took a beer out of the fridge and asked if I wanted one. When I shook my head he walked into the living room, speaking over his shoulder. "It's too late to do anything tonight, so just take it easy. We'll get started tomorrow." He picked up a tablet, settled into an easy chair and seemed to forget about me.

For a few moments I stood uncertainly in the kitchen doorway. My stomach still felt unsettled. I crossed through the utility room to the landing, picked up the ceramic jar and went to sit on the stoop again. Jonah must have heard the back door open, but he didn't say anything or make an appearance. I counted the bills, and sat with them in my hand until the cool evening air dispelled my queasiness. Then I returned the bills to the jar and the jar to the ledge, and walked through the living room to the hall. Jonah didn't look up when I passed.

My backpack sat on the chair where I left it. That bed sure looked more comfortable than the weeds in the parkette. I shut and locked the door, pulled my few clothes out of the backpack and hung them over the back of the chair, opened the window for a breeze, and fell into bed.

* * *

The next day Jonah took me shopping for some new clothes. "Looks like you need a few things, and I can give you an advance on your pay," he said.

"Thought the money in the jar was my advance," I said, looking up from my left-over dinner, which I'd heated up for breakfast.

"That's more like a deposit. If you don't use it, it's not anything."

I took a long hot shower, put on my one clean set of clothes, and followed him out to the car. The stores in the mall he took me to were a far cry from what I'd been used to with Tiran and Devlin, but I got everything I needed while Jonah sat on a bench with his tablet and a coffee.

"Don't you have to work?" I asked, as we drove back to his house.

"I pretty much keep my own hours," he said. "Figure I might as well get you set up today and go in tomorrow."

For the rest of that day, and over the next few weeks, Jonah showed me how to keep house for him. All of it was new to me. Aside from helping Jimmy load the occasional dishbot, I'd never done any domestic tasks. One of Tiran's paid staff had always cleaned our house, and Jimmy took care of meals, laundry and everything else.

Jonah started out slowly. He showed me how to sweep, vacuum and mop floors; how to do laundry; how to make simple meals. As I mastered the basic tasks, he taught me more advanced ones. I learned how to cook complex meals, operate kitchen appliances, manage meal planning, shop for groceries, change bed linen. Everything he expected me to do, he had no hesitation to do himself, often working right alongside me until I got the hang of things.

As he'd said, he worked long hours. At first he had to wake me up in the mornings to help him make breakfast and go over what he wanted me to do for the day. Over time, I came to understand his expectations and learned to meet them without being told. I got up before him, knew what had to be done each day, and would have dinner ready for him when he got home in the evening. He didn't give me orders, speak harshly, or treat me like a servant, but he had very specific routines, and I adapted to them.

Over the next few months we settled into a comfortable rhythm. Within the limitations of his schedule, I had pretty much complete freedom, and my work didn't take up the whole day. I could spend time sitting in the backyard with a coffee, or wandering the neighbourhood, or picking up essentials at the local mall. Jonah paid me every week, in cash until I eventually got a new comm and then by transfer. Occasionally I'd check inside the ceramic jar just to make sure the money was still there, but I never used it.

Jonah showed no sign of interest in me, and made no advances. We'd chat a little over breakfast and dinner, though he wasn't a big talker. He went out, to the gym or with friends, and often had visitors over, but many times he spent his evenings at home in the living room with a screen or tablet. Sometimes I'd join him to watch a vid on his screen. Other times we'd hang out in our own spaces, me in my bedroom or the backyard, and just leave each other be.

* * *

"So what do you do for a living?" I asked one morning. It had only occurred to me to wonder after a few weeks.

"I'm a consultant," Jonah said, taking a swallow of coffee. "I have my own company. I do freelance work with the vid industry."

I tensed, dropping my fork. "I don't—"

"I know you're not part of that scene any more. Me neither, for the most part. I do my work completely separate, during post."

I stared at my plate, fighting the urge to flee. *The jar; the back door; this was all a mistake.* But what did I expect? Hadn't he told me right at the start that we met at some industry event?

He took another forkful of the scrambled eggs I'd made for breakfast and went on. "I have my own studio. Mostly I work alone. Don't deal with anyone except the director or A.D. or whatever."

The coffee in my mug sloshed a little as I picked it up. "What do you consult on?" I asked.

"Well, military scenes mostly. I'm ex-military myself, don't recall if I mentioned that. I review footage to pick up errors, make adjustments for accuracy, that kind of thing."

"Sounds pretty specialized." I tried to breathe normally.

"It is. I'm the only one doing it, the only one with this particular expertise. That's why I can make a decent living."

"So...you just get footage, review it and send it back with suggestions?"

"Mostly. I do a bit of work myself on some of the effects. Explosives, mostly; there's a lot of that in my field."

I took a bite of toast. Something about what he just said rang a bell. Explosive effects... "You ever hear of a guy called Jack Van Valkenburg?" I asked.

Jonah's eyebrows lifted. "Course I did. He's a legend in that area. Why?

You knew him?"

"I...knew his brothers."

There was a long pause. Jonah had never asked me about my background, but now I could see him putting it together. "You're one of those kids that lived in Tiran Marx's compound."

"Yeah." I kept eating, bracing myself.

"Dusty St. Vincente's an old friend of mine," he said after a moment.

That took me by surprise. I set my forearms down on the table on either side of my plate, my hands making involuntary fists. "Listen. I don't want anything to do with—"

"I get it," he said.

"You say you aren't part of the scene, but I recall you telling me we met at some industry event. Which is it?"

He nodded and pushed his plate away, folding his arms on the table across from me. "I believe we first met at a movie opening. Once in a while I get invited to something I worked on, and once in a while I go. I don't go to industry parties as a rule, but sometimes when Dusty's hosting I'll show up. Might have been at one of his affairs where I met you another time; I seem to remember you being with some producer bigwig."

My mind whirred incoherently as I listened, still trying to analyze the danger. "Does Dusty ever...I don't want to see him."

"He doesn't visit here." Jonah tilted his head to the side, studying me. "I'm not going to tell you I'll never go to another industry event. I have friends who work in the field. But regardless, that doesn't involve you. You don't need to know where I go or who with. You don't want to see that crowd, you don't have to."

I took a deep breath, assessing his words. I'd much rather have forgotten the whole industry existed. But as long as I stayed here in New Ellay I'd never get away from those people completely. At least Jonah was straightforward about it; and from what I'd seen of him so far, he spoke the truth. Already I was half embarrassed at my reaction, as though I'd given away too much.

"Okay," I said after another moment, getting up to clear the table. "As long as I don't have to hear about it."

Gradually, as I grew comfortable around Jonah, I started spending more time with him. As far as I could tell, he had no romantic interest or partner, but he did have a small handful of close friends who would drop by the house regularly. They were all around Jonah's age, much older than me, but none seemed to be involved in the vid industry even peripherally. Len, for example, was a lively, outgoing bartender, and Malik, who seemed quieter and more introspective, worked as a robotics engineer. I sometimes joined the group of them for a beer, or even tagged along when they headed to the local bar to play pool or darts.

Like Jonah, Len had been in the military, and both of them saw action during the so-called Fractured Decade of the 2070s. Sitting around the house, or in the backyard when the overheated sun permitted, I'd listen to their stories in fascination and sometimes horror. Not just the civil war tales; many of their early experiences amazed me too. They'd both grown up poor and joined the military at a young age to escape, and much as I tried to avoid my own childhood memories, I couldn't help an occasional fleeting *If not for Jimmy and Tiran...*

Jonah would sometimes compare notes with Len, whose skin was a ruddy white, on their lives in the military. When I first heard the two of them casually discuss how Jonah's treatment had been impacted by his skin colour, the shock must have shown in my face. They saw my expression and laughed a little.

"Oh, I guess Barry bought into all the government propaganda about how *we've moved past race in this day and age*," Len said mockingly, repeating the line that ran in every history textbook as I was growing up.

"I suppose you didn't run into that bullshit so much, growing up in Marx's little kingdom," Jonah said to me. "You must've seen it in the industry, though."

"No," I responded instinctively, then stopped and considered. There'd never been anything overt, but a couple of odd comments or inexplicable reactions suddenly came to mind.

Jonah watched me as though he understood my thought process. "Might have something to do with why you left?"

I put my beer bottle down firmly. "I didn't make it as an actor because I was a shitty actor. I didn't work, I didn't study, I didn't even learn my lines." The last thing I wanted was to make excuses for my failures, or to start thinking of myself as a victim. "But I'm not saying that stuff never happened. Maybe it did."

"Well," Jonah said, going back to his drink, "just bear in mind you might run into it a bit more out here in the real world. This country never makes as much progress as it thinks it does."

That was no doubt good advice, but I wasn't quite sure I'd fully joined the real world yet, or that I wanted to. I rarely left the house aside from errands or maybe a run around the neighbourhood. Once, just out of curiosity, I'd gone alone to a nightclub where I wouldn't know anyone. I found it loud, irritating, and boring, and had no desire to try again. For now, Jonah and his friends supplied all the companionship I needed.

Chapter 16

On a bright June afternoon, with the heat pooling around me and sweat tracing lines down my face and neck, I sat in the shade on the back stoop with my comm in my hand, thinking about Jimmy. Now that I'd finally be telling him the truth when I said everything was fine, I could hardly bring myself to make the call. The weariness in his voice when we last spoke still hurt to think of, but it wasn't the whole problem. I'd had mixed feelings about contacting him ever since I left home.

Even at my lowest points I knew I couldn't leave the man who'd raised me to wonder if I were alive or dead; I owed him that much. And in the worst times, occasional thoughts of Jimmy had been a kind of comfort, something to hold on to. Hadn't he always been kind, or at least, meant to be kind, to me? I could hardly blame him for being right about Tiran. He'd tried to warn me, and yes, there was a big part of me that didn't want to hear *I told you so*. Not that he'd ever say it, but surely he must think it. He'd seen my humiliation just like everyone else, and I had no stomach to face any of them.

But other, confusing resentments mixed in with my memories of Jimmy. I remembered him telling me, during my affair with Tiran, that I could just move back home. Hadn't he always lacked faith in me? Perhaps I'd reached too far, perhaps I'd been over-confident and failed miserably, but at least I'd had goals once; at least I'd had ambition. Jimmy's life had always been so small, so confined to serving other people. A part of me used to find him a bit pathetic. I'd pitied him. Now that my defeat was complete, surely he must pity me.

I ran a hand over my damp forehead and thought back to rehab. Hadn't I made my peace with losing everything, with abysmal failure, back then? Why hold on to some stubborn idea of being above pity when I had nothing left anyway?

I called Jimmy. After a few rings, the voice that answered was unfamiliar—deep but adolescent.

"Uh, Jimmy?" I said, knowing it wasn't.

"No, he's sleeping. Wait—*Barry*?"

For a second I stared at my comm and debated hanging up. I should have done that as soon as I realized it wasn't Jimmy. Too late now. "Yeah. Who's this?"

"It's Ran—Randall. How's it going?"

"Oh my god, your voice is so deep!" I marvelled despite myself. "But where's Jimmy? Is he okay?"

"He's fine, just taking a nap, and I happened to hear his phone ring." Randall lowered his voice slightly. "He's been tired a lot since—you know about Lance, right? He's taken it pretty hard."

"Yeah, I heard. I'm sorry I wasn't around for the memorial or anything. I didn't find out in time."

"That's okay. It was nice, we had a little thing at the rec centre in Whittier with everyone, all his old friends were there."

Somehow, talking to Randall didn't seem as fraught as talking to Jimmy. "What happened, anyway?" I asked. "Jimmy just said he OD'd. Where was he?"

"Well, you know they were living downtown, right? Him and Steve, they moved out as soon as Steve left high school. I think Lance was pissed ever since he turned eighteen and didn't get a car from Tiran."

"Oh, shit." I'd forgotten all about Lance's Hummer. "He really believed that? He barely even spoke to Tiran."

"Wishful thinking I guess. Your little Alfa was pretty sweet. But it's not like Tom got a car either. I think Tiran gave him something, though, a—"

I didn't want to talk about Tiran, or Tom. "So Lance and Steve got a place together in New Ellay?" I asked. "What were they doing?"

"Lance was trying to do his music stuff, from what I heard. I think him and Steve just got paid to show up places sometimes, you know, cause of being quasi-famous. I guess they were indulging a lot. And then Steve found him one morning and couldn't wake him up…"

"Jesus, poor Steve. How's he doing?"

"Well, funny story about that," Randall said. I could hear him shuffle around a bit, as though settling into a new position. "After Lance died, we didn't know where Steve was. Like—he called an ambulance and met us at the hospital, and then he just disappeared. He wasn't at the apartment, he didn't answer his comm, we didn't know what happened to him. He wasn't even at the funeral. Jimmy was beside himself, losing all three—I mean, losing Steve on top of Lance. We didn't know what to do."

"But—but he's back now, isn't he?"

"Yeah, and you know who finally found him? Pasha. He used some kind of tech to pinpoint Steve's comm signal and then tracked him down to this…squalid little room in a bad part of town. Steve's, like, barely surviving, doing a bit of work for some shady mechanic. Turns out he's too scared to come home, he thinks everyone's mad at him for what happened with Lance. He thinks he burned all his bridges. But you remember how Steve was Pasha's buddy when we started school? Well, Pasha gets the whole story out of him. And then he goes up to Tiran and says *You need to give Steve a job.* Little Pasha! Just marches up to him. And Tiran does. So now Steve's working with Enrico and going to trade school, and he's got a sweet little apartment of his own above the garage here on the estate."

When the story ended I let out my breath in a whoosh. "Wow."

"Yeah, it was a wild ride."

"I'm so glad he's back. He's okay now, right?"

"He's better. You know I don't think he was ever into all that stuff like Lance was. He seems happy just hanging out with the kids in Whittier again."

I nodded. "How about you, Ran? How are you doing? And…how's Doc?"

He laughed. "Doc's doing okay, but he's getting older, you know. He's more than ten years old. He needs regular treatments from the vet."

"I'll send you money for them."

"Naw, man, it's okay. We got it."

"Are you done school?"

"Just graduated last week. I start college in the fall for tech design."

I leaned forward with the comm, head in my hand, feeling almost dizzy with the heat and the unfamiliar conversation. "Dee?" I asked finally.

"She's good. One more year of high school. She wants to be a doctor."

"She'll make a great doctor."

"Yeah, she will." There was a pause, then Randall said, a bit uncertainly, "Hey, Barr, what's up with you? How come you won't…see anyone?"

"Oh…" I let the word trail away into silence, knowing I couldn't answer. After a moment I said, "Look, I gotta go. But tell Jimmy I called, okay? And—and…I'll call again when I can."

"But is everything okay with you?"

"It's fine. Really. It's been great talking to you, Ran. Thanks for looking after Doc."

I put the comm down and sat for a long time on the back stoop with my head cradled in my arms, until the sky grew dark all around me.

* * *

I hadn't expected to stay with Jonah very long, but I didn't see many other options. Where else did I want to go, exactly? All the goals and ambitions I'd once chased had ended in total failure, and I had nothing to replace them with. This seemed like as good a place as any to stay, until I figured out some new plan.

My job didn't require great skill, though it took some organization and self-discipline to keep things running smoothly, as Jonah expected. I settled into a meditative rhythm, my mind focused on daily tasks and not dwelling on the past or other painful topics. Sometimes this life seemed like the most peaceful I'd ever known.

Weeks turned into months. It became a bit easier to talk to Jimmy, when I called him every couple of months to check in. I still blocked incoming signals on my comm, whitelisting only Jonah and one or two of his friends, but I did message Randall with Jonah's contact info, saying he could use it to reach me in case of emergency.

After a while, I noticed that Jonah sometimes disappeared into the basement with one of his friends. And occasionally there'd be a knock at the back door which he'd answer before leading the visitor straight downstairs. I'd never been down there, so I just assumed the basement housed some kind of hobby or game, a brew room or pool table perhaps.

It would have been in the early fall of that first year when I settled down in the living room to watch a vid with Jonah, Len and Malik. An hour or so later I happened to look up and notice Malik and Jonah had disappeared; Len and I were alone.

Len saw my puzzled glance and said off-handedly, "Yeah, they went downstairs, I guess Mal had an appointment."

I didn't understand. "Appointment?"

"Yeah, he's a client."

"Client?"

"Sure, one of Jonah's—Wait." Len sat up and looked at me. "You don't know? He should have told you. Jonah's a Dom."

The skin on my back rippled like a cold breeze had just run over it. "Dom?"

"Yeah, like…a service Dom. He takes clients. Here, in the basement."

I sat in silence for a moment, no longer hearing the vid playing in the background. Then I got up and walked into my bedroom, hardly aware of my actions as I threw clothes into my backpack.

When Jonah came upstairs a little later, letting Malik out the backdoor, I was alone. He found me pacing around the kitchen with my backpack in my hand.

"I have to go," I said abruptly.

"Why? What's wrong?"

"You never told me."

"About what? Oh." He stopped in the middle of the kitchen, his face suddenly still. "I guess Len told you. Look, I didn't mean to hide anything from you."

"It's a pretty big thing." I tried to keep my voice steady, wondering why

I hesitated now that the route was clear. I hadn't wanted to go down the stairs when Jonah might have been coming up them at any time. But nothing stood in my way now, and the ceramic jar was beside the door, right where we'd left it.

Jonah took a step toward the table. "Come on over here and let's talk about it. I'm sorry I didn't tell you earlier. I just didn't want to burden you with it at first."

"I—*don't want to play those games.*" The words burst out, more forceful than I'd expected.

"You don't have to," Jonah said. He pulled out a chair, sat down, and gestured at another one, across from him. "Have I ever given you reason to think I want you to?"

He sat waiting, allowing me time to think about his words.

"No," I said after a moment. "But..." I stopped, not even sure what my *but* referred to.

"I'm not looking for anyone else," he said. "I have plenty of clients and regulars. I told you before I'm not looking for company." He put his head to the side and gave me a long steady look. "Well, maybe a friend."

Is that why I hadn't left yet? It was true; the idea of a friend was tempting. I found myself pulling out the chair and facing him across the table. "I don't want to see anything."

"You haven't, have you?"

I shook my head, realizing that wasn't exactly it. "I don't want you doing it—here."

For a second I saw anger spark in his eyes. I didn't blame him; it was a big ask, and presumptuous for me to tell him what to do in his own home.

Then something changed, and his usual mild expression returned. "All right. I can probably take appointments at the studio."

I blinked. "Really?"

He shrugged. "I don't want you to be uncomfortable. It's your home too, I guess."

"I—I appreciate that." I struggled briefly, wanting to offer some kind of gesture in return. "It's okay if I'm not here. I can go out sometimes. Just let me know if you need me to."

"All right," he said again, with a nod. We sat for a moment, then Jonah put his hands on the table and started to push himself up. "Are we done?"

"What—do you do with them?" My words came out before I could stop myself. "Your clients."

He dropped back into the chair and gave me a slightly dubious look. "I thought you didn't want to know."

I leaned down to pick up my backpack, trying to hide the heat I could feel in my face. "I'm just wondering what you actually do."

"Whatever they want me to."

"But aren't you the…the Dom?"

Jonah's eyes narrowed a little. "So?"

It felt like I was missing something. "Well, doesn't that mean you're, like, in charge?"

"I am if they want me to be. They're paying."

I remembered the sub Devlin had once hired, and tried not to think of that scene. "So…the subs pay *you*?"

"Some of them." Jonah lifted his shoulders, still squinting at me. "I have a few regulars as well, just guys I like to play with."

"Well, are you in charge with *them*?"

"We have arrangements."

"So Malik—is he a client or a regular?"

Jonah laughed. "That's none of your business." He didn't leave though; just leaned back in his chair like he was waiting to see if I had more questions.

I did; more than I knew what to do with. "These appointments you have…is it just, like, a scene? Or do you…you know. Have sex too."

He made a visible effort to hide his annoyance. "Also not your business. Anyway, it depends. Sometimes…not always."

"It depends on what?"

"On what they want. What we negotiate. That's why it's called a service."

"But if you only do what they want, then…what's in it for you? Is it just for the money?"

"If it was just for the money I wouldn't have regulars."

"So—do you like doing what they want you to?"

"I like being a Dom. And I like giving people what they want. It works out."

I lapsed into silence, too confused to formulate any more questions at the time.

"Well," Jonah said after a moment. "If we're good here, I'm going to bed." He stood up and paused a moment, as though giving me chance to stop him, but I didn't. "Night," he said.

After he left, I stayed where I was for a long while, trying to process everything I'd heard. Finally I picked up my backpack and returned to my bedroom.

Jonah kept his word about moving appointments to his studio, and we managed around his secondary job with delicate care. He let me know when he'd be "working late" so I could hold his dinner; I didn't ask questions when he disappeared at odd hours. Though I still didn't socialize much, I made a point of going out occasionally—to a show at one of the few remaining public theatres, or to shoot some pool at the local bar—and letting Jonah know in advance so he could schedule a client at home if he wanted. Between us, we kept things running smoothly.

But my world wasn't quite as peaceful as it was before. That conversation with Jonah aroused something in me that I thought I'd purged. The shivery tingles of excitement at the idea of dominating another man had returned in a rush when we talked about his appointments. Only now they brought something else with them, confused reminders of my past. The old cravings had become tainted with memories of ugly experiences, noxious men, even the sordid vids I'd made at the end of my career. Everything I wanted to forget.

* * *

A year passed, and as June approached again it occurred to me that Mary-Dee would be graduating this month, the last of my siblings to leave high school. I hadn't been to any of their graduations. What might it be like to attend hers?

I missed my family—my brothers and sister, and the other kids from the estate. Those kids had once been the biggest part of my life; I'd thought of myself as responsible for them. Back then, it had never occurred to me that a time might come when I didn't see them every day, or when I thought they'd be better off without me.

Even now, when so much of my past remained a swollen, painful knot of impenetrable emotion, the kids stood out as untarnished in my mind. Aside from Tom, none of them had been part of that ruinous spiral of events I couldn't stand to think about.

I tried to imagine slipping into the back of some large convocation hall, watching Mary-Dee cross the stage in her cap and gown. Already I could feel the swell of pride in my heart. But would I actually be able to remain unseen? Jimmy would be there of course. And wasn't Curtis the same age as Dee? That meant his family, Pat, Dell, Phillip—and Tom.

For a fleeting moment I foresaw the reaction when someone spotted me, and cringed inside. Wouldn't it take the spotlight away from where it should be, on Dee and Curtis? But more than that, it would mean endless questions, and a need to account for my absence over the last four years. What could I say to explain why I'd left? Or how I'd spent those years? The kids had looked up to me once; the idea of letting them know what I'd done made me shudder. What good would it do them for me to suddenly reappear in their lives?

When I'd spoken with Randall a year ago, he'd sounded so normal, like any regular teenager. Recently, Jimmy told me Randall and his girlfriend had moved into the dorms at UC Berkeley. Now Mary-Dee seemed to be heading in a similar direction. Compared to the disasters the first three of us made of our lives, it seemed like Randall and Mary-Dee had a shot at ordinary, fulfilling futures. Why should I complicate things for them?

I abandoned the idea of attending the graduation, and ordered a pretty corsage to be delivered to Dee at the school with a card. *Love & admiration, B.*

The next time I spoke to Jimmy, I heard all about it. Dee had been offered a few scholarships, and would start pre-med at Stanford in the fall. I figured I'd made the right decision.

Life with Jonah stayed much the same, and aside from the turmoil in my own head I had no complaints. Sometimes when I thought back to the boy I used to be, I couldn't quite understand what happened to him. I remembered all the years of restlessness, the ambition and expectations, the constant craving for more. Now all I wanted was peace, and the soothing simplicity of my current life suited me. My brain seemed to slow down and lose its nervous energy. Occasionally, in this tranquil environment, I even thought I might be able to face my past one day.

In some ways, I was just as isolated here as I had been on the estate, or during my years in the insular, self-contained vid industry. I didn't really follow real-life events and hardly knew what might be going on in the rest of the world. Once in a while I'd hear Jonah and his friends discuss some current crisis, reminding me that the upheaval and disruption weren't over yet. But since I rarely left our small residential neighbourhood, none of it had much impact on me.

My social life remained limited. I didn't meet many people my own age, aside from a few regulars at the local bar, and that also didn't bother me. I'd always enjoyed other company in the past, but right now I felt more at ease alone. Maybe I'd try dating again sometime, but not until I figured out what I wanted from it.

Despite all my protestations to Jonah, I was embarrassed to discover how much I still thought about his work as a Dom. I'd look at his friends and wonder who was also a client, or get a message that he was working late and speculate over what he might be doing. Even with painful memories of my own past experiences corrupting my desire, I couldn't stop imagining the scenes.

What did all of this say about me? What did it mean for my future relationships? I used to envy people like Tiran, Dusty, Tom—men with power, even if they chose not to use it. After so many years in an industry where the strong were free to coerce and exploit the weak, how could I still be so intrigued by those exchanges? If I really wanted to dominate other men, if I wanted them to submit to me the way Tiran's subs or Jonah's clients did, why did my stomach turn over with a mixture of nausea, guilt and desire whenever I thought about it? What kind of man did I want to be?

I didn't have answers, but I always reached the same conclusion. I'd made enough mistakes in my life already. I wasn't going to try anything else until I had this figured out.

Chapter 17

"Hey," Jonah said after dinner one night, early in the new year. "Come here and sit down. I...want to talk to you."

I paused with a saucepan in my hand, hearing the momentary hesitation and then resolve in his voice. "Okay," I said. "Just let me finish cleaning up." I put the pan in the dishwasher and closed it up. "You want coffee? There's some ice-cream if you want it."

He shook his head. "I'm good. I just need you to sit down again."

I laughed, and pulled out my chair. "Okay, you have my attention. What's up?"

"I've been thinking," he said, clearing his throat slightly. "My company's been picking up more work lately and I need a helper. Well, you've shown yourself to be real reliable here. I figure I could look for a brand-new apprentice somewhere, or I could bring in someone I already know I can count on."

I listened with my hands in my lap. When he stopped, I put in gently, "You're talking about your vid company, right? The consulting work."

"Yeah," he said, catching my drift with a sheepish smile. "That's what I mean. Not the other."

"Well... it seems like that work requires a particular expertise."

He nodded. "It's true, a lot of it is based on my own personal experience. That's why I'll need to train someone one-on-one if I'm going to pass it along."

"So..." I said after another brief lull, "You're talking about me? You're asking if I want to start working with you?"

"Pay's better," he offered. "I could pay you twice what you're making now."

"But...Jonah, I can't do both. If I took that job, I'd have to stop doing stuff around here."

"You're right," he agreed. "You would. I figure in the short term I can help out. We can split the chores, and maybe some things won't get done, or not as often anyway. But if everything works out and we decide to keep going that way, we can look into hiring someone else to help out at home. Someone live-out."

I got up and went over to the freezer. "Maybe we need a little something to help us think this through," I said, scooping out two bowls of strawberry ice-cream.

When I returned to the table, sliding one bowl over to him, Jonah picked up his spoon and lifted an eyebrow at me. "You got some reservations?"

"A few," I said, taking in a breath. "I mean, for one thing, are you sure you'd be making enough money to cover all the extra costs? Double my current salary plus whatever it takes to hire someone at home—that's a lot. Do you really think you'll get enough new work to be worth it?"

"I've done the math. I'm not worried about that."

I dug into the ice-cream. "Okay. Well. What makes you think I'll be any good at what you do? I've never done anything like it, and I have no background in—"

"That's pretty much the same place anyone else would be starting at. I know you're steady and reliable, you work hard, you pick things up fast. I don't know what else I'd want in an apprentice that I don't already have in you."

I couldn't find a way to argue with that so I figured it was time to get to the main point. "Okay. But I told you right at the beginning...I don't want anything to do with the industry."

He nodded gravely, swallowing another spoonful of ice-cream. "I remember that. Well, the choice is yours. But I've got a couple things for you to consider. First off, you'll just be my apprentice at first. You won't deal with anyone but me. And even myself, I don't deal with many folks in the business. Most of the conversations get done by comm, and that's usually just a short discussion at the beginning and end of a project."

I scraped out my bowl and cocked my head a little. "I hear you, I guess. But—"

"And there's one more thing you might want to think about." Jonah gestured toward me with his spoon. "I don't know what your experience in the business was, but it seems like you don't have good feelings about it. I want you to remember that I'm proud of my work. It takes skill, knowledge, expertise, talent. What I do is valued in the industry, and I get treated with respect. I don't have to go looking for work; they come to me because they want what I have."

He stood up, and took our empty bowls over to the dishwasher. "Now you say you don't want anything to do with the industry," he went on, leaning against the counter. "But as long as you're living here in New Ellay, it's hard to get away from. I know this might mean facing up to some of your old demons—and God knows there's some choice devils in this town. Personally, I think the best way to stand up to the bastards is when you have something they need—something they value and respect. Something that doesn't depend on who you know or how you look."

I stared up at him, the muscles in my arms still tensing as I listened. When he stopped, I had to swallow a couple of times. "But," I said, forcing out a small laugh. "How does that help me? You're the one with the business. I'm not going to be starting up some kind of competition with yours."

"Well." His tone changed, and he reached up to scratch his neck. "I guess there's one more piece I haven't told you."

There's more? I pushed my chair back and turned to face him, where he stood against the sink. "What else have you got, man?"

He laughed a little, sheepish or contrite. "Here's the thing. I didn't mean to tell you this but...when I left the army, it's because I got a medical discharge. They told me I had a bum heart. I was twenty-three at the time, and they said I had maybe fifteen years before it kicked off for good."

My mouth fell open. "Oh, no..."

"Well, I'm forty-five now. Medical technology's come a long way, and I've had more'n a few pieces of titanium installed over the years. But when I saw my doctor last week, he said they can't keep it up much longer."

I was already on my feet, walking over to him. "How long?" I asked, reaching for his forearm. "Did they say?"

Jonah gave a dismissive wave of his hand. "I don't pay too close attention to what they tell me," he said, and then met my gaze. "They're talking about four to six years."

My vision blurred, and I wrapped my arms around him, the first and maybe only time we had any real physical contact. "Jonah, I'm so sorry."

He patted my back awkwardly. "Well, never mind about that. We'll see how it goes. The thing is, I don't like the idea of leaving my clients in the lurch. I'd really like to make sure I have someone to pass this work on to when I go."

"Yes," I said, my face still pressed against his shoulder. "I'll do it. I'd be honoured."

"Well," he said, still patting. "That's a relief."

* * *

Jonah and I worked together for almost five years. It wasn't always easy, working beside each other all day and living in the same house at night. Since our business depended almost entirely on information that existed only in Jonah's head, I had to be constantly at his side, absorbing technical details and intricate explanations for everything he did on a moment-by-moment basis. The work wasn't physically demanding but it required intense and continual concentration. Inevitably, we got on each other's nerves. Small irritations flared into major altercations, and minor disagreements into massive debates.

Jonah could be difficult, with his demands for precision and perfection, and he was used to working alone and doing things his own way. It took time for him to adapt to the requirements of partnership, and of course my endless questions annoyed him. I was often frustrated by his insistence that everything had to be done just right even though he was too impatient to provide all the details I needed to meet his standards.

"It was your fucking idea!" I'd yell, standing beside him in the small editing booth in his studio. "You wanted to share your—your *divine knowledge* so fucking share it!"

Many times I threatened to leave—if not the job, at least the house. With a decent salary and nothing major to spend it on, I had enough savings to move out on my own if I wanted to, an option I considered at least once a week.

But when the aggravation became too much, when I was a breath away from ditching the whole thing, I'd remind myself of all the other men I'd once tolerated. Men who didn't deserve space in the same world as Jonah. Here was something that would always make sense. I didn't know how much longer I'd have with Jonah, and I didn't want to regret a moment of it.

In any case, he had other qualities that made him bearable. He was even-tempered for the most part, which helped to balance my own over-the-top tendencies. He worked hard, and never expected more from me than he was willing to do himself. His pride in his work was contagious, and I soon found myself adopting the same high standards he held.

"I like to think," he mused once, as we worked together on a particularly harrowing sequence, "if I just get this right, I can show people what war is really like, and maybe we'll have less of it."

Slowly, over the years, I found myself building the specialized knowledge base and expertise I needed to be effective at the job. It was gratifying to master arcane details that almost no one else in the world, besides Jonah and me, would ever know. At first, when clients asked technical questions I passed them on to Jonah, but gradually I discovered I could answer myself. Then clients began contacting me directly, sometimes even when Jonah was available, looking for my advice and assistance. The satisfaction I got from being needed and valued is hard to describe. In some odd way, it reminded me of home.

* * *

We did re-organize the housework, and after a year or so we hired a local woman to come in every couple of days. Jonah and I mostly shared the shopping and cooking, and we ate a lot of take-out. We lived together more as friends or room-mates than as employer and employee.

On a breezy Friday evening in the spring of 2106, more than four years after I started training at Jonah's business, I headed out to one of our local bars for an evening of pool and darts. I'd let Jonah know my plans earlier, per our usual protocol.

"The casa's all yours," I called to him as I left.

It wasn't a date or anything; I was just meeting one of my friends, a technician I'd met at the dentist's office. As Jonah had said, we didn't deal with many people at his job, so working there hadn't done much to expand my social network. But I'd slowly befriended a few people in the neighbourhood.

I'd had no romantic relationships or even interest since leaving rehab; nothing beyond a couple of brief hook-ups. It didn't bother me much at all. If anything, I actively avoided dating-related activities. Sometimes I thought I'd had enough physical contact in the three years before rehab to last the rest of my life.

Walking to the bar, I imagined how I might have reacted ten years ago, if someone told me that the highlight of my future week would be beer and darts at the local pub with a dental technician.

But apparently even that was too much to hope for tonight. My friend messaged me shortly after I arrived to say something had come up and she wouldn't be able to make it. We re-scheduled, and I stayed to finish my beer. Drinking was no longer a big deal for me. I didn't abstain completely, though I rarely had more than one or two at a time.

I walked home under the streetlights, arriving around nine o'clock to find the house dark and Jonah shut up in his bedroom. A few minutes later, as I rummaged in the kitchen for a snack, the doorbell rang. Jonah was still in his room so I went to answer it.

I pulled the door open and caught a brief glimpse of a striking male figure on the front step, unfamiliar to me at first. The figure reacted before I did, jumping back abruptly with a hand flying to his mouth, while I only had an impression of silvery luminescent skin and shimmering blue eyes in the glow of the porch light.

"Barry—" he gasped.

I wondered how he knew my name, then took in the full sight of the young man in front of me. "Oh my god. *Pasha.*"

"I—I'm not stalking you," he said in a rush.

I tried to close my jaw. "But...how—?"

At that moment, Jonah came up behind me. From over my shoulder, he said, "Oh, hi, Pasha. I guess we should—"

I whirled around and stared at him, light slowly dawning. "Ohhhh, *no,*" I breathed in disbelief.

"You said you were going out," Jonah said to me. "It's okay, we can—"

But I'd turned back to Pasha, who stood frozen on the steps. "What are you doing here?" I demanded, and barely paused for his answer. "You'd better not be here for Jonah. You'd better not be his—*client.*"

When Pasha only stared at me with huge, stricken eyes, I took a step or two forward and clutched his shoulders with my hands. "Are you out of your mind? What do you think you're doing? You have *no business* being here. You need to leave, *now.*"

From behind me I faintly heard Jonah. "Whoah, whoah, hold on..."

"Barry, I—" Pasha began, trying to gather himself.

"You have no idea what you're doing!" I clenched my fingers harder in his shoulders, forcing him away, toward the stairs. As he took a step backwards I followed, still half-pushing. "Go on home! You have no business messing around with this. I don't want to see you here or—or anywhere like this, ever again!"

"Easy, Hawkins," Jonah said, putting a hand on my shoulder. He slid past me and reached out to Pasha. "It's okay, Pasha, I—"

I lunged at Jonah, ramming my hands against his chest. *"Don't you touch him!"*

Jonah almost lost his balance on the steps and Pasha gasped, watching him flail, while I heaved a breath and braced myself.

Then Pasha spoke up, before anyone else could. "It's okay," he said, retreating to the bottom of the stairs, almost disappearing in the darkness outside the pool of porch light. "I'll go. I'm sorry."

Jonah recovered and planted himself by the front door, arms folded across his chest. "Fine," he said. "I apologize for this lunatic, Pasha. Just call me later."

"Don't you fucking dare," I raged.

We both stood on the steps as Pasha turned and faltered his way through the dusky shadows along the path to the street. Then I stalked past Jonah into the house. "Don't talk to me," I said, slamming the door to my room.

* * *

That night I barely slept, unable to slow my rushing pulse and spiralling brain. I paced around the room for a while, wishing I had a drink and trying to figure out what had tripped the danger sensors in my limbic system so wildly. The alcohol was in the kitchen, where I might run into Jonah, so I did without. Eventually I threw myself onto the bed, shoved a pillow over my head and asked myself why I saw Jonah as such a threat to Pasha, when I trusted him so completely myself. *It's not Jonah,* I found myself thinking as I finally dropped off to sleep. *It's the game…*

When I woke in the morning, my mind had settled a bit and embarrassment overtook me. My first instinct was to try and avoid Jonah, but you can't dodge someone you both live and work with for very long. *Might as well get it over with,* I figured.

"Well," Jonah drawled, when I straggled into the kitchen. "If it isn't Mr. Holier-than-thou himself. What's the matter, buddy, you just find Jesus or something?"

I figured I deserved all that. "No," I said, going over to the coffee machine. "Uh… you want another cup?"

"No thanks. I guess I should get out of the kitchen before I contaminate your breakfast."

"All right," I said, leaning against the counter as the machine made my cappuccino. "You can stop with that. I'm sorry I over-reacted."

"Over-reacted?" Jonah said, not placated. "Maybe you weren't disapproving enough. I'm obviously some kind of demon."

"Okay, seriously, I'm sorry. It wasn't about you. Look, can we—I guess we should talk about it."

"I guess we should." He eyed me from the table, an empty mug and plate in front of him, and I wondered how long he'd been waiting for me. "You told me you were going out last night," he said. "How was I to know you changed your mind? I didn't—"

"I'm not blaming you for that."

"Well, what *are* you blaming me for? Is it my fault he—I take it you know Pasha."

"I grew up with him," I said. "I'm sure you're aware he's Dusty's son." I picked up my coffee and pulled out the chair across from Jonah. For a moment I cradled the mug in my hands, trying to pull my thoughts together. "Okay, listen. You know I love you and respect everything you do, Jonah," I began at last. "Obviously I don't…disapprove of you or—or judge you or anything like that…"

"Could've fooled me."

"But I don't want you seeing Pasha again."

Jonah pushed his chair away from the table and folded his arms like he did the evening before. "I think that's up to Pasha. He's a grown adult, and believe me, I always confirm that."

"You always confirm that when?" I said, the skin on my arms prickling.

"When I take on a new client."

"So he *is* your client!" For some reason that almost set me off again. "For how long? What do you *do* with him?"

"That is none of your business," Jonah growled. "I respect my clients' privacy."

I dropped my head into my hands and tried to recover my breath for a moment. "All right," I said finally. "But I don't want you seeing him anymore."

"I told you, that's up to Pasha. What is your problem with him, man?"

Fire crackled in my brain again. "I don't have a problem with him! I have a problem with you—or *any* Dom getting their hands on him."

"I didn't fucking force him into anything," Jonah seethed. "He came to me."

I found myself with my hands over my ears, like a five-year-old. "I don't want to hear about it!" I shoved my chair back and began pacing around the kitchen, trying to control the rage welling inside me. "Look," I said finally, my voice almost back to normal. "I'm not trying to blame you or suggest you did anything wrong or ever would. But Pasha…" I turned to face Jonah and searched for a way to make him understand. "He can't be part of this whole Dom-sub game. He's the sweetest kid I've ever known."

Jonah still glowered at me, but I could see a few thoughts crossing his mind. After a moment he tilted his head. "First of all," he said, and stopped, as though he didn't know where to start. "How old do you think he is?"

I had to pause and consider. Last time I'd seen him, Pasha was fifteen.

"Twenty-four," Jonah answered himself. "He's twenty-four years old. That's old enough to decide for himself what he wants."

I took in my breath, and tried to answer rationally. "That may be so. But he doesn't—"

"And second," Jonah went on, not listening. "What do you mean, *game*? Do you think what I do is some kind of game?"

"Isn't it though?" I said, bitterness seeping into my voice. "Isn't it just a way for old men to amuse themselves?"

"You think my clients pay me to amuse myself?"

"I don't know what they pay you for. I've never understood subs. But Pasha *isn't* one. He's an innocent kid. He's not like me, he hasn't been through all this shit. He doesn't know what he's getting into."

"How do you know what he is or isn't?" Jonah burst out. "How do you know what he's been through? When's the last time you saw him?"

I sat back down, caught off-guard by his vehemence. "I—I guess it'd be almost ten years ago. Nine years."

Jonah didn't speak for a minute, letting that settle with me. My mind darted back to the moment I saw Pasha at the door yesterday. It was so unexpected and stressful at the time, I'd had no chance to process his appearance. Now I recalled how unfamiliar he'd seemed at first. He'd grown but not filled out like I had, so he appeared tall and very lean; a runner's build.

His face had changed the most, the soft roundness I used to know replaced with visible cheekbones, an angular jaw and a short, straight nose. But his moonlight skin and eyes like the ocean, the sweetness in his voice—all those remained as I remembered them.

"You don't know anything about what he wants or needs," Jonah said, more quietly, bringing me back to the present.

"Maybe not," I mumbled. Something about those mental images left me a little dazed. "But I still have to keep him safe."

Jonah reached across the table and seized my arm in a firm grip. "Listen, Barry. I don't know what you went through before I met you, though I gotta say I'm starting to get an idea. But you have to remember: That's your story. It's not his. It doesn't have to be his."

I looked down at Jonah's hand and swallowed a couple of times, then put my own hand on top of his and held it. "You may be right," I said, trying to keep my voice steady. "About everything. And I really am sorry. But this is non-negotiable to me. If you keep Pasha as a client, we're finished. I'll leave and never come back. I don't mean it like a threat, I just won't be able to stay. It's him or me."

Jonah gave me a long level look and held it for several seconds. "All right," he said at last. "I'll talk to him."

Chapter 18

With the promise I'd extracted from Jonah and the assurance that Pasha wouldn't show up on our doorstep again, I assumed I'd be able to rest easier. But as it turned out, resolving the most immediate issue only left more space in my brain for other fixations. All of which seemed to revolve around Pasha.

Since it was Saturday, I didn't even have work to distract me. I spent the weekend walking around the neighbourhood, pacing circles in my bedroom or hunkered motionless on a chair in the backyard as my mind endlessly replayed that brief encounter, and my mind whirled with questions.

What was it Pasha said when I first opened the door—that he wasn't stalking me? What did that mean? And how would that be worse than having an appointment with Jonah? I could still hardly believe he saw Jonah *professionally*. He probably hadn't been to the house before, since Jonah's regular clients knew to use the back door. But even if it was his first visit here—had they been meeting previously at the studio? How long had it been going on for?

And *why*? What would make Pasha want to seek out a Dom? Could he really be a sub? But why? And why *Jonah*? Well, perhaps he knew Jonah through his father, since they were friends. Dusty had always been so protective of Pasha, though—did he know Pasha was *hiring* Jonah? What would he think about that? How could he allow it?

Of course, Pasha was an adult; Dusty couldn't stop him. Did Pasha still live on the estate? Maybe he'd left home, like I did—although I couldn't imagine him going through the same kind of excesses I had. I wondered what he'd been doing over the last nine years. How had he ended up at Jonah's front door? Who was looking out for him now?

Part of me wanted to just forget the whole incident, but that seemed impossible. My old protective instinct had mixed with some new kind of curiosity. I kept recalling the moment I saw Pasha on our doorstep—that first arresting appearance, the way his newly defined face fit with features that were once so familiar to me. Why couldn't I stop thinking about seeing him again? Because I missed the Pasha I used to know, or because I wanted more of the current one? Either way, could I really bring myself to face this representative of a past I'd been avoiding for so long?

Surely I should just dismiss the whole thing, force myself to let it go. And what would happen to Pasha then? He wouldn't see Jonah again, but would he hire some other service Dom? Or worse—seek out random encounters at the kind of clubs I used to go to? Meet men like the ones I'd once known? The thought made my stomach churn. How could I sit back and let that happen?

On the other hand, what business did I have to stop him from anything? Jonah was right—Pasha was an adult now. And who was I to him? Someone who walked out of his life ten years ago without explanation. Why should he listen to me? What right did I have to interfere, even to stop him from seeing Jonah?

That night I lay helplessly in bed, turning everything around and around in my mind and agonizing over what to do. Did I owe it to Pasha to take Jonah's advice? Should I just let him form his own future without imposing the burden of my own past mistakes on him?

What must he think of me, I wondered—the way I spoke to him? Scolded him, berated him. I winced at the memory. He didn't deserve to be treated that way, especially not by me. Didn't I owe him an apology at the very least?

I reached for my comm and started a message to him. *I'm sorry.*

That was all I really needed to say, wasn't it? Let both of us move on with our lives. My finger hovered over the send button.

Then I deleted the message and formed a new one. *Can I see you?* Hurriedly, I pressed send, dropped the comm, and tried to force myself into sleep.

CHAPTER 18

* * *

When I woke up a few hours later, Pasha's response was waiting. *Of course. The Sentinel, Tuesday evening?*

Relief flooded over me. Not only did he respond, but the Sentinel—a well-known club in downtown New Ellay—seemed like a fine, neutral choice. If we met after dinner, there'd be no commitment for any length of stay. *Yes. 9pm?* I messaged back, and a couple of hours later got his confirmation.

Tuesday was two days away. I appreciated having the time to get my emotions under control and prepare myself for this first in-person encounter with my past. It made me nervous, and yet seeing Pasha's response also filled me with a kind of jubilance.

Meanwhile I tried to be as nice as possible to Jonah. I hadn't exactly been fair to him, and even if I didn't mean to threaten, it surely came across that way. It wasn't the first time I'd issued an ultimatum or threatened to leave either, was it? I'd always been a little dramatic. Sometimes I wondered why he had so much patience with me.

I spent Sunday cooking Jonah's favourite meals and asking if I could bring him anything. He growled at me and went out for a bit, but otherwise seemed forgiving. We worked together Monday and Tuesday, as I grew steadily more apprehensive and jittery. Jonah must have figured something was up, but I didn't mention my upcoming plans to him and he didn't ask.

On Tuesday night I arrived at the Sentinel just before nine, anxious to assess the scene before Pasha arrived. I might have been there once or twice before but I didn't remember it. As it turned out, the club had a relatively quiet front room that overlooked the main dancefloor, with small tables and chairs and a more muted sound system that would allow for conversation over the music.

I found a table in an uncrowded corner and ordered a drink to calm my nerves while I waited. From my position, I could see the front entrance and the dancefloor, though not many people were on it yet. My table held a small lighted candle that I positioned and re-positioned as I wondered how we'd greet each other and what we might talk about.

Pasha arrived right at nine, pale as always but dressed well and with a bright eager look as he searched the room. I found myself on my feet, my hand half-lifted, watching him. He'd been agitated and dazed when I saw him the other night but now, as he caught sight of me and headed over, I only saw pleasure and a kind of restrained anticipation in his delicate features.

When he neared the table where I stood, he put out his hands with a hint of uncertainty. "Barry..."

I wrapped my arms around him almost in a daze, hardly able to believe the moment had come. Before Pasha's unexpected appearance a few days ago, I hadn't seen anyone from the estate in almost ten years. No matter how stunted and tangled my memories remained, this was a reunion with one of the few untainted vestiges of my past. I held Pasha in a wordless grip as warmth and relief unfurled inside me, only slightly tinged by something darker or more complicated.

He returned the embrace without reservation as far as I could tell, fine strands of hair brushing my cheek as his arms tightened around my back.

I pulled away finally, but continued standing with my hands on his shoulders. "Pasha—I'm so glad you..." I trailed away, half-choked, not sure what I meant to say. *So glad...you came? you're not mad at me? you're safe?*

His brilliant eyes glittered back at me. "Me too."

The words didn't really matter, it seemed. I laughed and gulped in a little air, pulling him down to his chair as I slid back into mine. "No, really, thank you for coming," I said, willing my pulse to slow to a normal rate. "Especially after the way I spoke to you last."

A faint tint touched the top of Pasha's cheeks. "It's okay," he said.

For a moment we sat staring across the table at each other, like we both wanted to drink in ten years of changes. He was stunning, I realized; no wonder I'd wanted to see him again. That pliant delicacy of his youth, now mixed with the sharp angles and evenness of his adult features and the pale bloom of his skin, gave him an almost other-worldly quality. He met my gaze with slightly parted lips, as though waiting to be guided by my next move.

"I'm sorry," I said at last.

Pasha made a tiny tilting movement with his head. "For what?"

"Everything."

His quiet smile promised grace. "Don't be. I'm just so happy to see you."

"Me too. I didn't know how much I wanted this." I almost laughed at myself, then took a long deep breath, like I could inhale the peace and stillness that surrounded him. "There's so much to catch up on. I don't know where to start. But wait, let me buy you a drink."

A servingbot had just appeared beside us. Pasha ordered a glass of red wine, then turned his attention back to me. Once again, he seemed to wait for me to take the lead. I recognized his complaisance from our youth, but it had a livelier, more decisive quality now—like it came not from passive nature but an active choice.

"So how are you, Pasha?" I asked, and then followed in a rush with more questions. "Where are you living? What are you doing? Are you working? And—and all of that."

He laughed, and tucked a few strands of silver-blond hair behind his ear. "Well, I left home a while back. I have an apartment in Echo Canyon. And I'm an art teacher at the elementary school there."

"Wow, really? What a perfect job for you."

"Do you think so?" He smiled. "I mean, I love showing the kids how to make things on their own. Most of them have never made anything by hand in their lives, when they show up in my class. I run a specialized program that focuses on manual creation, without technology."

"That must be so satisfying."

"It is."

Pasha's drink arrived, and I ordered another beer, then returned to my questions, leaning a bit closer to be heard over the music.

"So did you go to school—I mean, college? To be a teacher?"

"Two years of art school, two years of teacher's college. I moved out when I graduated, got the job last year."

"How'd your folks feel about it when you left?"

"Well—" He hesitated. "They couldn't expect me to stay at home forever."

There seemed to be more to the story than what he'd revealed. I did the math since he'd finished high school and noticed a missing year or two in there. I wondered if any of it related to hiring Jonah, but didn't want to bring that up just yet.

"Do you live alone? Are you—" I broke off.

"I live alone. And I'm single." He answered me without hesitation.

A flood of relief washed through me. No one had managed to gain control of him yet, at least. My drink arrived, and I took a sip. "How—how's your mom and dad?"

"They're fine. Not sure if you heard, my dad won an Oscar a couple years ago."

"Yeah, it was hard to miss." Did that come across as bitter? I added hastily, "Well-deserved, I'm sure."

There was a pause. Pasha hesitated, as though unsure whether it was his turn or he was allowed to ask questions. Then he fixed his clear blue eyes on me more firmly and reached across the table to grasp my hand.

"I'm so sorry about Lance," he said.

"Oh...yeah. That was pretty awful." I looked down at my glass and turned it around in my fingers. "Especially since..." I forced myself to meet his eyes and swallowed down the bile rising in my throat. "I wasn't there for it. I only found out months later. I didn't go to the funeral or even the memorial."

His hand tightened on mine. "They tried to reach you. They wanted you to—"

"I know. I don't blame them. I blame—" I choked, and changed direction. "I should have been there for Jimmy."

"I guess it's been pretty hard on him," Pasha said, and then, as though not wanting to sound accusatory, he added, "But I think he's doing a bit better now."

I remembered the story Randall told me. "Thank you for finding Steve," I said. "You were a hero."

He flushed a little, releasing my hand. "I don't know about that."

"From what I heard..."

"They—" Pasha jumped in and then stopped abruptly, like he'd almost lost his nerve, before pushing on. "They all miss you. They'd love to see you too."

Seconds ticked by. "I don't think that's a good idea," I said.

I could see him start to ask, the *Why...?* almost reaching his lips before he stopped himself. "Can I ask," he said instead, more gently, "what you've been up to?"

Of course I'd known that question would come up, and I'd tried to plan a response, but nothing ever seemed right. Now I had to wing it. "I—well, I…I've done a few different things…"

Pasha saw my discomfort and tried to help. "Well, what about right now? What are you doing now? I know you live with Jonah, but…"

"I'm working with him, too." I stopped, wondering what Jonah might have told him. "At his consulting company."

"You're kidding!" His surprise seemed genuine. "I didn't know that."

"Yeah, he brought me in as a kind of trainee; I've been doing it for over four years now." I hesitated, not sure if Pasha was aware of Jonah's medical condition. "I think he likes having someone to share all that obscure knowledge with."

"I don't really know what he does, exactly. Something in the—in the vid business?"

I gave a short explanation, thinking about the way Pasha had just hesitated, as though not sure he could mention the industry to me. I understood he was feeling his way around with delicacy, trying to identify safe topics for us to talk about. Part of me wanted to continue in the same way, like we were on some kind of blind date and just getting to know each other. But there were harder subjects I knew I had to get to at some point.

When the serverbot came around again I ordered one more drink. I hadn't had this many in a long time, and I'd probably feel the effects soon. In the background the music changed tempo, a more pronounced beat tempting dancers to the floor.

"How's Phillip?" I asked, once we'd exhausted the discussion about Jonah's business. "And Curtis?" These days I got regular updates from Jimmy so I already knew the basics, but I wanted to hear Pasha's version. "Are you still in touch with everyone from—with everyone?"

Pasha nodded. "They're all good. Let's see—Pip's in South America right now, travelling around with his Brazilian boyfriend. I think they're planning to start a revolution or something..."

We both laughed; some things never changed. It felt good to share this small moment of mutual childhood intimacy.

"Curtis is fine," Pasha continued. "They prefer *they* now. I guess they went through some stuff, but they're doing much better now. Did you know they got married? It's like a traditional, old-fashioned arrangement, but she seems really good for them."

Another life event I'd missed. I looked down into my beer glass and tried not to show anything. The sound system played a bouncy pop number, and the dancefloor started to grow more crowded.

"And Tom—well, Tom's pretty much living with Paul now, I think. They work together at the Foundation, from what I understand."

I didn't want to hear about that. "What about Ran and Mary-Dee—do you ever see them?"

"Dee's pretty busy with med school. But I see Randall all the time. He lives just outside of town, he's got a great job and seems really happy. I go over there for barbeques in his backyard. He's got the sweetest new pup. Hey, how's Doc?"

"Doc's with Jimmy for now," I said. "Randall couldn't take him to college so he stayed at home. I really thought about bringing him to Jonah's place but it seems cruel to disrupt his life at this age. He must be...what, sixteen? Almost seventeen?"

"New technology's been a miracle for dogs. He should have a few more years. So...have you seen him since..."

"No." Having a beer with an old friend, listening to him talk about the childhood gang—that was lovely. But this started veering into dangerous territory.

"What about...Jimmy?" Pasha asked gently, pushing in a little further.

"I talk to him every month or two." Did I sound defensive?

"Have you ever thought of, like...meeting him in—"

"No." I sat up and spoke more harshly than I intended. "If you're here because you think you can arrange some kind of—"

"I'm not." He reached across the table to wrap his fingers over my fist. "I promise that's not why I'm here. I just wanted to see you."

His light touch and pliant tone appeased me. But the exchange reminded me we had other topics to get to.

"So." My voice was still slightly discordant. "What were you doing with Jonah anyway?"

The abrupt change of topic didn't seem to surprise Pasha. He smiled faintly with what might have been a touch of embarrassment, brushed a bit of hair away from his eyes again, and took a sip of wine before answering.

"I mean, you know what I was there for," he said at last. "But I want to make sure you understand," he went on, pushing his wineglass aside so he could lean forward, arms on the table in front of him. "I didn't expect to see you. I wasn't stalking you or anything. I know you—you didn't want us to do that."

I recognized the words from our doorstep encounter, and it dawned on me he was thinking of what I'd said to Tom in the rehab center parking lot ten years ago. "I didn't think you were," I said, half-laughing. I signaled to the serverbot for one more round. "But you must have been awfully surprised to see me at Jonah's."

"Not exactly," he said, and his fingers trembled slightly as he reached for the candle and slid it back and forth on the table. "I knew you were living with him. I mean, he told me that before."

"Oh." I tried not to frown, not wanting to repeat my previous outburst. "So—so you're in touch with him?"

"Not often. I mean, I know him through my dad and—well, I talked to him a bit." He looked away from me, down at the table.

"When you hired him, you mean."

Pasha's lips remained half open but he didn't respond right away. Over on the dancefloor, a rhythmic electro beat started up, and the lights pulsed in time.

"When was that?" I pressed on. "How long have you been working with him?" I could hear my voice, how stern it sounded. Like I had some right to be interrogating him. "And what do you *do* with him?"

He tried to hide a faint smile. "It's not sex, if that's what you're wondering."

I forced my jaw to unclench, and made another attempt. "Look, I know it's none of my business, Pasha, but I—I—I worry that you might be in over your head. And I don't get what you're—why you'd want to do that."

He sucked in a small breath through his lips and hesitated again. "Is it...Jonah in particular you're worried about?" he asked after a moment. "I mean, is there some reason why..."

"No, no. Jonah's a great guy. Totally reliable."

"Yeah, that's why I called him." Pasha nodded in agreement. "He's, like, an old family friend and I figured I could trust him so..."

"But he's a *lot* older than you. Why can't you stick to someone closer to your own age?" I made an effort to sit up straight, but with more alcohol in my system than I was used to, it was harder than I expected. "And I don't understand why you want a Dom in the first place."

Pasha tilted his head with a very slight look of amusement. "You don't understand why I'd want a Dom?"

"I mean, I get how you might be—curious. Or want to experiment or whatever." I shook my head, then tried to keep from swaying. "But you have to be really careful about...where you go or—or who you do it with. They're not all like Jonah. Have you ever...done things like that with other guys?"

The flush creeping up Pasha's throat seemed to glow in the dark room. He stopped and started a couple of times before he got his next words out, but when he finally spoke his voice was clear. "Jonah's not the only one," he said. "I've had other experiences."

My fingers tightened around the glass in my hand, and I fought to contain the visceral rush of anger that left me even more dizzy. "I told Jonah not to see you again," I rasped. "And I don't want you going to other Doms either. I don't trust any of them."

I thought I saw dismay in his eyes, and something else too, but surprisingly not resentment. "Look, Barry—" he began, almost cajoling.

"I know I have no right," I said defiantly.

"It's all right. You were always a little bossy," Pasha said, and he made it sound like that wasn't such a bad thing. "But I don't want to give you the wrong impression. I'm not …*experimenting*."

"What do you mean? You're—"

The rosy tint had disappeared, leaving his face as pale as sakura blossoms. "I know who I am," he said, holding my gaze as he spoke. "I know what I want. I'm a sub."

The word ricocheted in my brain, sending some turbulent mix of arousal, guilt and revulsion to my stomach and making it twist almost painfully. "How do you…" I whispered, hardly able to breathe.

"I went through plenty of experimenting in the past. I used to deny it or whatever, but that never really helped. I'd rather just face it head on. It's not so terrible, is it? To be a sub?"

I swallowed, trying to hide my reaction. "No," I said, and then quickly, "I mean, of course not. But—"

"Barry." Pasha slid his hand across the table to grasp my wrist. When I stopped speaking his eyes met mine with a long searching look. "It seems like…" He hesitated, and his brow furrowed as he held my gaze. "You seem to have a really strong reaction to this subject. I mean, even when I first showed up to meet Jonah, you…" He paused again. "It just makes me wonder if you've had some kind of…experience or something."

I closed my eyes for a moment, and for the first time wondered if this might have been a mistake. "Not…exactly," I said finally. "I mean, not like yours. But I—I mean…sort of. Yeah. Look—I don't want to—"

He squeezed my wrist with his hand, then let go. "It's okay. I don't mean to pry. I just wondered where it was coming from. But you don't need to tell me anything."

"It's just…I've seen things." I said, trying to get a grip on myself. "It's not always good."

"I know." He nodded gravely, his hands in his lap. "I've seen things too."

"So many men are gonna try and take advantage of—"

"Yeah, well," he sighed, "that's why I wanted to work with Jonah. Someone I trust."

What have I done? I wondered. Had I taken away Pasha's only safe option? "I can't," I said at last, hoarsely. "I can't have you working with him."

He nodded, with sympathy or understanding, maybe even trust. "I get it. But—well, I'm just not sure what I'll do now."

I leaned forward and grabbed his arm before I knew what I was about to say. "Look, if you need someone—if you need a Dom—let me. I could do it. Couldn't I? If you want me to."

Pasha held himself completely still for several long moments, and I froze, transfixed by the intensity of those crystalline blue eyes. "I…" he breathed, and then seemed to gather himself. "I don't think you're ready, Barry."

My alcohol-addled brain couldn't make sense of his words just then, but somehow I knew they were true. "I know," I mumbled. "I just wanted to—"

"I appreciate the offer," he said, his voice still soft. "I know you want to keep me safe."

The music changed again just then, to an old '90s song I recognized from my youth. Pasha pushed back his chair and got up suddenly, grabbing my hand.

"C'mon," he said. "Let's go dance."

"Dance?" I followed him in a bit of a daze. "All right. I guess we aren't really so much like brothers that it's weird."

"Brothers!" he said. "No indeed."

He led me onto the dancefloor, where the alcohol was a blessing, and we shimmied and twisted, laughing and shaking our hips until the tension and awkwardness had been forgotten. After a few fast songs the music switched to a ballad, and Pasha moved closer to me. I pulled him into my arms without thinking about it much, and we swayed together, his head on my shoulder. I reached up to run my fingers through his silky, shoulder-length hair and felt his hands press against my back. How long had it been since I'd had contact like this with anyone?

When the song ended, Pasha stepped away, looking more serious. He brushed the hair off his face, then leaned in to be heard over the music. "I'd better go," he said into my ear. "I have to work in the morning."

I nodded, and we left the dancefloor, walking to the entrance at the front of the club.

"Did you drive?" I asked.

"Yeah." He pointed to his car in the parking lot across the street. "You?"

"Uh-huh." I saw him glancing around and added, "No, the convertible's long gone. I have a sensible four-door now. It's just around the corner."

"Okay, well..." Pasha hesitated, then threw his arms around my shoulders in a quick hug. "I'm so glad we did this, Barry."

"Me too." I put my hand on his arms just before he let go. "I—I want to see you again. Can we meet up another time?"

He smiled. "I'd love that. Just let me know when." He headed across the street, turning back once with a wave.

I watched him leave, then walked around to my car and headed home.

Chapter 19

I didn't make another plan with Pasha right away. My overtaxed brain needed time to sort out and process what had already happened. When I woke up the morning after, slightly hung-over and confused, I didn't immediately remember everything from the night before, but over the next couple of days it all came back to me.

Some of the memories made me wince. *What* did I say? Had I really propositioned Pasha so absurdly? What was I thinking? And what must he think of me?

Still, once I got past the immediate cringe factor, I thought the evening hadn't gone too badly. Pasha was as sweet as I remembered him but so much more radiant now, and with subtle changes in the way he carried himself that made him more intriguing. And how lovely it had been to hear all those updates about my childhood compatriots, even if uncomfortable memories had occasionally encroached.

I didn't necessarily have to go through it again. I'd made my peace with Pasha, satisfied my curiosity, and resolved the immediate issue. Any new meeting with him would increase the risk of confronting uncomfortable topics, awakening memories I didn't want to re-visit, pulling at threads that still knotted painfully in my brain. Did I really want to keep taking those chances?

Except there was no doubt in my mind. I had to see Pasha again, and not just because I enjoyed staring into that exquisite face. There was something both comforting and exhilarating about spending time with him, and I knew I wanted more of it.

Even so, I didn't set anything up right away. I messaged him a few times, first to thank him again for meeting me and apologize for my inappropriate comments, then just to check in periodically. But I held off on suggesting we get together, and he didn't push.

My mind kept returning to our conversation, finding new things to dwell on. I'd woken up thinking the immediate issue had been resolved—but had it really? All I'd done was tell Pasha to stop seeing other Doms. But when he asked what he was supposed to do instead, what solution did I give him?

Why did Pasha need a Dom anyway? Remembering what he said about being a sub still left me uncomfortable. Why did it bother me so much? I knew that dominance appealed to me; all my life, no matter how much I tried to deny it, any thought of power over another person had triggered that little thrum of excitement in my core. But the idea of submission left me uneasy and repulsed. Where did that come from?

Society generally perceived submission as weak, distasteful, even pathetic. It was hard to rid myself of the mindset. Who would want to spend their life serving another person? Why would Pasha identify with that? And how did it make me feel about him?

"What's the deal with subs, anyway?" I asked Jonah abruptly. The question filled my mind so much that it came out almost involuntarily.

Jonah and Len exchanged glances. We were sitting around the living room, sharing a couple of beers, with a screen playing in the background. I'd managed to keep the thought inside until Malik left, since it seemed like an impolite topic to raise with one of Jonah's clients.

"What do you mean, what's the deal with them?" Len asked.

"I mean...I get Doms, I see the appeal. But why would anyone want to be a sub?" I tried to take a playful tone, to give myself an out if I needed it.

Jonah narrowed his eyes at me, usually a sign of mild irritation. "Sounds like you don't think very highly of subs."

"Well," I said, laughing. "Most people don't. I mean—do you?"

"You can't be a Dom if you don't respect subs," Jonah said.

"Huh." I stored that away to think about later. "But why do they do it? Why does anyone choose to be a sub? What's the fun of it?"

"Choose?" Len asked.

I waved my glass around, not understanding their confusion about what seemed to me such an obvious question. "Yeah, *choose*—why would a person choose to let someone else dominate them? Why would they give power *away*?"

Jonah leaned back, his forearms resting on the sides of his easy chair, and gave me a long look. Beside me on the couch, Len took a swig of beer and watched Jonah with a kind of amusement.

"I thought you *didn't want to play those games*, Hawkins," Jonah said at last.

"Who says I do?" I asked, trying not to sound defensive. "I'm just curious. I've never understood subs."

"But you think you understand Doms," Jonah said.

That took me aback. I glanced over at Len, who still looked entertained, and then back at Jonah. "What's to understand? Doms like to be in charge. I should know, I grew up with the biggest Dom in the country, maybe the world."

Jonah's eyes darkened as his eyebrows lowered over them. "And who would that be?"

"You know who I mean. Tiran." I didn't generally like talking about him, but they'd provoked me.

Len choked on his drink, and Jonah positively vibrated in response. "Tiran Marx?" he snarled. "A *Dom*?"

"Well..." I turned my glass around in my hands, shooting looks back and forth between them. "Sure. I mean, everyone knows that."

Len elbowed me lightly. "Now you've done it," he said, his voice low and laughing.

"Tiran Marx," Jonah began, very slowly and deliberately, "is a self-centred, self-indulgent asshole who's been kicked out of every Dom club in this town and several others. He's an embarrassment to the entire community. He's the *exact opposite* of a Dom."

I stared at him, mouth agape. "What—what do you mean?"

Jonah put his glass down on the table beside him, and leaned toward me in his chair. "Tiran Marx is not a Dom, no matter what he likes to think.

He's just a selfish jackass with too much money."

"Well..." I shook my head and stored his comments in my brain to think about later. "I mean, he's got subs..."

"That doesn't make him a Dom. People make all kinds of arrangements, for all kinds of reasons. But he has no discipline, no training; he gives them nothing."

"He's got money and influence and power," I said. "That's what he gives them."

"Money and influence," Jonah growled, "do not make you a Dom. And that's not what subs want. It's about trust, not power."

The whole conversation was muddling me. "But if you *don't* have money or influence or whatever, why would anyone want to submit to you?"

For a moment Jonah shut his eyes. When he opened them again, I saw his usual patience returning. "Power doesn't come from any of those things, Hawkins. It's inside. A real Dom's power comes from within. That's what people submit to."

I listened to Jonah in silent confusion, not knowing how to respond. Somehow his words made sense, but didn't answer my question.

Len nudged my leg with his. "I guess you've figured it out by now. Jonah has *opinions* about Megabucks Marx."

"That's because I've had to deal with him," Jonah said with resentment. "I'm in some of those clubs he tried to join. We're the ones who have to manage the fallout and pick up the pieces. We're the ones that had to get rid of him."

"He said he doesn't like to...hurt people," I said.

"I never said he did. If he was dangerous we would have stopped him. He's just lazy and selfish."

It was strange, even after all these years, to hear Tiran treated with so much disdain. I'd grown up in a world he ruled, however benevolently, and that he chose to populate with people who served him one way or another. No one spoke badly about him on the estate; even Paul Armstrong kept his antipathy to himself. I'd seen countless breathless media stories about him, and watched endless streams of industry professionals fawn over him. It had never crossed my mind that other people, out in the real world, might think differently.

* * *

I held out for a few weeks before I asked Pasha to meet me again. He agreed promptly, and proposed a Sunday picnic on the beach, while it was still possible. These days, staying out under the intense rays of the sun for any length of time was only feasible a few months of the year. By the end of April it would be impossible again.

Can you bring wine? Pasha messaged. *I have the rest.*

I picked up two bottles, then put one back and grabbed some soda instead. I didn't need a repeat of last time. We met at the parking lot of a beach he recommended, calling it the prettiest one in town. I carried the drinks and a banana loaf I'd made the night before, while Pasha brought a picnic hamper and sun umbrella. Our hands were too full to hug hello.

As we followed the path out of the parking lot toward the water, Pasha nodded at my outfit. "Guess we had the same idea," he said, smiling.

We both wore loose wraps tied around our hips, the kind I'd always favoured for the beach. Pasha's usual satchel was slung across his top and he wore a broad-brimmed straw hat for protection.

"I have my swim shorts underneath," I said. "Hoping we can go for a dip."

"Me too," he said. "Let's do that first, before the sun's right overhead."

"I don't think I've been swimming since—" I paused. "I left home."

He shot me a delicate glance. "Don't you miss it? You used to be in the ocean all the time."

"I never really thought about it...but now I can't wait."

This was a crowded urban beach, a far cry from the peaceful sands of the estate or even the small Whittier beach. Though the experience was new to me, I found something companionable about joining so many strangers, the picnicking families and exuberant children, the dogs and babies and teen lovebirds. A savoury aroma of grilled meat drifted from small kerosene broilers as seagulls circled overhead waiting for leftovers.

CHAPTER 19

Pasha and I dropped everything on a picnic table near the edge of the grass, pulled off our wraps and kicked off our shoes, and ran straight into the water.

It's funny how everything comes back so quickly. The momentary chill of the ocean sending a shiver down my back, the pull of the current, the salt on my lips, the faint tang of fish and seaweed, even Pasha splashing beside me…it all felt instantly familiar. I could almost believe I'd been transported back fifteen years to a time when this was the only way I could imagine spending a steamy afternoon.

We both dove under the waves at almost the same time, and for a while I just swam straight out, long neglected muscles in my arms and legs rejuvenating in the surf. I only made it a few meters before reaching my limit, and then I turned onto my back and let the waves carry me in toward the shore.

Pasha swam well, much better than I remembered. After a few laps he re-joined me, and we splashed silvery spray at each other and body-surfed in the waves until hunger tempted us back to land.

At the picnic table we shook water out of our hair and re-tied our wraps. Pasha spread out a tablecloth, then unloaded bread and cheese and fruit from the hamper while I opened the wine and poured glasses.

"You were right, this is a pretty beach," I said.

Pasha nodded. "I come here often to paint. It's my favourite for sunsets and night views."

"You still paint a lot? I'd love to see your work."

"Any time," he said, slicing a loaf of ciabatta.

I sat across from him, watching the sunlight glint off the ripples in the sea. "I don't know why I haven't done this for so long," I said. "The water's not even as cold as I remember."

Pasha looked up from making us plates with a small smile. "Do you remember that time…I must have been, I don't know, seven or eight…when I got swept out by a wave, and you saved me?"

"No," I said, surprised. Why didn't I recollect that?

"I'm sure it wasn't as big a deal for you as it was for me," Pasha said, answering the question I hadn't asked. "The current started pulling me out—like, way out, and I was so scared I couldn't even say anything. But then you were just—*there* beside me, and you grabbed my arm and pulled me back to shore."

I took a bite of the bread and cheese he'd handed me, shaking my head a little. "If you were seven or eight, I would've only been eleven or twelve. I shouldn't have let you go in with me."

"I think someone was with us, one of the grown-ups. But they were on the beach, they probably didn't even see it. You were right there."

"Hm." Thinking back, that didn't sound so unlikely. The adults had always kind of taken a light approach to supervision. I guess they'd relied on me to pick up the slack.

Pasha picked up his wine glass. "We used to spend so much time outside, running around, in the water, on the cliffs...you always made everything so fun. What about our midnight feast, do you remember that?"

"Oh yeah. That I do recall," I said, tossing back a handful of raspberries.

"I'll never forget that night! It was so exciting—the bonfire on the beach, and all the food we stashed away, roasting marshmallows...in the middle of the night with no adults around! You planned it all, and it worked perfectly. I can't believe no one noticed us."

I ducked my head, laughing. "Well, I have a confession to make. I mean, I knew we wouldn't get away with it—all those cambots patrolling everywhere. So I worked it out with Reshmi ahead of time—remember her?"

Pasha shook his head. "I didn't know the staff like you did."

"She was head of the night shift for security. So I told her what we wanted to do—it was right after we all got out of detention for something, remember? I told her it was our celebration of freedom and talked her into not telling anyone."

"Oh my god, really? So all the guards knew?"

"C'mon, you couldn't do anything there without being seen." I shrugged and brushed away the gathering sweat that mixed with sea water on my brow. "But I wanted them to know anyway, just in case. To make sure nothing went wrong—you know, with the bonfire and everything...." Something in

Pasha's eyes made me pause with my hand halfway to my plate. "What?"

He smiled as a ray of silver-white sunlight fell across his face, turning his pale skin almost translucent. "You always kept us safe, Barry."

After we'd finished most of the food and wine, Pasha tossed a blanket onto the grass under the shade of a nearby camphor tree. We brought over plates of my banana loaf and leaned back against the tree trunk, side by side. The warmth of his bare shoulder against mine reminded me of our slow dance at the Sentinel, and I found myself acutely conscious of his hip brushing mine as he ate.

"You ever think," I said after a while, stacking our empty plates on the grass, "what a funny coincidence it is that I'm living with Jonah, and you just happen to know him through your dad." It occurred to me as I spoke that Pasha had never asked how I came to end up there.

He didn't answer right away, and when I turned toward him he looked away.

"I…have to confess some things too, actually," he said after a moment. "I don't want you to—to be upset."

"It can't be that bad," I said, though my stomach muscles tensed a little as I spoke.

"I hope it's not." He moved away from the tree and re-positioned himself, cross-legged, facing me, with his clear blue gaze fixed on mine. "But…I mean, it wasn't a coincidence."

I didn't compute. "What do you mean?"

Pasha took in a long breath, then let it out slowly. "I mean I asked Jonah to look out for you."

"What? When?"

"When you were in rehab."

"But—how did you—" I stopped, too confused to react.

"Barry," Pasha said, and paused. "There's a few things I have to tell you. Did you never wonder why no one went after you? When you left the estate?"

"What? No. I didn't expect anyone to." My voice grew progressively harsher as small threads of bitter memory gathered and tangled in my stomach.

"But you were only nineteen. Did you really think your dad wouldn't go looking for you?"

"That was the last thing I wanted."

"It doesn't matter. He was devastated. He tried to reach you at Devlin's place but security would never let him in. Even my dad tried, he knew Devlin, but—"

"I don't want to hear about Devlin." It was getting harder to breathe.

"I'm sorry. Anyway, in the end we hired someone to keep track of you..."

"*We?*"

Pasha nodded. "*Everyone* was worried about you, Barry. We were all involved. I guess you know the detective found you at that first rehab centre. The staff wouldn't let Jimmy in, so...that's why Tom staked it out." Pasha rushed his words, like he wanted to avoid this part of the story. "And he told us what you said, that you didn't want us stalking you. After that Jimmy said we had to leave you alone. He didn't want to drive you away completely."

My back teeth ground against each other. I unclenched my jaw enough to say, "So? What's any of that got to do with Jonah?"

"Well, I couldn't—I mean I couldn't just forget about you. Tom said you left that first program without finishing, but I always knew you'd figure it out one day and want to clean up for real. And I was worried because...I know you have to pay a lot for those places."

The muscles in my arms and shoulders had grown stiff with tension. I pulled my legs up and wrapped my arms around them, then dropped my head on my knees, watching small drops of sweat fall onto the red plaid of the blanket below my legs.

"I didn't have any money of my own. So..." Pasha hesitated for several long moments. "I went to Tiran."

My head jerked up. Pasha was looking away from me, out over the water. "I told him it was his fault anyway. All of it." He shook his head. "The *least* he could do was pay for you to get better."

"Oh, fuck, no..."

But Pasha turned to me with a sudden fierce, defiant look. "He *owed* you that. *More* than that." He must have caught my reaction, because the brilliant blue of his gaze disappeared again as he looked down. "Anyway, he didn't care. He just said fine, bill it to him."

"You had no right." I could hardly force the words out. "I would never have taken his money if…" I started to get up, to leave, then forced myself to stop. Despite the rising nausea and dread, my revulsion at the idea of unwittingly accepting help from Tiran, I had to hear the end of the story. "But—Jonah?"

Pasha spoke quickly again, like he wanted to get it over with. "I called all the rehab centres in town and told them to bill Tiran if you ever contacted them. When the accountant finally told me he got a bill, I figured you'd be getting out soon…and I didn't want you to be all alone when you left. I kept looking at maps trying to figure out who I might know in the area, and finally I saw the name of Jonah's company. I mean, I really don't know him well but I know what his company's called."

"So you asked Jonah to pick me up." I couldn't keep the dull rancor out of my words.

Pasha's voice had been low and clear, but now it wavered a little. "Not to pick you up. Just to… keep an eye out for you. To make sure you were safe."

I turned my head away from him, toward the blue-green shimmer of the ocean. *Why did I come here,* I thought vaguely. *Why did I set myself up for this? I should never have messaged Pasha again.* And then another dim thought followed behind. *Sixteen. He was sixteen when he did all this.*

"Like you always did for us, Barry. Couldn't I do that for you?"

I could hear a growing despair in his voice but nothing penetrated the fog of turbulence and outrage that had apparently swamped my brain.

"I don't even know what happened," Pasha went on rapidly. "Jonah just messaged me and said you were okay and living with him for now. Once or twice he told my dad you were okay. When I asked to—to hire him…I didn't know if you were still there, and he said we'd meet at his studio. I wasn't trying to spy on you."

I had stopped processing his words, unable to add anything else to the turmoil in my mind. Almost without realizing, I'd risen and pulled my backpack off the table. "I…have to go," I said.

"Barry, I'm—wait, let me go with you. Maybe I can—"

But I didn't stop or wait for him, just walked back to my car and drove home alone.

Chapter 20

For the next couple of days I stumbled around in a daze, when I got up at all. I spent long hours in bed, staring at the ceiling and trying to process the jumble of information Pasha had given me.

So…everything I thought I'd gone through on my own had been orchestrated by others? Was I some kind of marionette with strings pulled by puppeteers in the background?

Knowing that Tiran had paid for my recovery, after I'd walked away and refused to look back, hurt the most. Even in the worst of times I'd been able to salvage a scrap of defiant pride at having made a clean exit, at going it alone. Everyone had seen my colossal failures, my public humiliation, Tiran's complete indifference—but at least I'd scraped together some dignity in my escape. And now I had to be indebted to him for rescuing me? I knew they'd all pitied me back then, but Tiran's was the hardest to bear. How could Pasha do that to me?

I'd always thought I made things easier for Jimmy by walking away. For Jimmy and me, both. I didn't have to face him, and he didn't have to clean up my mess. If the other kids missed me at first, Jimmy could shield them from my worst mistakes, and they'd all gradually realize they were better off without me.

But—*devastated,* Pasha said. Trying to see me, afraid of losing me completely. And not just Jimmy—apparently everyone was involved. None of the adults had thought of me as a child for years before I left the estate. Why would any of them worry about my ability to fend for myself? It took a long time to adjust to the idea that they might have been looking out for me even after I left them all behind.

And Pasha—he'd done more for me than all the others. What if I'd never been able to get into rehab? What if Jonah hadn't found me? I'd never stopped to fully appreciate my good luck. Only it wasn't luck, was it? Pasha, at sixteen, had almost single-handedly saved me from the life that surely would have awaited me otherwise.

He was fifteen when I last saw him, with the same sweet earnestness and delicacy he had now. People sometimes mistook his pliancy for timidity, but I'd always known he was no push-over. I remembered Randall's story about Pasha marching up to Tiran after Lance died. Maybe he knew what to do then because he'd already done it once for me.

The thought of Pasha asking Tiran for a favour on my behalf still made my stomach churn. What was it he said, about Tiran *owing* it to me? But he didn't know what really happened. He had too much faith in me; he didn't understand my complicity in the whole debacle. No doubt he believed I was Tiran's victim. What would he think if he knew the whole truth?

I shook my head and pushed myself out of bed. It was Wednesday—no, Thursday now, and I had to get through another day at work even if I'd spent all night awake and brooding.

My comm showed a new message from Pasha. He'd already sent a couple, but I'd been ignoring them. A sudden remorse washed over me. No, he should never have approached Tiran on my behalf—but stacked up against everything else he did for me, what business did I have blaming or resenting him? He probably saved my life.

Jonah banged on my bedroom door. "Get your ass in gear, Hawkins!"

I didn't have time to figure it all out right now. But I couldn't leave Pasha hanging, thinking, perhaps, that I'd hold this grudge forever. I grabbed my comm and sent a quick message. *Sorry for the awkward exit. Talk soon.*

If there was one thing I knew for sure, amidst all the swirling tumult and uncertainty I still had to sort through, it was that I needed Pasha to be there at the other end of it.

* * *

"So I just got the whole story," I said to Jonah as we drove to work together in his car. With business booming, he'd finally traded in his ancient manual drive for a brand-new model. "Finally. Pasha told me."

"The whole story about what?" Jonah asked, focused on his comm as the car took care of its own navigation.

I rolled my eyes. "How many stories are there? About how we met. Because he asked you to baby-sit me."

"Either he told you a lie, or you weren't listening. He never asked anything like that; just for me to let him know if you were okay."

"If that's true then why did you approach me? Why talk to me at all?"

"Because I needed someone to keep house for me," Jonah said.

"But why me? I guess you knew who I was all along, but you didn't know anything else about me. Unless Pasha told you—"

"Pasha told me nothing about you. He just wanted to know you were safe."

Safe. There was that word again. "So then why?"

Jonah shrugged. "I thought you might need a job."

"Really?" I looked over at him, trying to see through his usual terseness. Jonah didn't usually volunteer more than he was asked, but that didn't mean he never had more to say. "That's really the only reason?"

He finally turned his head slightly, to give me a rare smile. "Well…" he drawled. "I'd seen you around. Thought you might be having a rough time. And I had an empty room in my house. I just thought, you know…maybe we could help each other out."

Strange to think of yet another person wanting to help me in those darkest days. I reached over and squeezed his arm. "I hope I did."

* * *

Later, when we got home, I went through all of Pasha's messages. As always, they weren't pushy or demanding, only concerned. He apologized once—I wasn't sure what for—and asked if we could meet again when I was ready. *I know you might need some time,* he said.

In truth, I did. It took a few weeks to recover, to take apart my whole life since I left home and put it back together again with all this newfound knowledge.

So many small details in Pasha's story kept flooring me over and over. Jimmy trying to see me at Devlin's house and being rebuffed…how had I not known? Those harsh words I'd spoken to Tom in a moment of resentment—I'd never realized how much impact they had. That woman at Harmony; she must have been the only one to put together my name with some note in their system from years earlier. And she'd never mentioned Tiran's name. Pasha must have left instructions not to.

I wondered what Jonah thought when he got Pasha's request out of the blue. Did he put my name together with the person he'd seen around, met at industry events and probably heard a bit about through the rumour mill? How long had he watched me at the coffee shop, waiting and debating, before he finally approached me?

And Pasha. Everything he'd done for me, quietly, in the background, over years. Confronting Tiran, calling all those recovery centres, hunting for someone to look out for me. I imagined him waiting and hoping for the message from Jonah—the message telling him I was fine, he didn't need to worry any more. His job was done.

And then…

For—what, six years?—he'd heard nothing from me, nothing about me besides perhaps the occasional word from Jonah through Dusty. If Pasha's actions had been motivated by some misguided sense of obligation, he must have known he'd paid back his debt in full. Did he ever think of me again, once he'd fulfilled his duty?

What was it he said right at the end—something about not spying on me? He and Jonah both claimed that meeting at the house was unplanned, and I believed them. Pasha didn't hire Jonah because he wanted to see me—did he?

But if not—why *did* he hire Jonah? What did he mean about being a sub? I still didn't understand the appeal of submission. Even when I'd asked Jonah and Malik, they hadn't explained anything, they'd only talked about what it meant to be a Dom. What they said was slowly starting to make sense to me, but the rest was still a mystery.

Why did it matter, though? Why did I care so much about Pasha's choices or how he lived his life? Of course I was grateful for everything he'd done for me. And maybe I'd never really stopped feeling responsible for the kids on the estate, even when I thought the best thing I could do for them was disappear.

But it wasn't obligation or duty that kept Pasha constantly on my mind these days. Something had changed in the way I thought of him. He wasn't a child; he didn't need my protection or guidance, I could see that now. If anything, it sometimes felt like he was leading me. There was so much more I wanted to learn about him, or maybe from him. Did he see the way my feelings had shifted? What would he think if he knew? He seemed to have seeped into my consciousness, into my chest, my core, deep into my bones. Already I couldn't imagine life without him in it.

* * *

"Hey Mal," I said, opening the front door on a Saturday night. "C'mon in. Jonah's just running a little late, but Len's here."

Malik stepped inside and we headed to the kitchen. "Want a beer while you're waiting?" I asked.

"Might as well get a head start," Malik agreed.

The three of us sat around the kitchen table with our drinks. I was starting to pull myself together by now, at least enough to carry on a conversation, though I'd declined to join this evening's planned pub crawl. I preferred to keep my drinking moderate anyway.

"The idea," Len explained, when I asked about their proposed route for the evening, "is to get sufficiently stewed before we reach the Plover, where all the real cute bottoms hang out."

"For whose benefit?" I asked, grateful for the distraction from my still obsessive thoughts. "Who's looking?"

"Well, *we're* looking...for Jonah," Len said.

"It's just one more shot in the ongoing quest to find him the right guy,"

Malik added.

"Really?" I was a bit surprised. "What for? Doesn't he get anything he wants from his clients?"

"What?" Len stared at me with his mouth half-open. "That's work. We're talking about fun."

"I thought his regulars are for fun."

"Ok, sure," Malik said, "but those are just scenes. Jonah needs a partner."

"Like you guys do?" I tried not to smile. Len and Malik were always going through relationship drama; falling in love, swearing this was the one, breaking up messily.

"No," Len said haughtily. "*Not* like us."

"What's Jonah's deal, anyway?" I asked. "I don't think he's been involved with anyone since I met him."

"He hasn't. That's the problem. Not since Isaiah," Malik said.

"Isaiah?"

Malik and Len exchanged looks. "You never heard about Isaiah?" Len asked

"I don't think so. Doesn't sound familiar."

"Can't believe he's never said anything in—what, is it five years you've been here? Six?" Len grimaced slightly over his beer bottle. "I guess he really doesn't like to talk about it."

"Well, don't break his confidence or anything..." I said, a bit awkwardly. "But now I'm curious."

"He'd probably rather we told you than talk about it himself. It's still pretty raw for him, even after—what's it been, Len? Almost ten years?"

"Eight and a half."

"That's when Isaiah left—eight and a half years ago," Malik said. "Isaiah was his boyfriend."

"More than boyfriend," Len put in.

"Partner. Sub. Houseboy. Everything, really."

"Yeah. He was everything to Jonah," Len agreed.

Didn't Jonah mention a houseboy, that first day we met? Yes, he said he'd had one once, and didn't want another. "How long were they together?" I asked.

Len and Malik consulted again. "Sixteen years?" Malik suggested.

"At least, maybe more. Seventeen? Yeah, I think it would have been seventeen years. Right after Jonah got out of the army."

"How old was Isaiah?" I asked.

"About our age. A year or two younger. Jonah really thought they were in it till they end."

"What happened?"

Len shook his head slowly, sweeping the table with his beer bottle. "No one really knows. One day Isaiah was just gone. Jonah's never wanted to talk about it."

"I think," Malik said, gesturing faintly with his free hand, "well, my theory is...you know about Jonah's medical thing, right?"

I nodded. "Yeah, he told me."

"I think Isaiah couldn't handle it. Waiting around for his partner to get sick, and...well. I think he wanted to leave first. But that's just my theory."

"Kinda tracks with Isaiah though," Len added.

"Anyway..." Malik shrugged in conclusion. "Jonah's never dated since."

For a moment we were silent, and then Len shot me a sly look. "When he brought you home, we all thought, maybe..."

"Really?" I said. "Because he was pretty clear to me about it not being like that. He's a lot older than me."

Malik gulped his beer, then reached over to pat my hand. "Honestly, man, I'm glad it worked out like this. I think you were just what he needed. A friend."

I laughed, half-embarrassed. "But you guys are his friends. All of you."

"Yeah, but not like you are. You know, sharing his home and learning his work...letting him be a kind of mentor to you. I think he really needed that."

Mentor was a funny word for it, I thought. Outside of work, Jonah had always been a little taciturn and reserved; he didn't give a lot of advice or even speak more than a few words at a time, and he rarely offered anything without being asked. But I'd learned some things from him, things about discipline and effort and quiet self-respect.

Malik broke the mood with a little laugh. "Some of us were hoping though."

"What?" I said. "Hoping what?"

"You know." He bumped my leg under the table with his knee. "That you'd be playing our game."

I almost choked. "Really? You thought I might be one of you? A—a *client*?"

"Naw, man." Malik glanced at Len with a half-guilty grin. "Not one of us. One of *him*."

For a moment I couldn't make sense of his words. Then the meaning hit me, and my face glowed red-hot in an instant. "You mean—" I took a swig from my beer, too afraid of being wrong to finish.

"C'mon, man, look at you." Malik seemed amused at my embarrassment, or maybe that wasn't his first beer.

"Tall, brooding stranger...." Len picked up the theme. "Mysterious, tragic past. Nice build. Strong, firm, sometimes just a *little* over the top. You can't blame anyone if it crossed our minds."

I tried to play it off coolly, hoping the flush in my cheeks would recede. "I'm ten years younger than all of you, at least."

"What's age got to do with it?" Malik demanded. "I've had Doms half my age."

The heat returned with a vengeance. "I spent two years cooking and cleaning for Jonah," I reminded them. "Hardly the kind of work for a Dom."

"Ahh," Malik said, leaning across the table toward me, "but you forget about the *service* part of a service Dom."

The front door opened at that minute and Jonah called out, "Sorry I'm late, boys..."

Malik gave me a final wink, while Len chortled on his way out.

I gathered up the empties as they went to meet Jonah. Alone, I grabbed a couple of cold drinks out of the fridge and held them against my cheeks to cool myself down. Were they trying to provoke me? Surely that was just some kind of harmless flirtation or dumb joke. But if I wasn't careful, my reaction would give my innermost secrets away. I stayed in the kitchen until the three of them left.

* * *

By early June I'd recovered most of my equilibrium. My mind had stopped whirling around, turning the past over and over, and mostly settled on Pasha. How long till I could see him again? Wasn't I ready yet?

We'd messaged a few times, simple check-ins. I wanted him to know I wasn't angry, even if I needed a bit of time to pull myself together. On his part, he seemed content to wait.

But I was out of patience myself. I gave in and messaged him on a Tuesday night, lying in my bed and unable to sleep. *Can I see you this weekend? I'll try not to freak out this time.*

As usual, his response came back promptly. *Dinner Friday?*

I let out my breath in a rush of relief. *Sure. When do you finish work?*

This time there was a brief delay before he answered. *Just remembered, the kids at school have an exhibit Friday night.*

Was he begging off? I hesitated over my comm, not sure what to say. Another message arrived before I came up with anything. *Their year-end artwork display! Would you be up for it? We could get dinner right after.*

I recoiled instinctively at the idea, then stopped myself. Why not? How hard would it be to check out some kids' paintings? I'd get to learn more about Pasha's work and his students. And then I'd have him all to myself for dinner. *Sounds great,* I said.

We worked out the details, he gave me the address, we said good-night. I turned out the light and fell asleep, dreaming of Friday.

Chapter 21

The exhibit took place at a community centre in Echo Canyon, a neighbourhood south of downtown. I parked my car on the street about a block away. While Echo Canyon included a few nice residential blocks, this was not one of them. As I walked, I noticed boarded-up buildings, broken streetlamps, and an abandoned car against the curb.

In the dusk shadows, light glowed from the community centre windows. Inside, chaos reigned, as small children of every shape, size, gender and background chased each other through the wide halls while parents and teachers chattered in clumps around a series of colourful, handmade paintings that lined the walls. Slightly older kids staffed tables laden with raffle tickets, snacks and drinks, loudly plying their wares to raise funds for some kind of school program.

I stood in the entrance for a moment, a little lost. Then Pasha found me, grabbing my arm and giving me a quick hug of greeting.

"Hey, there you are," I said. "Listen, about last time—" I'd meant to apologize again, but it was hard to get a serious sentence out amid the cacophony.

Pasha squeezed my forearm. "Never mind that. Come and let me show you around."

I needed a few minutes to adjust to the lively energy and hyper kids, but I soon found myself enjoying it all. We made our way through the crowds, admiring the bold designs and sometimes startling images in the artwork on the walls. Pasha told me he'd been working with his students on abstract expression. As someone without much understanding of art, I was amazed at the raw emotion some of the pieces contained, incongruous and striking in a world where immaculate perfection was the norm.

As we walked, Pasha was bombarded non-stop with questions and comments from young and old alike. The kids called him *Mista St Vista* and demanded his opinion on their work, appealed to him to settle arguments, or brought their parents over to meet him. The other school staff, holding tiny cups of grape juice posing as white wine, stopped him to make joking comments and acerbic observations.

Pasha responded easily to all of it, patient and encouraging with the kids, affable and receptive with the adults. I could see how his aura of tranquility drew people to him and made him everyone's confidante.

We stayed for a couple of hours. Toward the end, once the kids and parents started to dwindle away, the teachers and admin staff fell into animated discussion. As Pasha joined in, I stood on the outside half listening to the conversation, which seemed to be about local politics, budget cuts, and funding for the school's special projects.

Later, as Pasha and I walked down the street to a family-run Italian restaurant he knew, he filled me in a little more. The public school where he worked was in the same neighbourhood as the community centre. It offered a number of critical services for low-income kids and families, including an after-school art program he ran, which cuts to government funding for *undesirable projects* now jeopardized.

Pasha gave me a curious glance as he explained it all. "Haven't you seen this on the news?"

"Well...no." I rarely followed the news, aside from whatever Jonah and his friends happened to be talking about. It had never been relevant to me. Growing up on the estate, we'd been untouched by the outside world, and the vid industry had its own insular information stream. Now, living my quiet life with Jonah, I still largely ignored anything that didn't directly affect me. "Um...maybe I should."

"Everything going on in this country has a big impact on us at the school, and the kids and families I work with," Pasha said. He led us into the restaurant, saying a few words to the owner and then showing me a small secluded booth near the back, lit with a candle. "Is this okay with you?"

"Sure."

As we settled in with drinks, he told me about a series of summer workshops he was planning for local kids. Without funding, he'd be doing it all for free, relying on volunteers to assist him.

"Hey, uh…maybe I could help out," I said. "I don't know anything about art but…" I was going to say I could look after children before I stopped myself.

Pasha shot me a bright, hopeful look. "That would be amazing," he said. "You were always so good with kids. You'd make such a difference."

Would he still think so if he knew everything I'd done since I left home? I studied the menu, wondering again what I ought to tell him.

"You practically raised me and the others," he added. "This'll be nothing for you."

I laughed uncomfortably. "Pasha, you never needed me. Your folks love you. Your dad was always very protective."

His face clouded a little. "Maybe too protective."

"He treated you like a precious thing," I said, leaning forward. "Because you are."

"My dad—" Pasha paused. "He had his own ideas about me. But you were there with me every single day. You did so much for me. For all of us."

I turned away to signal the serverbot and mumbled, "If you knew what—"

"I don't care what you've done or where you've been since you left home," he said. "I'm talking about all those years on the estate. You made everything magical for me. I have nothing but good memories of my childhood, and that's because of you."

The bot arrived and as we placed our orders I took a few long breaths to try and steady the pulse throbbing erratically in my neck. This conversation felt less safe than previous ones, but I didn't want to run away again.

Once we were alone, Pasha lifted a hand to brush back a few stray blond strands, then pinned his ocean blue gaze on me. "What about you, Barr?" he asked. "Do you have good memories from your childhood?"

"I..." How could I explain what I could hardly bear to think about? "I did once. But then it...it got messed up."

He had a way of looking at me like he understood, or at least had an inkling of what I meant. "While you lived there?" he asked. "Or just when you look back on it?"

He was pulling at the knotted tangle of threads in my brain. "Uh...a little of both, I guess." I shifted my legs back and forth under the table as the aching coil twisted and resisted. "You know, I loved that life at first...the freedom, the space, all the other kids. It was a little paradise. But then it's like...I wanted more." I tried to hide my embarrassment. "I don't know what was wrong with me. I had so much, but..."

"You took on a lot of responsibility," Pasha said. "And that was great for me and the other kids. But the adults expected an awful lot from you."

I didn't see it that way, exactly. "I mean, I *liked* being in charge of things."

"I know. And you were great at it. Only the more you did the more they expected from you."

Our plates arrived, and I focused on my meal. But when I looked up, Pasha was still watching me. "They treated you like an adult when you were just a kid, Barry."

"You make it sound like I was some kind of victim," I said, swirling the pasta around my fork. "But I knew what I was doing. I was in control."

"Were you?" He seemed to hold his breath for a moment before plunging on. "What about with Tiran? Were you in control with him?"

I almost dropped my fork, almost snapped that I didn't want to talk about Tiran, that if he continued I'd leave. It was all in my throat and I saw Pasha bracing for it, but somehow I managed to catch myself before the responses overflowed. "Pasha, I really don't—"

"He was a grown man and you were just a boy. Do you honestly think you were in control?"

"Look, I know now that I wasn't, but I thought at the time I could—"

"You thought you could handle him like an adult because everyone *treated* you like an adult. But you were just a kid."

I sighed. His words offered a kind of comfort; it was tempting to believe in them. But he didn't know the whole story. "Pasha, you don't understand. I was no innocent. He didn't exactly seduce me."

Pasha's steady gaze didn't flicker. "What does that matter?"

"He didn't even want me." My throat felt thick, and I had to push my words through it. "He tried to say no. I was the one that—I forced him into it."

"*Forced* him?" I'd never heard such vehemence from Pasha. "*Forced*?" He leaned across the table and pointed his fork at me. "He was thirty-four years old, one of the richest, most powerful men in the world. You were a nineteen-year-old kid, pretty much dependent on him. You really think you could make him do *anything* he didn't want to?"

He paused, but I could only stare, fascinated at his sudden ferocity.

"All he had to do," Pasha said more quietly, "was say no."

I still couldn't respond. My head started to spin, like I was looking through a rear-view mirror and all the cars had turned upside down.

"I think you've been carrying that around for years," Pasha said after a pause, his usual mildness returning. "When he's the one at fault. You say he resisted you at first, so he knew it was wrong. He was just too weak to do the right thing."

Weak. What a strange way to describe Tiran. I wanted to believe him, but Pasha still didn't fully understand my role in it all. "The thing is, though..." I toyed with my fork in the dish, then pushed it aside, unable to stomach any more. "I wasn't in love with him. I—wanted things from him. You know, I had these dumb ideas about..." *power*, I thought, but I couldn't bring myself to say the word. Pasha already knew I didn't understand those dynamics, no need to make it even more apparent.

"You wanted to make it in the vid industry, I know," Pasha said. "You had ambitions. No one blames you for that."

I choked out a small laugh. "Maybe you don't, but plenty of people did."

"Who?" He looked surprised. "Who would hold that against you?"

Jimmy, I thought. *Your dad*. I half opened my mouth, then shut it again. "I mean," I said finally, "They all tried to warn me."

Pasha's clear eyes narrowed a little. "Who did?"

I rushed on, trying to get the worst of it out, like purging a wound. "They all disapproved, and when they saw me fuck everything up, well—they knew they were right."

"Wait..." A slow awareness had started to grow in Pasha's gaze. He reached across the table and clasped my hand in both of his. "Do you think my dad and the others were mad at you for your thing with Tiran?"

"Why wouldn't they be? They all warned me. They knew how stupid I was."

"They weren't mad at *you*." He squeezed my hand. "They were mad at *him*. All of them—Jimmy, my dad, my mom, Rocky—they were furious. Everyone blamed him when you left home. Believe me, we all knew who was responsible."

Once again, I could hardly take everything in. I lifted my arms, squeezing my head between my hands. "What are you saying..."

"No one blamed you for being a kid, Barry. I mean, I guess they kinda did once, that time with the intruders. They gave you no grace then. But they knew you were out of your depth with Tiran. I think it made them finally see what they'd done."

I moved my hands to cover my eyes, trying to give my brain time to catch up. When I finally lowered my arms, Pasha was leaning back in his chair, waiting for me.

"Didn't you—didn't you go through some kind of therapy in rehab, Barr?" he asked. "I thought you might have worked through some of this."

"God...no," I said. "I basically refused therapy. I couldn't handle it."

He started to say something, then paused, and seemed to take a different tack. "I understand. I wonder if it might be a little easier now?"

I knew what he was getting at, but didn't want to make any commitments. "How..." I started, as a way to change the subject, "how did *you* figure this all out? You were just fifteen when it was happening."

"I saw you with Tiran. I always knew he wasn't good enough for you." Pasha spoke with such simple assurance that I found myself thinking, again, about his faith in me.

"Pasha..."

The serverbot whirred up to take our dishes away, and I ordered a coffee to postpone the end of our meal.

"You say that," I pressed on, "but you don't know what I did after I left home."

"That doesn't matter," he said with the same certainty. "It doesn't cancel anything out." His hand moved up to tuck some hair behind his ear, paused mid-movement and then continued. "If you had a rough time for a while... well, so did I. Sometimes that's just part of growing up."

"Some of the things I did..."

"You don't have to explain anything to me." He said it like he wanted to save me from discomfort, not like he wasn't interested. "It might be easier with a therapist. I could help you find one, you know."

Maybe I should give it a rest, I thought. I'd been so afraid he'd find out about everything later and be appalled, but I was starting to get the impression nothing would shake his belief in me.

"You know, I—I didn't start out working at Jonah's company," I said. The serverbot brought my coffee and I held the warm mug in my hand for a moment. "I spent two years keeping house for him."

Pasha smiled like that didn't surprise him. "You were always good at looking after people," he said.

Once again, I had that sensation of being guided; coaxed onward or, perhaps, backward, to some once familiar place. A place where I knew what I wanted, and didn't run away from it.

I took a gulp of coffee, then put the cup down with a bit more force than I intended. "Listen," I said.

Pasha's face grew still as he watched me, waiting. In the low light of the restaurant a kind of silvery light shimmered away from him, like moonlight through clouds. His lips parted slightly with that delicate patience I had started to recognize as his way of ceding the next move to me.

"I still don't know exactly how this all happened," I said. "You being back in my life like this. I can't tell you how happy it makes me."

He smiled slightly. "Me too."

"Not just because it's fun to reconnect and everything. Pasha, you talk a lot about the past and what I used to be like, but...the truth is, I'm not sure

I'm the person you remember."

"I think you are."

The conviction in his voice made my breath catch for a moment before I forced myself on. "But I've changed in some ways for sure. I mean—about you. We used to be like brothers but...well, that's not how I think of you now. Not even close." I struggled to hold his unblinking gaze. "Maybe you've noticed it—the way I'm feeling. Or maybe you haven't. I don't want to make you uncomfortable. If you don't want to hear this, you can say the word and I'll never bring it up again. It's just that...I don't see these feelings going away anytime soon so I—I thought you should know."

There; the truth was out. I stopped, trying to read Pasha's reaction as he sat motionless across from me.

"I..." His voice came out in a low rasp, and his eyes glinted, brilliant in the candlelight. His whole body seemed suspended in a kind of vibrating stasis. "Thank you for telling me that," he whispered at last.

I blinked, not sure if there was more to come. When he didn't say anything else I pushed the coffee cup away and leaned back in my chair. "I know I'm not—what you want. I know I can't give you what you need. I don't know how..."

"No," Pasha began, as I faltered. "It's okay. Listen, Barr..." His body seemed to re-animate as he reached some kind of decision. "You asked about seeing my art. My apartment's not too far from here. Why don't you come over now and I can show you?"

That was a bit unexpected, but I didn't blame him for wanting to change the subject. At least this way we could get over the awkward moment. "Okay," I said. "Sure."

* * *

We took my car, since I didn't want to leave it on the street, and he'd walked to the community centre. He directed me to his apartment building, in a nicer part of the same neighbourhood. We didn't talk much on the drive, my mind still overflowing and Pasha's movements constrained with what I read as tension.

I didn't exactly regret telling him how I felt; he had to know the truth—and so did I. Only now it was out there, and we were both forced to live with it. If he didn't want me to mention any of it again I wouldn't. But I still needed him in my life, and that meant finding a way to work around it all—the awkwardness for him, the pain for me.

Pain. A world where Pasha didn't think about me the way I did about him hardly seemed endurable. But I couldn't dwell on it, not now, while he was still here beside me trying to salvage what was left of our relationship. I just had to make it through the rest of this night; there'd be time for self-pity later.

"Here," he said abruptly, pointing me to a mid-rise complex just ahead. "There's parking at the back."

I followed where he indicated and parked the car. Pasha led me through the building's back door and into an elevator. He stood beside me stiffly, as though holding himself in check, with a careful, fixed expression that I didn't know how to interpret.

When we got out, he led me along the hall to his apartment, unlocked the door and stood aside to let me in first. I entered a small foyer, then paused and glanced back at him. He motioned me forward, now with a small smile of anticipation or resignation, I couldn't tell which.

The room in front of me was dark, with outlines of a sofa and chairs just visible in the grey light from a window straight ahead. Pasha clicked something and two large floor lamps illuminated the space.

I started to glance around but my eye was drawn immediately to the far wall, where a single large, painted canvas filled the space. *His art,* I thought, and moved toward it.

At first I took the painting for a portrait, before I got closer and recognized the image: an enormous lion, in brilliant amber and bronze, with a rippling flaxen mane, just like the one on the birthday card Pasha gave me all those years ago. Its watchful golden eyes stared straight into mine, one massive paw half-raised to shield the small cub that nestled between its front legs.

For a few long seconds I couldn't move, trying to take in the sight before me. Then I stepped forward and lifted my hand to trace the curves of the mane with my fingertips.

"I have other pieces," Pasha said in a low voice behind me, "but this is the one I wanted you to see." When I looked back, he still stood near the entry with his hand on the light switch, watching me. "I thought it might be the easiest way to tell you."

"This is...me?" I managed at last, my fingers brushing the canvas in front of me.

"It's always been you," he said.

I stared at him, then back at the painting, a sudden panic welling up in my stomach. "But—" For some reason I needed urgently to tell him. "*Your card,* Pasha. I carried it around with me for years and then..." The tears erupted suddenly, like a burst balloon filled with water instead of air. "And then I threw it away."

"Oh, Barry..." He stepped forward, arms outstretched. "That's okay."

I shook my head almost frantically, my eyes awash. "It's not, it's not..."

"It's okay." He took me in his arms. "I'll make you another one."

But I could only collapse against him, boneless and weak, overtaken by the relentless purge of grief. My tears drenched his shoulder, at first for the lost card, the gift I'd loved and valued and discarded, and then for all the lost things. For Lance not making it to twenty-one, for Steve alone and scared and hiding, for Jimmy thinking he'd lost us all. For Doc growing old without me, all the missed graduations and weddings, the years Jonah wouldn't see, the life Jimmy gave up for us, even the stupid convertible. For failed ambitions and unmet desires, mistakes, confusion, and a prince's kingdom forever tainted with shame and confusion.

Pasha held me close, without words, his fingers stroking my back. Every time the surge started to ebb, some new thought would launch another release, and my limbs would buckle again. I'm not sure how long it lasted but it seemed to go on for hours, my whole world channeled into that long black tunnel of loss.

At some point I guess Pasha must have led me to his bedroom and got me into the bed, and eventually I fell asleep.

Chapter 22

Sometime in the night I woke up, disoriented and briefly alarmed, before I recognized Pasha's dim outline in the bed beside me. I leaned up on an elbow and watched his faint breathing in the pre-dawn light. He didn't stir, and after a moment I fell back on my pillow. Between the two of us we must have removed most of my clothes, as I was only wearing my shorts. I turned onto my side, my body curved a couple of inches away from his, and fell back asleep.

In the morning, light movements broke through my sleep and I opened my eyes to find Pasha starting to slip out of the bed.

I seized his arm, barely awake. "Don't go."

He stopped and looked back at me, smiling. "I was just going to start the coffee."

"Later."

He slid back under the covers without protest. I released his wrist so he could lie on his side, facing me. The hair tumbling over his face partly obscured his eyes, and my fingers crept across the small distance between us, brushing a couple of strands aside and then back, behind his ear. The blue oceans came into view, fixed steadily on me.

"Is that…okay?" I whispered.

His chin moved in a tiny nod, and his lips parted. "More than okay."

"I—I don't exactly remember what happened last night," I said, though I could still feel the dried salt on my cheeks. "Except for the crying. I'm so sorry about…"

"Shh," he said, and his hand darted out to stroke my cheek. "Seems like that's just what you needed."

I reached up and circled his wrist with my hand once more. "Did we...agree on anything, or—"

"We didn't do much talking," he said, and after a moment's hesitation added, "but...it seems like we both want the same thing."

That was how I remembered it too. I let go of his wrist and moved my hand through his fine soft hair to the back of his neck, pulling him closer. He lowered his eyelids when I leaned in to kiss him, his lips tasting just as full and soft and sweet as I'd imagined.

"This, right?" I breathed.

He nodded, and I kissed him again, reeling with relief and anticipation, joy and desire. I guided him onto his back and slid over top of him. As he so often did, Pasha let me take the lead, and I was grateful. I wanted to make this last, to savour him slowly and revel in each touch. My fingers skated over skin as smooth and pale as the seashells we used to find on the beach, and I set out to taste every inch of it. He responded to each breath and movement with a tightened grip or press of his lips against whatever part of my body he could reach, but for some reason I needed more.

"Is this okay?" I'd murmur, with every new position, every tug at his clothes, every slide further down the bed. *Yes*, he'd moan, and *yes* and *yes* again.

When I took him in my mouth, I had a fleeting memory of all the tricks and techniques I'd learned, everything I'd been taught to please men or perform for the cameras. But none of that mattered. I was attuned only to Pasha, to the gasps and hitches in his breath, the clench of his fists in my hair, the clutches and spasms and arching that told me everything I needed to know.

* * *

"I guess we could have coffee now," I said later, as we lay motionless on our backs, hands intertwined and hips brushing against each other.

"But what about you?" Pasha asked, turning his face toward me. "I didn't have chance to..."

I kissed his forehead. "We can do that later," I said. "We have all day. Unless you have somewhere to be?"

"No." He laughed and sat up, swinging his feet to the floor. "Not likely. Stay there, let me bring it to you."

I didn't need much persuasion. Exhilarated as I was, last night's breakdown seemed to have sapped some of my energy. I hoped the coffee would wake me up, because however much I wanted to just spend the day in bed with Pasha, some anxious part of my mind was warning me we still had things to figure out.

He returned in a few minutes with a tray of coffee and toast and we sat up to eat, leaning against the headboard behind us. For a second it took me back, a quick flash of mornings in bed with breakfast trays and Tiran beside me. I shut my eyes instinctively, then changed my mind and opened them. Those memories had too much power when I kept running away from them. I glanced at Pasha, his radiant eyes meeting mine over his coffee cup, at the small double bed, the narrow rays of sunlight brightening the modest room, the view of concrete buildings through the window, the single shared tray between us. This would be a new memory, different in every way from the ones in my past.

As we finished breakfast, both of us grew quieter, and Pasha lingered a little over his plate as though not quite sure what would happen next. I wondered if he shared my uncertainties. Either way, the hesitation lingering at the back of my mind had to be addressed.

"Listen, Pasha…" I put my empty coffee cup back on the tray and turned toward him, cross-legged under the covers. "I'm so happy to be here with you. I hate having to bring this up. But…" I paused, praying I wouldn't regret my words. "But I think we both know there's things we have to figure out."

He glanced down for a second, like he'd half-expected this, then moved the breakfast tray onto a night table and reached over to squeeze my hand. "What things?"

"Well, to start with…I don't want you settling for something that's not—complete. I know I'm not enough for you."

Shadows darkened the clear blue eyes. "Why..."

"Because you told me what you need, and we both know I don't...I can't ..."

Pasha gave a sudden tug on my hand, pulling me toward him. "Are you sure about that?"

"You already said it. You said I'm not ready."

"Not ready now," he said, "doesn't mean you'll never be."

I froze for a second, then leaned back a bit so I could see him better. "But—"

"The real question is what *you* want," he went on. His eyes searched mine as I stared back, trying to decipher his meaning. "If it's something that even appeals to you."

"What do you..."

He released my gaze, as though freeing me from the intensity of his need, and looked down again. "When we talked about this before, you seemed uncomfortable," he said. "Like you might have had...your own experience. Like maybe you've tried it and don't want to try again. If that's it, then...then I totally understand. I won't push you into anything you don't want." His voice dropped so I could barely hear him. "I've made that mistake before."

Something seemed to be squeezing my stomach. I had to fight for the breath to answer. "I do. I do want to. I've always wanted to but—but I don't know how." I pressed my hands over my stomach. "Pasha, I don't want to mess up with you."

He watched me intently, as though trying to see through my words straight into my heart. "So...you have tried?"

"Being a Dom?" I felt the flush in my face, but it seemed critically important to allow for no ambiguity in what we were talking about. When Pasha nodded I went on. "I've tried some things. At clubs or...whatever. But I'm not good at it, and—and everything always goes wrong. I don't know what I'm doing."

For a moment we were both silent, and then Pasha spoke, slowly. "When I said you weren't ready...it's not because I thought you wouldn't be good at it. It was more because you seemed so—unsure. Like you might have lost something you used to have."

"Yeah." I almost laughed. "My confidence."

"Not exactly," Pasha said, tilting his head to study me. "I got the impression you don't feel the same way about...well, being in charge. It always came so naturally to you, but when we talked earlier you seemed to—kind of hold back. Even when..." He half smiled. "You were ordering me around."

"Sorry." The warmth in my face intensified. "But...yeah, I think I know what you mean. I guess it's because I mostly feel like a fraud now. Like an imposter. What business do I have telling anyone else what to do when I fucked everything up myself? Why should anyone listen to me?"

Pasha looked a little amused at that, and he leaned over to give me a quick kiss. "I think those doubts are probably good for someone who's always been a leader...like you."

"But it's not just that." I stopped. There was something else, some unformed fear still trapped in that tangled knot in my brain. I grasped at the threads I could reach, trying to unravel it. "I mean...I used to like power. I thought it was what I wanted, to have control over someone else. I envied people with power, only... when I met them I found they—weren't what I thought. They hurt people who don't want to be hurt. And when I met people who *did* want to be hurt, *I* didn't like it. It got all mixed up and...ugly, and painful."

"Oh..." Pasha hesitated. "I think I've seen that too. Sometimes I've been part of it. But..." He reached for my hands and held them in both of his. "You said you still want to try it, so...is it possible there *are* things you'd like to do? With me?"

Oh, yes. The question seemed to turn on some tap in my brain, my mind instantly flooded with inarticulate desire. I wanted to explain, but the familiar rush of desire swept my words away. The old cravings, those searing memories of intimacy, service and surrender, electrified my flesh and filled my chest with heat and hunger.

Pasha's fingers tightened their grip, as though the current surging through my body had begun to flow into him through our joined hands, and after a moment I felt a kind of answering thrum. "I think..." he said in a whisper, "we can make it whatever we want. We can find a way that works for both of us."

"Can we?" I breathed.

"You might be more ready than I thought."

I squeezed his hands and took in a breath. "I wanted power because I thought that's what you need to be a Dom. But Jonah says it's about trust, not power. That it's what's inside that counts. Do you think I have..."

"I know you do," Pasha said. "Maybe it got a little lost over the years, but I bet we can find it again...together."

I remembered his quiet patience in our conversations, the way he always seemed to bide his time and let me take the next step. I'd thought he was deferring to me, and maybe in a way he was, but now I wondered if he'd always been a step ahead, waiting for me to catch up.

"Pasha..." I pulled him into my arms, overwhelmed with relief, covering his face with kisses, then his long throat and soft hair. When we moved apart, I saw serenity in his eyes.

What would it be like to have a kind of dominion over this man? Some mutually agreed right to command, safeguard, succour him? My body shivered against his at the thought.

"I don't know if I'll ever be good enough for you," I said at last. "I have so much to learn."

He smiled, like that struck him as funny. "All these years you've been living with Jonah—a *professional* Dom—and it never occurred to you to ask him?"

I didn't know how to explain. "By the time I got to Jonah, I didn't want anything to do with that world. I thought it was always going to be messed up. That's why I—"

"That's why you didn't want me getting involved with him."

"Yeah. But now I can't wait to ask him for help."

"So I'm not allowed to work with him but you are?" Pasha teased.

I pulled him against me again. "We can both work with him, if that's what you want."

He nuzzled into my neck as we wrapped our arms around each other. Fears allayed, and my heart full of anticipation and desire, I kissed him again, already starting to think about round two. But before I could adjust my position, Pasha slid a hand over my thigh and breathed into my ear.

"Is it my turn now?"

"You don't have to..."

"You said later. You promised."

It wasn't what I had in mind; I'd been thinking of something more mutual. I didn't want to make any assumptions about what he might like, what roles or positions he preferred. But he was already kissing his way down my chest, and the last thing I could say to him was *no*. His movements were so sure and persuasive and irresistible, I soon lost all ability to think rationally. I had a brief thought of stopping before release but he quickly brought me past the point of no return.

Afterwards I held him tight against me while I recovered, breathless and in awe. "I had no idea you'd be so good at that," I told him, and his rosy skin glowed with pleasure.

When we eventually agreed to get out of bed, Pasha pulled on a robe and picked up the tray from the table. This time I followed him out of the bedroom to explore the rest of the apartment.

The main living area was a good-sized room, with a dining table in one corner, an easel set up beside the window, and a comfortable seating area. Bright mid-day sunlight glinted off the brilliant golds and tawny bronze of the lion on the wall. When Pasha came out of the kitchen he found me in front of it.

"When did you paint this?" I asked.

"Oh..." He went over to the sofa, ducking his head a little. "A long time ago. It's not the only one I did. They were all packed away in a closet until I...until I saw you that night. I hung this one up after we got together the first time."

"So..." I still couldn't fully parse out the meaning of it all. "You...you..."

"C'mere," he coaxed. "Let me tell you all about it."

When I joined him on the sofa, he curled up beside me, his shoulder nestled against my chest as I wrapped an arm around him.

"I'm sure you've figured it out by now," he said, not quite looking at me.

"That I was in love with you before you left home. In fact I don't really remember a time when I wasn't."

"Honestly, Pasha—I had no idea."

"I know." He looked a little amused at my obliviousness. "It's probably just as well. It would've been weird back then. Twenty-four and twenty-eight is a lot different from fifteen and nineteen."

"It's not like I ever had any hold over you. We weren't even buddies in that system I set up." I slid my hand along the warm skin of his chest, under the robe. "And you were always way smarter than me."

He laughed. "Well, I never had any illusions. I knew you didn't have the same kind of feelings for me. I was happy when you left home because I wanted you to get away from Tiran, and I knew you had all those big dreams. But even so…" Pasha pressed his fingers into my thigh and went on, more slowly, "It was hard when you left."

I could see him treading carefully, not wanting to trigger any guilt or sound like he blamed me. "I'm sorry," I said, wishing there was a way to pull him closer than he already was.

His fine hair brushed my cheek as he shook his head. "Don't be. I was happy for you, just sad for me. That's when I started painting lions. I mean, it was all I could think about. I made it through high school but when I started at art college in the fall I just couldn't focus. I didn't know what I wanted."

"It's hard to imagine you that way. You always seem to know what you're doing."

"It took me years to figure things out, Barr. You and I might have gone through some of the same things."

I tightened my arm around him. "At least Dusty had the sense to keep you out of the vid industry. I can't imagine what would've happened to you there."

"I'm not sure that made much difference." Pasha moved away from me and leaned forward on the couch, forearms resting on his thighs. "I gave up on school and lived downtown for a while, and I probably went to all the same places you did. Even those clubs where you said you tried things out—I know those places. And, I mean…everything you said about men taking advantage of me—it's true, there were men like that. But it's not like I was any better. I used them just as much."

"What do you mean?" I reached over to brush the loose hair out of his face, trying to read his expression. "How could you…?"

"I mean I made a lot of mistakes back then," Pasha said. He pressed his hands together between his knees, and kept his gaze on the floor. "I didn't know what I was doing or what I wanted. I took risks and manipulated people, and I pushed people for things they couldn't give me."

"I can't believe that."

"It's no use thinking of me as pure and innocent," Pasha said, raising his head until his clear eyes met mine. "Because I'm not. If you ever want to tell me some of your story, I'll tell you more of mine, and you'll see it's no prettier."

"But, Pasha…" I could hardly process his words. "I thought you said you were a sub."

He laughed, and this time there was a touch of bitterness in it. "You think subs can't hurt people? We have power too, you know…and we can misuse it just like anyone else. I was frustrated and angry a lot of the time, and I found ways to take that out on the guys I played with. I knew how to get into a person's head. I could mess with their mind until they were just as unhappy as me."

I remembered all those encounters I'd had, the ones that ended with dissatisfied partners. They'd had good reason to be dissatisfied, of course, but it still did a number on my self-confidence. When I looked at Pasha's sharp profile, his lucent skin and pointed jaw, and tried to imagine his disdain, I had to suppress a shudder.

"Look, I'm not proud of any of this," he said. "I'm telling you because I don't want you to think you're the only one who's ever made mistakes. As far as I can tell, the main difference between you and me is that I eventually made peace with who I am. And I feel like you're still trying to get there."

I moved my arm to his shoulder and tugged him back against me. "How did you do it?" I asked, after a moment. "Make peace with yourself?"

He shrugged. "It wasn't one big moment. I finally just realized I had to face facts. I know being a sub means some people will despise me or think I have no self-respect. I understand the stigma—I guess that's why I resisted for so long. But in the end…none of it can change who I am."

Listening to him speak, I recognized my own lingering prejudices with growing dismay. It had never occurred to me to think about the impact my biases had on people like Pasha.

"Once I figured that out, I moved back home and started teacher's college," Pasha went on, more lightly. "I figured teaching is a kind of service, which is really what appeals to me, so it seemed like a good fit."

"Teaching is perfect for you."

"And I packed away all the lions. I had to make peace with that, too—that I might never see you again. So after I finished school, got a job, moved out for good…I decided to work with a pro Dom. I needed a safe space to figure out what kind of sub I was, and what I wanted from a Dom. I figured, that way I'd be ready if I ever found the right man."

He tilted his head to look up at me with a faint smile. "I always knew who I was waiting for," he said, in a lower voice. "A man who's kind and protective and exciting and brave, who's good with kids and animals, who makes me feel safe and valued and…loved. I knew it was possible to find someone like that because I already did, once."

"Pasha…" I took his face in my hands and pressed my lips against his.

When I moved away, he left his arms around my neck. "I avoided Jonah at first," he said, like he wanted to finish his confession, "because I really wanted it to be about improving myself and not hoping to catch a glimpse of you…but it was hard to find anyone else I could trust. I only had a couple of sessions with him, and I still feel a little guilty. Maybe my motives weren't so pure. Maybe all I really wanted was to run into you."

"Thank the gods," I said, kissing him again, "for impure motives."

I hadn't meant to start anything, but he kissed me back, insistently, with open lips and his tongue darting against mine. My hands tightened around the back of his head as I opened my mouth to respond. In a moment he was straddling me, his knees on either side of my thighs on the sofa.

"Pasha—" I gasped, cupping his face again. "Are you—do you—it's getting hard to—"

"Yes," he said, and pushed my hands away so he could lean forward to reach my lips again.

"So soon?" I dropped my hands to his hips to support him, then raised them again, sliding my fingers over the smooth flesh of his back to the angular curve of his shoulder blades. "Already?"

"I just told you," he said, in quick breaths between kisses, "how long I've waited."

I stopped protesting and focused on following his lead. Pasha lowered himself onto my lap, and as he began to move I matched his rhythm, my hands on his back and fingers curved over his shoulders, his hands holding my face, our mouths pressed together as our breathing grew faster and more erratic. At just the right moment, as I gasped and clutched at him convulsively, he reached down to take us both in his hand and brought us to our first mutual climax.

* * *

"I'm starving," Pasha said, quite a while later, when we'd more or less recovered.

"Me too. I guess all we've had today is toast."

"Want me to make something?"

I sat up and glanced around. The room had grown a bit dimmer, lit only by the deep amber light of late afternoon. "Why don't we go out? It should be cool enough by now."

We took a shower together, then headed out to a diner he knew nearby. Over our late lunch, or early dinner, we talked about everything from the other kids on the estate to Pasha's art to my life with Jonah and some of what led up to it. Pasha didn't ask prying questions, but I tried to give him a general idea about what happened to those once grand ambitions.

All the while, the back of my brain buzzed with a persistent awareness of that new role Pasha might one day entrust me with. But I was careful to avoid making any allusions to it, determined to learn what I needed from Jonah before I even approached Pasha with any kind of intent. I'd made enough mistakes in my life; finally, finally, I had a chance to do one thing right.

After our meal we got ice-creams and walked around the neighbourhood while Pasha filled me in on the issues affecting his school. He talked about climate and war refugees fleeing unstable parts of the country, about the increased desperation of people displaced by advanced robotics and technology, about oligarchs with money and power who stoked cultural and racial divisions and reduced public investments.

"It all impacts my school," he explained, "because New Ellay is one of the few stable urban areas left, so it's a magnet for everyone who's been displaced. Most schools here are private now; mine's one of the only ones left in the public system, so refugees flock to us. We try and accept everyone and offer programs that help kids and their families—art for the kids and skills training for adults. But there just aren't enough of us, so it's a constant struggle."

I listened in wonder, amazed at how I'd been able to stay unaware of all this for so long.

"You know, growing up on the estate, I never really heard about anything going on outside," Pasha said.

"Me neither," I agreed, relieved he understood. "We were completely isolated from the real world." And I'd never made any effort to change that, I realized as I spoke.

"Even at school, I didn't learn much," he said. "It was kind of a shock when I left home and suddenly found out about everything going on."

I knew what he meant. I'd had a similar feeling when I heard Jonah and Malik talk about growing up, and their lives in the army during the civil war years. But even that was in the past; what Pasha faced was here and now.

By the time dusk turned into darkness, I'd committed to volunteering not just for the summer arts class but for whatever programs I could contribute to, year-round. I figured if Pasha could live out there in the real world, so could I.

"Are you...staying with me again?" Pasha asked, looking up hopefully, as we decided to head back.

"If you let me."

He did. At his apartment we tumbled straight into bed and didn't get out until the next morning. By then I'd learned much more about what Pasha liked, and discovered that his preferred positions aligned perfectly with mine.

Just after we finished our shower, when Pasha went to the kitchen to rustle up some breakfast, my comm buzzed with an incoming voice call. Those were rare, and I'd only whitelisted a few contacts, so I checked it curiously. Malik.

A creeping tendril of fear spread in my belly as I answered. "Mal?"

"Where've you been?" His voice was raw, and harsher than usual. "You need to meet us at the hospital. Jonah's been admitted, and they don't think he's coming out."

Chapter 23

Jonah had warned me once that the end, when it came, would be fast. He lasted just over a week, conscious and lucid for most of it.

When he saw Pasha and I together that first day, he managed a short barking laugh. "So here's what you've been hiding lately," he rasped. "Always figured that's how you two would play out."

The hospital room had an extra bed so Malik and I both stayed by Jonah's side, taking turns to get a few hours of sleep. We'd step out to the waiting room to give other friends privacy for their good-byes. Though I knew how well-loved and respected Jonah was, I hadn't expected the sheer number of people who turned up once the news got out; a steady stream of friends, personal and professional clients, and colleagues. Many of them I'd met, but most, especially the clients, were strangers to me.

A couple of days in, Pasha pulled me aside and told me his father wanted to see Jonah. Of course I didn't begrudge Dusty a final visit; they'd been friends for almost as long as I'd been alive. But I couldn't face seeing him again, for the first time, in that situation.

Pasha took care of it, meeting his father at the hospital while I seized the opportunity to run a few errands outside. I dealt with a couple of emergencies at work, picked up some odds and ends for Jonah, checked in at the house and grabbed a change of clothes. That was the only time I left the hospital.

Toward the end, as the pain meds amped up and Jonah spent more of his time knocked out, it became apparent how quickly the chance to communicate with him was slipping away. From then on, I spent Jonah's waking moments telling him what he meant to me, promising to protect his company and his work, and thanking him for everything he'd done. It seemed urgent to tell him about the impact he'd had on my life. But looking back on it, I think he already knew.

Sometime after midnight on an early Wednesday, while Malik dozed on the bed behind me, I sat next to Jonah, holding his hand. In the dim light, I didn't notice right away when his eyes opened. But I felt the faint squeeze of his hand and looked over to find him watching me with that increasingly rare spark of consciousness.

I leaned over to kiss his cheek, not sure if he'd be able to speak. As I started to move back, he reached up with his other hand and grasped the back of my neck. "*Don't let the bastards win*," he breathed. I half-choked and half-laughed, taking his face in my hands and resting my forehead on his until his eyes closed again. He left us a few hours later.

* * *

Always a perfectionist, Jonah provided detailed instructions for every aspect of the end of his life. He didn't know exactly when the day would come, but he must have meticulously prepared for it months or even years in advance.

Malik and I had agreed to be his executors awhile back, and I was grateful for Jonah's organization in the immediate aftermath. He'd already arranged and paid for his own cremation, so we put most of our energy into planning a memorial service for him in early July.

I went into the office as soon as I could, knowing he didn't want to leave his clients in a bind. Picking up the pieces of his work and making sure nothing got lost seemed like the best way to honour his memory in the short term.

A lawyer reached out to us about the will, so we set up a telecon and Malik came over to join me for it. We already knew Jonah had no immediate family, his parents long gone, his only sibling lost in one of the coastal upheavals decades ago, and no other relatives he was close to. Even so, I wasn't quite prepared for the contents of the will. Aside from a few small legacies to

Malik and a couple of his long-time regulars, Jonah left everything to me—his business, house, car, and savings.

"You seem surprised," Malik said, after the lawyer signed off. We sat beside each other on the living room couch, where we'd been facing the big screen.

I didn't know how to react. "Aren't you?"

"No," he said, laughing. "He didn't talk to you about this?"

"I mean, I knew about the business. He basically asked me to take it over. But the rest..."

"What else was he going to do with it?" Malik asked.

"But I'm not his only friend. What's everyone going to think?"

"Trust me, no one expected anything else."

"Are you...sure it's going to be okay?" I said finally. "I don't want anyone feeling like I..."

Malik leaned over to hug me. "Listen, we're all grown up, we have jobs and homes and cars. He knew you're the one who needs this the most, and we know it too."

I blinked a couple of times. "What about Len, though?" I said. "That ancient piece of junk he drives is always breaking down, couldn't he..."

"Sure," Malik said with a smile, "give the car to Len if you want. But stop worrying about the rest of it."

"I gotta admit, keeping the house will make things easier for me. I don't really want to think about finding somewhere else to live."

"Just don't be surprised when you get the odd client knocking at the back door. I'm sure there's a few that haven't got the news yet."

For the first time, I remembered my plans to learn from Jonah. "Oh *no*, Mal," I said, choking up for probably the hundredth time in the last week. "I missed my chance! I—I thought I'd have more time! Now I'll never..."

"What? You'll never what?" Malik asked.

I paced around the room, my hand over my eyes. "Learn how to be a Dom."

"Uh...since when did you want to be a Dom?" Malik sounded a bit amused. "I thought you rejected that idea pretty hard when Len and me brought it up."

"Since—since..."

"Oh, never mind. I get it. That little blond hottie you found knows what he wants, am I right?"

"It's not a game, Mal," I said, stopping in front of him.

"No, it's not." He grew serious. "I totally agree. Listen, you might have missed your chance to learn from the best. But I bet me and his other clients can tell you a few things about what makes a good Dom. I tell you what, I'll get a few of the boys together after the memorial's over and see if that helps." He reached up to squeeze my hand. "What do you say?"

"I..." It was hard to keep my emotions under control these days. The wave of relief and gratitude his words produced threatened to capsize me. "Thank you," I said. "I can't wait."

* * *

The memorial seemed to grow bigger every day. So many people wanted to attend, speak or perform in Jonah's memory. At first we'd planned to hold it at the house, but the size of the guest list soon made that impossible. Every day Malik and I got more enquiries—from friends and clients, former army buddies, fellow Doms, industry professionals. I wondered if we'd hear from Isaiah, but as far as I know we never did.

After some discussion, we switched the venue to the Echo Canyon community centre, where the kids' art exhibit had been hosted. Pasha knew all kinds of small businesses in the area, run by people who'd attended his school's training programs. I used some of Jonah's savings to hire local caterers, music services, florists, event managers, and everything else we needed.

At some point I stopped reviewing invite requests and let Malik handle them so I could focus on the rest of the planning. As the event drew near, it occurred to me to take a closer look at the guest list. That was when I realized with a shock that many of the attendees would be people I knew from my early days in the industry—not just from Jonah's work but my own erstwhile acting career. Dusty, to my relief, had left immediately after his hospital visit for a long, isolated shoot somewhere in northern Asia, and wouldn't be able to return any time soon. But several other names on the list were painfully familiar to me—some had been guests at my nineteenth birthday party, others I'd worked with, and some I'd even briefly lived with after Skylar pawned me off. In fact, Skylar himself had just sent a request, which I promptly denied.

But as for the rest of the guests, I had to wrestle with my instincts. I'd always known Jonah was widely respected in his field, and this only told me how widely. In my early days with him, it seemed absolutely critical for me to have no contact with industry players. Now those same players wanted to show up in person at the memorial I was hosting in his honour, and I still recoiled at the prospect of meeting them face to face.

These men and women had seen me at my worst. They'd watched me trade favours for access or position, and some of them had taken me up on it. Others had exploited my incapacity and helplessness during those final days before rehab. How could I look them in the eye and make civil conversation?

In the end, Jonah's words got me through it. I remembered him telling me the best way to face your enemies is with something they need. All these powerful people wanted to pay their respects to Jonah because his work had been vital to them. They might not realize it yet, but I was now the only one who could give them what they needed. Soon they'd be working with me, and paying me well for my services. All I had to do was stand strong and face them with that knowledge, not the memories that still made me cringe.

Malik and I hosted the memorial, with Pasha by my side. It was everything Jonah might have wanted, and a solace to the hearts of those of us who loved him. The lushly decorated space, overflowing crowds, moving tributes, and stirring performances seemed almost worthy of the man. Pasha took care to publicly credit the small companies that provided services, and many of the guests expressed interest in working with them in the future. I was especially happy about the venue. Secretly, I believed that Jonah, like me, would have enjoyed forcing all those rich industry types to walk by the burnt-out streetlights and boarded-up buildings of this run-down yet vibrant neighbourhood they'd like to forget the existence of.

* * *

A few days later, Pasha and I ate breakfast together in the kitchen of his apartment. We hadn't had much peaceful time together since that call from Malik. Both the community centre and Pasha's school were located in this area, so we'd spent many nights at his apartment as we geared up for the memorial. But now school had finished for the year, and though we'd be back often for the summer program, we'd agreed that Pasha would pack up a few things and stay with me at Jonah's—now my—house for a while.

"How much is your rent here, anyway?" I asked, over pancakes and bacon. "I thought public school teachers don't make that much."

"They don't," Pasha replied. "I'd never be able to afford this place on my own salary. My folks are helping me out; they give me a monthly allowance."

"Oh, that's nice of them."

Pasha looked down at his plate, but I caught the small frown. "I'd rather not have to take it," he said.

"Listen…" I remembered Dusty's visit at the hospital. "I know it's awkward that I don't want to see your dad right now. It's not fair for you to be in the middle. I promise I'll work on things. I don't want you to feel estranged from anyone you love."

"I know you will," he said.

Something in his tone made me wonder if I still wasn't quite getting it. "You know, I always thought you and your dad were close," I said. "But I'm starting to get the feeling you…"

"My dad has a problem with who I am," Pasha said. His voice was firm, but he picked up his coffee cup like he wanted to shield his face with it.

I stopped, my fork frozen horizontally over my plate. "He what?"

"Actually they both do. My mom too. I guess that's the last part of my story, the part I didn't tell you yet."

"Are you saying…they don't like you being a sub?"

"Yes." Pasha put his mug down and resumed eating.

I watched him for a moment. There was no hint of a flush on his silvery skin, though the slender fingers that held his fork had tightened a little.

"But..." I said at last, "Dusty's a sub himself. Why doesn't he—"

"No he's not."

"What?"

Pasha kept eating with the same slightly clenched grip. "He acted like one, but he's not a sub by nature, not like I am. Did you know he left Tiran?"

"What?" I said again. After a moment I set the cutlery down, pushed my plate aside, and leaned forward on my arms. "I—I didn't know any of this. What happened?" A thought came to me before he could reply. "Wait—was it because of me?"

"Not really. Though I don't think that helped. He wasn't happy about what happened with you, but he didn't leave till a few years later."

Pasha went on eating with the same dogged focus, and I started to get the impression this was his version of that tangled knot inside my own brain.

"Hey..." I said, remembering how carefully he always treated me. "If you don't want to talk about it, it's okay. We don't have to."

"It's not that." He sighed, and unclenched his fists to set the cutlery down on his plate. "It's just sort of complicated. The thing is, my dad's actually a Dom, he always has been. He told me some of this when I turned eighteen; he said I was old enough to understand then. This was after you left, and I was already pretty confused."

I reached across the table, and he let me take his hand.

"So apparently," he went on, "when dad first moved out west with Tiran, he had a sub of his own. Then he hit it big right away—like, he became this big star overnight. He says he let it get to his head, he was young and drinking too much—whatever. And one night he did something to his sub. I don't know the details, but the sub got hurt pretty bad, and it could've been worse, he could've been permanently injured or killed."

"Oh, no..." I breathed.

"So my dad figured he wasn't ready to be a Dom. And that's why he asked Tiran to take him on. He figured that was the best way to learn; like, from the other perspective. You know?"

"But..." I let go of Pasha and raised my hands in baffled confusion. "You mean all that time he wasn't really Tiran's sub?"

"I don't know exactly what arrangement they made. I think it was real, though. I mean, I don't think Tiran was just playing; I think he really liked my dad belonging to him. And I think my dad really wanted to learn from him."

"But Jonah said Tiran's a terrible Dom!" I burst out.

Pasha smiled a bit sardonically. "No shit. He *is* a terrible Dom. I guess that's what my dad finally figured out. Or else he just decided he'd learned enough. Anyway, for whatever reason—my folks moved off the estate four or five years ago. They live downtown now, with dad's original sub, who apparently forgave him."

"That is...so weird," I said. "I never would've guessed about Dusty. Wait, isn't your mom a Domme? Why didn't he learn from her?"

"Yeah, I asked him that...he said they thought it would be too hard on their relationship. You know, they really love each other."

"And they both love you. I don't get why they'd have a problem with you being a sub."

Pasha's lips tightened. He got up, taking our plates to the sink, then leaned against the counter. "I came out to them when I moved back home, after I'd come to terms with everything. And they were both appalled. My mom tried to hide it, but my dad didn't. He kept saying he was worried about me, he was afraid I'd get hurt—"

"Well maybe..." I put in, hesitantly, "I mean, maybe he is worried about that. Look what happened to his own sub."

"If he was worried about my safety, he could have taught me how to protect myself. He could have told me what to look out for, or how to recognize a good Dom. But that wasn't really his problem. He'd start off talking about safety and next thing I knew he'd be saying *Everyone will look down on you! No one will respect you!*" Pasha's fingers gripped the countertop behind him. "And my old favourite, *No son of mine...!*"

"Jesus, Pasha!" I jumped up and seized his shoulders, pulling him against my chest. "He didn't...throw you out or anything, did he?"

"No." Pasha steadied himself in my arms, looking up into my face with a small smile. "He's not a monster, just—biased. Like a lot of people. I told him I can't change who I am and he eventually adjusted to it, or at least pretended to."

"You're being way too kind."

"Maybe it'll get better over time. Anyway…I only told you this so you won't feel bad about not wanting to see him. I don't want to see him that often either." He stepped away from me and glanced around the kitchen. "Now let's finish cleaning up so I can pack some clothes and we can get out of here."

We cleared the table and looked after the dishes while I brooded over Pasha's story. It was easy to be angry and outraged at Dusty for his prejudices, but didn't I share some of them? Was I so sure I'd rid myself of them?

"I wonder what…" I began without thinking, as we headed into Pasha's bedroom.

"What do you wonder?" Pasha asked when I paused.

"What your dad would say if he knew you were with me." I stopped, and grabbed his wrist. "Wait—did you tell him? When you saw him at the hospital?"

"No." Pasha stroked my arm. "I thought you'd rather I didn't. But I bet he'd be thrilled to have you for a son-in-law."

"Really? Even if I was—" I clamped my jaw shut to stop myself from finishing the sentence, but Pasha wasn't fooled.

"If you were my Dom?" He went over to the bureau and started sorting out clothes. "Why wouldn't he be? He was happy enough to let you take care of me when I was ten."

I sat on the end of the bed beside Pasha's travel bag, watching him work. "It's so funny to think of us as kids, now. I *really* never thought about you like this back then."

"You never thought about me at all back then."

"I thought you were a sweet kid."

Pasha stacked a pile of shirts in his bag and gave me a playful smile. "So when *did* you first think of me…this way?"

"Oh my god." I fell backwards on the bed. "Honestly, I think it was the very first moment I saw you on the porch that night. Afterwards I kept wondering why I couldn't just forget about the whole thing, and then when you walked into the Sentinel…I think I knew."

"So it was lust," he said, half-laughing.

"Only at first." I sat back up on the bed so I could see him. "By the end of that night, I couldn't imagine not having you in my life. Every time I saw you after that, it just…felt like my soul was at rest."

He stopped his work to smile at me over his shoulder. "I think I know what you mean."

"What about you?" I asked. "Did you know what I was feeling?"

"Not right away. I thought at first you might just be missing home. But I started to hope when you kept—" He broke off, staring down at something delicate and gold he'd just pulled out of a drawer.

"What is it?" I asked.

Pasha turned, holding the object out to me. "I forgot all about this. Tiran gave it to me when I asked him about paying for rehab that time. He said you left it at his place."

The gold chain, the one with the theatre mask pendant, glimmered in his hand. I stared for a moment, then slowly reached out for it.

"It's yours?"

"Yes," I said huskily, my fingers brushing against his as I clasped my fist around the chain. "Jimmy gave it to me on my eighteenth birthday."

He understood. "I'm so glad you got it back."

"Me too," I said.

Chapter 24

Malik kept his word. Soon after things settled down, he arranged a kind of small group discussion with some of Jonah's clients, which turned out to be the first of many. We held it on an evening when Pasha was out. Len agreed to act as facilitator, and I stocked up on pizza and beer.

The clients were all close to Jonah's age, and most had been friends as well, so I already knew most of them. I expected to be a little embarrassed at presenting myself to these men as a would-be future Dom but no one seemed surprised. We sat around the living room while Len asked questions about why they'd all wanted to work with Jonah.

That day, I heard a lot about trust and respect, communication, consent, safety and boundaries, and also a bit about how hot Jonah was, which I could understand. Several of the guys talked about bad experiences they'd had with other Doms, and emphasized all the things that made Jonah different. We didn't get into specific guidelines or technicalities that night, but the general discussion was enlightening for me.

After a couple of hours, as the conversation began to wind down, I asked the question I'd been wondering about all these years. "Why do you do it? What's in it for you?"

The men exchanged looks, as though asking who should take that one. To my surprise, Len spoke up first.

"Well, I don't know about the others, but for myself—"

"Hold on a minute," I said. "What do you mean, for yourself? You weren't a client. You're not a sub."

Len laughed. "That's not the same thing. Jonah and I were friends since we were kids. We didn't want to complicate things by adding a business relationship. But that doesn't mean I'm not a sub. I just work with a different Dom."

I gaped at him. "But you're—you're—you were in the army."

Everyone laughed, as though I'd made a joke, and I realized how ridiculous that sounded. There it was again; the old stereotype, my old bias. I started to understand how deeply those beliefs had been ingrained in me, and how much work it would take to root them out.

"You know that's got nothing to do with it, man." At least Len didn't seem annoyed. "Or maybe it does in this case, since that's kinda where it started for me. Like I was saying, for me it's about wanting to let go of responsibility. So the more I'm in charge of in real life, the more I want someone else to take charge of me in private. You know?"

A couple of the others nodded at that, but everyone had a slightly different take. Malik described submission as a kind of adrenaline rush for him, a thrill ride, while other men talked about finding peace and security in service. Some described it a bit like Pasha did—as not a choice, but an immutable part of their character that couldn't be denied. And a couple just said that giving up power was *hot* and added an extra current of excitement to their desire, which sounded a lot like how I reacted to the idea of being in charge. If I couldn't fully explain where my cravings came from, maybe I couldn't expect them to fully explain theirs.

What struck me most was how these men differed from all the prevailing stereotypes about subs. None of them were weak or outwardly servile; in fact, they were all successful, confident men, many of whom I knew well. Some, like Malik, had well-paying, successful careers while others were like Len, fun-loving and laid-back. They all acknowledged their needs and desires without shame or embarrassment, and made it clear that their taste in this area had no bearing on the rest of their lives.

That evening was the first of many conversations and discoveries Malik helped guide me through over the next few months, which finally broke down my old prejudices.

CHAPTER 24

* * *

Over the summer I started working with Pasha on the art program he ran for children in his neighbourhood. I had no art skills to offer but enough experience with kids to be able to help manage the classrooms. The work was challenging but fun and eye-opening for me.

The more I learned about the plight of families in places like Echo Canyon, and the more I saw people struggling against the forces stacked against them, the more impressed I was by the school and community centre. Pasha and the other instructors often talked about new projects that would meet local needs if they could find funding for them. I offered up some of Jonah's savings to support a couple of programs in the fall, but that felt like a drop in the bucket.

"I'm thinking of approaching the Foundation for some grants," Pasha said, on our way home from the community centre at the end of another day. As usual, I took the driver's seat, but there wasn't much to do in the way of driving.

"What Foundation?"

Pasha shot me a quick look, as though to check my reaction. "You know. The one Paul Armstrong runs."

I almost choked. "*Tiran's* Foundation?"

"It's one of the biggest funders in the world."

"What? Isn't it just what he calls his *do-gooder* thing?"

"I don't know what he calls it," Pasha said. He had a way of speaking about Tiran with disdain, which I found soothing, though sometimes I wondered if it might have originally stemmed from jealousy. "But Tiran has nothing to do with how it's run. Paul has complete control."

"Well...what does it do?"

"They used to just focus on international work. That's Paul's background, from what I understand. I heard he's always been pretty radical. But lately Tom's been pushing for more domestic projects."

"Tom Van Mertz? What...have you been in touch with him?"

Pasha nodded. "I hope you don't mind. I met with him last week."

I wasn't sure how I felt about that. "How come?"

"Well, you know he works with Paul at the Foundation now."

"No. I didn't know."

"Oh...well, he does. And apparently he wants the Foundation to take on more projects here, in this country."

"What kind of projects?"

"I guess they're just trying to figure that out. You remember Tom came from one of the old wastelands. There aren't many of those left, but he's been working on some reclaiming programs. He's also interested in support for the displaced kids, and you know we have a lot of them here in Echo Canyon. He's supposed to put in some proposals to Paul, and I have a few ideas I think I can sell."

"Huh." As usual, I was left with a slight sense of awe at how much went on in the world that I didn't know about.

Pasha slipped his hand over mine, interlocking our fingers. "I want to make sure you're okay with all this, though. Before I go any further."

"Oh, Pasha. I'd never try to stop you from something like that. I don't want to see Tom, but if you really think you can get funding from them, you should."

He nodded. "I think I can get a lot."

We rode in silence for a minute, before I asked what I really wanted to know. "Did you...tell Tom about me?"

"No. I figured you didn't want me to."

I sighed, and clenched my fingers more tightly around his. "It seems so stupid, still being afraid to see people. It's not fair to you either. I can't keep going like this."

"If you're not ready..."

"It's time I did something about it." I thought about Pasha's story, the way he'd made a conscious decision to improve himself after everything he went through. *Don't let the bastards win.* "Listen, if I...if I make an appointment with a therapist, would you come with me? At least the first time?"

He squeezed my hand. "I'll go anywhere with you."

In the end Pasha didn't just join me for the appointment; he helped find the right person and make the first contact, as well. Fortunately I could adjust my work hours to make time for the sessions. Therapy was a long, slow process. It took me a while to warm up and once I did many of the conversations became painful and difficult. While Pasha had coaxed a few threads loose from the mass that blocked my memories, the rest was still an impenetrable tangle. I had a lot of work to do. But after a few months I began to think I was making progress.

* * *

I didn't start wearing Jimmy's chain right away, after Pasha gave it to me. Something about the theatre mask pendant bothered me; it made me think of old ambitions and misguided beliefs.

"Can we stop at the jeweler's, here?" I asked Pasha on a whim, as we drove back from an appointment.

"Sure. Why?"

"I want to see about…getting something changed on this." I showed Pasha what I was holding. Though I didn't wear it, I carried the chain around in my pocket at all times.

It only took the jeweler a couple of minutes to remove the pendant. He asked if I wanted to add anything instead, which I declined, and then handed me the two pieces separately.

As we walked back to the car, I put the pendant back in my pocket. Maybe I'd tuck it away somewhere in my bedroom, a memory of a long-lost era. But the chain alone I fastened around my neck as soon as we got in the car, and it felt instantly familiar and comforting.

When we arrived home, I stopped in the foyer to glance at my reflection in the mirror. My face had changed a lot in the last ten years. I'd recovered from some of the ravages of the worst times; I'd gained some weight back and improved my health. With the chain, I thought I looked more like my old self than ever.

Pasha paused behind me. "I bet your dad would be happy to see you wearing that," he said, leaning over my shoulder to peck my cheek before heading to the kitchen.

"Uncle."

"What?"

"Technically, he's my uncle," I said, wondering why I'd suddenly felt compelled to point that out.

"You never called him Uncle Jimmy."

I followed Pasha into the kitchen, but instead of helping with supper I found myself sitting down heavily at the table. "I know. I always call him Jimmy or dad. But he's not my dad. He's my mom's brother."

Pasha shut the fridge door and turned to look at me, then came over and pulled up another chair. "No one talks much about your mom," he said.

"I remember her. I was six when she died. I have memories."

"What was she like?"

"Wild. Chaotic." I let my mind drift back to those faint fragments of memory. "Rebellious. I guess it's more like impressions than memories. Whenever she was around, things felt exciting, but...I don't know what kind of life we would have had with her."

"Didn't Jimmy ever adopt you?"

"No. I guess he never thought about it. You know, he was just nineteen when he inherited the five of us."

"It must have been hard for him."

"I never understood why he stayed." I'd often thought this, idly or in passing, but now it struck me as the central question. "He could have just put us all in care. Maybe he should have. He gave up his whole life for us."

"Did he ever...seem like he regretted it?"

"No, never." I propped my elbows on the table and leaned my head on my hands. "I think I...always expected him to."

"What do you mean, Barr?" Pasha asked, touching my arm. "You expected him to regret it?"

"I mean...not in so many words. But when I was little I think I...always half-expected him to wake up one day and realize he didn't have to be there. Like, he could just walk away."

"You were afraid he'd leave?"

"Not exactly afraid. He just always seemed so—so overwhelmed. Harried. I kept wanting to make things easier for him. Maybe underneath I thought that might keep him from leaving."

"Maybe that's why you spent so much time looking after your siblings."

"Oh...I don't know. I mean, I also liked being in charge of everything. But I remember thinking—" I stopped, half laughing. "It sounds stupid, but I'd always think, *I* don't need him, but the little ones do. So maybe if he didn't have to worry about me, he'd be more likely to stick around for them."

"Oh Barry." Pasha threw his arms around my neck. "No wonder you grew up so fast."

I returned his embrace, my mind still elsewhere. "I think in some way I kind of despised Jimmy for staying. That's the worst part—that I almost saw him as pathetic, giving up his life to take care of a bunch of kids when he didn't have to. I knew what he did for us but I was always a little—impatient with him. Like, why spend your life in service to other people?" I shut my eyes, not wanting to make the obvious connection. *That's how I used to think of subs.* Had that bias bled into my feelings about Jimmy, or perhaps, vice-versa?

"The funny thing is..." Pasha said slowly, "you spent so much of your own life in service. You looked after all of us on the estate—even the adults, in some ways. And Jimmy. You looked after Jonah. Now you're helping the kids at school."

"I wonder if that's where all those aspirations came from, the big ambitions," I said. "I never wanted to be like Jimmy, with such a small life. I guess he always kind of suffered in comparison to Tiran."

"Well, Tiran did a lot for us," Pasha said, as though trying to be fair. "But it cost him so little."

I knew what he meant. Our house, Jimmy's job, our school fees, even the convertible and the party he threw for me—all of that was just money, and Tiran had more than he'd ever use. Jimmy gave up his life to make us a family.

All of that was fodder for my therapy sessions. Meanwhile, Malik and the others continued running their own type of therapy for me. Every week they joined me to discuss their experiences and let me ask the questions that continued to haunt me. How could a sub know who was safe to trust? How did a person know if they were a real Dom? What would make them fit for the role? What rules, guidelines or principles distinguished a real Dom from someone like Tiran?

The men spoke about negotiations, limits, safewords, personal choice and responsibility, mental health and resilience, subspace and aftercare. I would listen in fascination as they talked amongst themselves, sharing their stories. Once people started bringing up specific activities I remembered, again, how much technical skill was involved in practising safely.

"Did Jonah know how to do all these things?" I'd ask in amazement. It still hurt to think of what I'd missed by not asking him about his work when I had the chance.

Len suggested I meet with his own Dom, who introduced me to others. They invited me to join their club as what they called an *initiate*, which meant I wouldn't be allowed to practise but could observe, learn and ask questions. When I started going to events, I asked Pasha if he wanted to join me, but he declined.

"I've been to those places many times," he said. "I don't need the education. We can go together when we're…ready."

We both knew what he meant, and the words sent a sharp tingle of electricity through my belly. *Soon*, I thought.

The men at the club were welcoming and supportive, but they never replaced Malik, Len and Jonah's other friends and clients. That group became not just a safe space for me, where I could ask all the dumb questions I was afraid to share with the pros, but also a kind of living memorial to Jonah.

"So, have you ever…thought any more about our suggestion?" Len asked as the others were starting to leave after one of our sessions.

"What suggestion?"

"You know." He nudged me and glanced at Malik.

"No pressure," Malik said. "But the guys have all been talking."

"I don't understand," I said, though I thought I was starting to.

"You know how you took over Jonah's vid business?" Malik began.

"Well, some of us have been hoping…" Len added.

I frowned a little. "Is that why everyone's been so helpful? Because…"

"Don't be a chump," Malik said. "It's not like that. The others just reached the same conclusion we did. That you'd make a great service Dom."

"Thank you," I said, gratified despite myself, "for the vote of confidence. But there's only one person I'm interested in working with right now."

When I told Pasha about the conversation later, he laughed and wrapped his arms around me. "I can't blame them for taking a shot," he said, "but I don't want to share you. At least not anytime soon. Maybe they can try again in a few years."

* * *

Did I want to dominate Pasha? I wanted a companion, a partner, a lover—all those things first. I wanted to make him happy, to meet his needs. If the best way to do that was through an arrangement that would fulfill my own deepest cravings…well, that had to be some kind of miracle. The details hardly mattered to me. I would do whatever he wanted; I would give him whatever he needed. I remembered Jonah once telling me how he did what his clients asked him to. For the first time, I understood the service part of his job.

But I had some idea, by this time, of the range of activities that might be involved, and how specialized they could be. Many of the techniques I saw at the club required practice and great skill. I needed to know where to focus my training. It was time to find out more about Pasha's interests.

I began tentatively, asking him questions like the ones we'd covered in the group sessions—what appealed to him, what he wanted in a Dom, what he liked and didn't, his tastes and preferences. We didn't get into specifics like boundaries or limits; I just wanted to see where our tastes aligned and where I might need to expand my newly-developing skill set.

It was no surprise to me that Pasha knew exactly what he wanted—or that his preferences dove-tailed so neatly with mine, since I'd already concluded we were made for each other.

"I want to serve," he said, threading his fingers through mine as we lay under the covers in the dark. "Not just in bed, but always. I want to honour and obey, and I want to feel protected and valued. I feel like that's all I've wanted my whole life."

"So a...what they call a total power exchange?" I asked, trying to keep the nervous tremble out of my voice.

He propped himself up on one elbow and looked down at me, drawing small circles on my chest with the fingers on his other hand. "I'm not sure I ever want to be completely powerless. I like the idea of someone taking charge of me, but I think I'd always reserve the final right to decide for myself."

"I get it," I said. "You want to obey because you choose to, not because you have to." I was already familiar with Pasha's particular style of surrender, which came so naturally to him that I often caught glimpses of it even outside of a formal arrangement. He had a very deliberate way of listening, considering and following direction. I understood that meant he could also choose not to, if circumstances required.

Over the next few weeks I learned more about what Pasha wanted specifically. To my relief, he had only mild interest in things like bondage, pain or humiliation. What he mainly craved was the chance to give up control to someone he trusted. Restraints, edging, toys—those appealed to him, and he thought he might want to explore a few other areas. I listened to him closely so I'd know exactly what I needed training in, and where I needed to keep learning.

As our conversations went on, I think we both felt the unspoken tension increasing. Our lives fit together almost perfectly, and sex already took my breath away, but this added a new current of anticipation that promised so much more. We'd catch each other in little knowing glances and smiles, small moments of suddenly loaded silence when we were both obviously thinking the same thing.

I asked him to go shopping with me, making it clear what type of items I had in mind. He agreed, and I took mental notes as he carefully made selections that told me more about his preferences.

You can't be a Dom if you don't respect subs. Did I think less of Pasha for his need to submit? It was impossible; I knew him too well for that. He was a full, whole person–brave, strong, kind, talented. His desires were just one part of him, like mine were just one part of me.

In September, on my twenty-ninth birthday, Pasha presented me with a small box from the jeweller we'd visited weeks earlier. Inside was a new pendant, a golden sun intertwined with a silver moon, engraved with our initials. As much as I adored it, nothing matched my euphoria later the same night when he knelt at my feet and asked me to be fully his, in the way he most desired. That was the gift I cherished most of all.

* * *

Pasha let his apartment go and moved in with me. We turned the guest room into his studio, and hung the lion and cub painting over the bed in our room. He continued teaching but gave up his parents' allowance.

I kept working at Jonah's company. There was plenty of business, enough to comfortably support us both. I learned to face past acquaintances with confidence and pride, and even attended a few industry events where Jonah's work was recognized and honoured.

On the whole, though, I preferred Pasha's world. I spent time with him in the community, learning about the students and families and what they needed. After a few months, I began offering vid editing programs, and we used Jonah's savings to set up a small bursary in his name, for students who wanted to pursue it as a career. Malik ran robotics engineering projects for kids and adults, and Pasha used grants from the Foundation to set up business and employment opportunities.

Our lives were exciting and rewarding and often messy. We frequently hit roadblocks, barriers or opposition that left me stressed and frustrated. Once in a while we encountered old prejudices, and I learned that some people still clung to bizarre and hateful ideas about the colour of my skin. But even with all that, I knew I'd rather live in the real world than hide forever in isolation.

I continued my therapy sessions, and the knotted tangle started to release its threads. My support system outside of Pasha—Malik, Len, Jonah's other friends, the other Doms and the rest of the community—kept me grounded and safe. It became easier to think about my past—through the mistakes and regret, to the people and places who helped shape what I became.

"I wish I hadn't wasted so much time with Tiran and the others," I told Pasha. "Sometimes I feel like they got me at my best."

But Pasha only shook his head. "Everything that happened to you is part of who you are. And you're at your best right now."

By this time, I was okay with Pasha telling people we were together. Someday I'd be willing to see Dusty, maybe even Tom. Tiran didn't loom so large in my mind now that I saw him as a weak and selfish man. Still, I sometimes remembered the way he talked to me that one time, the kindness he'd shown when I was hurt and confused. Tiran could have been a friend to me once. He might have helped me, back when I needed it, if he'd had more personal integrity. But he didn't, and I knew I never wanted to see him or the estate again.

* * *

Early in the new year, before the temperature became unbearable once more, Pasha told me Randall was having a cookout in his backyard and we were invited.

"He'd really like to see you," Pasha said.

With a small shock, I realized how much I ached to see him too. "I'll go," I told Pasha, "but there's something I have to do first."

And so, on a bright and sunny day in March, Pasha and I pulled up near a coffee shop in Whittier, with an outdoor patio and a small wrought iron paling. There was Doc, tied to one of the pickets. As we walked closer he recognized me, throwing himself onto my chest with as much force as his ancient body could muster. I dropped to the ground, gathering him into my arms and letting him climb all over me for a few minutes. When I could tear myself away, I stood up and walked onto the patio where Jimmy stood, watching me.

"Dad," I said, and fell into his waiting arms.

THE END

About the Author

M.E. Samm lives, writes and reads in Canada. Sign up for her extremely occasional newsletter, or contact her at mmmesa@gmail.com.

Subscribe to my newsletter:

✉ https://mesamm.carrd.co

Also by M.E. Samm

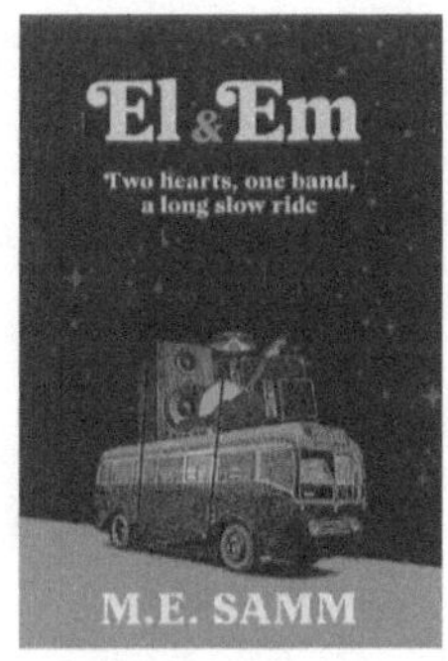

El & Em

Philadelphia, 1972: All Luke wants is to share his music with the world. When an imposing, slightly older trumpet player called Emmett joins his band, Luke is fascinated – and a lifelong friendship is born. Love and loyalty are forged in the slow burn of tours, shows and recording sessions. Over the years, Luke's curiosity and Emmett's indulgence slowly push the two of them into complicated new territory. Emmett tries to keep them safe – but Luke wants it all.

In this monumental romance spanning more than twenty years, there are no heroes and no villains – just people doing their best in a messed up world.

Content Notes:

- Open relationships
- Period-realistic racism
- References to AIDS and period-realistic homophobia
- Mild Dom/sub power dynamics
- No use of slurs, no sexual violence, no cheating

Available on Kindle and Kindle Unlimited at https://www.amazon.com/dp/B0DH8CM54Q

www.ingramcontent.com/pod-product-compliance
Lightning Source LLC
LaVergne TN
LVHW091123080826
845145LV00008B/2019

* 9 7 8 1 0 6 8 9 7 2 2 4 9 *